PRAISE FOR LEE

Malibu Burning

"*Malibu Burning* is a blistering thrill ride full of Southern California thieves, cops, and firefighters, all facing high stakes and imminent danger. Superbly researched and told, fast-paced, and downright fun, this is Lee Goldberg at his best!"

—Mark Greaney, #1 *New York Times* bestselling author of the Gray Man series

"By turns tense and rambunctious, wildly entertaining, and breakneck-paced, Lee Goldberg's splendid *Malibu Burning* is pure storytelling pleasure from beginning to end."

—Megan Abbott, Edgar Award–, Anthony Award–, Thriller Award–, and *Los Angeles Times* Book Prize–winning author of *The Turnout*

"*Malibu Burning* is classic Lee Goldberg at the top of his game: a fast-paced, funny, and deeply satisfying page-turner."

—Jess Lourey, Amazon Charts bestselling author of *The Quarry Girls*

"An inventive, twisty, and funny caper from one of crime writing's true pros. Elmore Leonard and Donald Westlake would've loved this wild heist."

—Ace Atkins, *New York Times* bestselling author of *Robert B. Parker's Bye Bye Baby* and *The Heathens*

"This is a book I couldn't put down. Lee Goldberg is a master when it comes to building tension and writing heart-pounding action scenes. *Malibu Burning* is a roundhouse kick of a thriller, a true nail-biting race against time."
—Simon Gervais, former RCMP counterterrorism officer and author of *The Last Protector* and *Robert Ludlum's The Blackbriar Genesis*

Movieland

"Bestseller Goldberg's strong fourth Eve Ronin mystery . . . [has] assured prose [that] matches the tight plot."
—*Publishers Weekly*

"Goldberg's compelling follow-up to *Gated Prey* is a fast-paced, riveting police procedural influenced by actual events in California. A character-driven series entry that skillfully depicts Hollywood corruption."
—*Library Journal* (starred review)

"A beautifully cinematic novelist who strikes a precise balance between darkness and humor."
—*Bookmarks* magazine

"A tense, gritty, and engaging novel with wit, suspense, action, and some great twists."
—*Mystery and Suspense Magazine*

"Murder, politics, and deception in the heart of Hollywood . . . oh my! *Movieland* brings the heat and packs a punch like a shotgun blast to the face."
—Steve Netter, Best Thriller Books

"Well-written, page-turning pacing and relatable characters make this a must-read series."

—J. Todd Wilkins, Best Thriller Books

"The fourth book in Lee Goldberg's splendidly compelling Eve Ronin series."

—*Mystery Scene*

"An intelligently written series with memorable characters and intriguing plots. Lee Goldberg is one of those authors with natural-born storytelling gifts."

—*Deadly Pleasures*

"It's an entertaining and twisty tale of murder and long-held secrets in a picturesque portion of Southern California."

—Bookgasm

"The fourth book in Lee Goldberg's series is his most ambitious and best realized yet . . . *Movieland* is crime writing of the highest order. Goldberg's style touches on both Michael Connelly and Robert Crais, in whose company he now squarely belongs."

—*The Providence Journal*

"*Movieland*, Lee Goldberg's fourth novel featuring Ronin, is every bit as good as the first three. The characters, including victims, suspects, and an assortment of lazy, hardworking, honest, and corrupt cops, are quirky and well developed. The depiction of police procedures feels authentic. The writing is vivid and precise. And with startling twists around every corner, the suspenseful tale unfolds at a furious pace."

—Associated Press

"Goldberg's work conjures up the same authenticity and mood as Michael Connelly's Bosch novels . . . *Movieland* is a must-read for anyone who enjoys compelling crime fiction with a strong sense of place."

—Crime Fiction Lover

"*Movieland* is a fast-paced mystery with interesting and well-developed characters and plenty of twists and turns. If this book and this series aren't on your radar yet, they should be!"

—*Kings River Life Magazine*

"Totally loved Lee Goldberg's new Eve Ronin book, *Movieland*. This series just keeps getting better."

—Nick Petrie, Thriller Award–winning author of the Peter Ash series

"Lee is fantastic at combining clever plotting, humor, and thrills in his stories."

—Boyd Morrison, #1 *New York Times* bestselling author

"LA noir is real; so is Malibu noir, and no one does it better than Lee Goldberg."

—Luanne Rice, *New York Times* bestselling author

"Finished this on the plane home. Typically classy police procedural from Lee Goldberg—giving Michael Connelly a run for his money . . ."

—Ian Rankin

Gated Prey

"The seamy side of California dreaming . . . Goldberg not only ties up . . . but links some of Eve's investigations in ways as disturbing as they are surprising."

—*Kirkus Reviews*

Bone Canyon

A *Mystery and Suspense Magazine* 2021
Best Book of the Year Selection

"Lee Goldberg puts the *pro* in *police procedural. Bone Canyon* is fresh, sharp, and absorbing. Give me more Eve Ronin, ASAP."

—Meg Gardiner, international bestselling author

"Wow—what a novel! It is wonderful in so many ways. I could not put it down. *Bone Canyon* is wrenching and harrowing, full of wicked twists. Lee Goldberg captures the magic and danger of the Santa Monica Mountains and the predators who prowl them. Detective Eve Ronin takes on forgotten victims, fights for them, and nearly loses everything in the process. She's a riveting character, and I can't wait for her next case."

—Luanne Rice, *New York Times* bestselling author

"*Bone Canyon* is a propulsive procedural that provides high thrills in difficult terrain, grappling thoughtfully with sexual violence and police corruption, as well as the minefield of politics and media in Hollywood and suburban Los Angeles. Eve Ronin is a fantastic series lead—stubborn and driven, working twice as hard as her colleagues both to prove her worth and to deliver justice for the dead."

—Steph Cha, author of *Your House Will Pay*

Lost Hills

"A cop novel so good it makes much of the old guard read like they're going through the motions until they can retire . . . The real appeal here is Goldberg's lean prose, which imbues just-the-facts procedure with remarkable tension and cranks up to a stunning description of a fire that was like 'Christmas in hell.'"

—*Booklist*

"[The] suspense and drama are guaranteed to keep a reader spellbound."

—Authorlink

"An energetic, resourceful procedural starring a heroine who deserves a series of her own."

—*Kirkus Reviews*

"This nimble, sure-footed series launch from bestseller Goldberg . . . builds to a thrilling, visually striking climax. Readers will cheer Ronin every step of the way."

—*Publishers Weekly*

"The first book in what promises to be a superb series—it's also that rare novel in which the formulaic elements of mainstream police procedurals share narrative space with a unique female protagonist. All that, and it's also a love letter to the chaos and diversity of California. There are a lot of series out there, but Eve Ronin and Goldberg's fast-paced prose should put this one on the radar of every crime-fiction fan."

—National Public Radio

"This sterling thriller is carved straight out of the world of Harlan Coben and Lisa Gardner . . . *Lost Hills* is a book to be found and savored."

—BookTrib

"*Lost Hills* is Lee Goldberg at his best. Inspired by the real-world grit and glitz of LA County crime, this book takes no prisoners. And neither does Eve Ronin. Take a ride with her and you'll find yourself with a heroine for the ages. And you'll be left hoping for more."

—Michael Connelly, #1 *New York Times* bestselling author

"*Lost Hills* is what you get when you polish the police procedural to a shine: a gripping premise, a great twist, fresh spins and knowing winks to the genre conventions, and all the smart, snappy ease of an expert at work."

—Tana French, *New York Times* bestselling author

"Thrills and chills! *Lost Hills* is the perfect combination of action and suspense, not to mention Eve Ronin is one of the best new female characters in ages. You will race through the pages!"

—Lisa Gardner, #1 *New York Times* bestselling author

"Twenty-four-karat Goldberg—a top-notch procedural that shines like a true gem."

—Craig Johnson, *New York Times* bestselling author of the Longmire series

"A winner. Packed with procedure, forensics, vivid descriptions, and the right amount of humor. Fervent fans of Connelly and Crais, this is your next read."

—Kendra Elliot, *Wall Street Journal* and Amazon Charts bestselling author

"Brilliant! Eve Ronin rocks! With a baffling and brutal case, tight plotting, and a fascinating look at police procedure, *Lost Hills* is a stunning start to a new detective series. A must-read for crime-fiction fans."

—Melinda Leigh, *Wall Street Journal* and #1 Amazon Charts bestselling author

"A tense, pacy read from one of America's greatest crime and thriller writers."

—Garry Disher, international bestselling author and Ned Kelly Award winner

MALIBU BURNING

OTHER TITLES BY LEE GOLDBERG

King City
The Walk
Watch Me Die
McGrave
Three Ways to Die
Fast Track

The Eve Ronin Series

Lost Hills
Bone Canyon
Gated Prey
Movieland

The Ian Ludlow Thrillers

True Fiction
Killer Thriller
Fake Truth

The Fox & O'Hare Series (coauthored with Janet Evanovich)

Pros & Cons (novella)
The Shell Game (novella)
The Heist
The Chase
The Job

The Scam
The Pursuit

The Diagnosis Murder Series

The Silent Partner
The Death Merchant
The Shooting Script
The Waking Nightmare
The Past Tense
The Dead Letter
The Double Life
The Last Word

The Monk Series

Mr. Monk Goes to the Firehouse
Mr. Monk Goes to Hawaii
Mr. Monk and the Blue Flu
Mr. Monk and the Two Assistants
Mr. Monk in Outer Space
Mr. Monk Goes to Germany
Mr. Monk Is Miserable
Mr. Monk and the Dirty Cop
Mr. Monk in Trouble
Mr. Monk Is Cleaned Out
Mr. Monk on the Road
Mr. Monk on the Couch
Mr. Monk on Patrol
Mr. Monk Is a Mess
Mr. Monk Gets Even

The Charlie Willis Series

My Gun Has Bullets
Dead Space

The Dead Man Series
(coauthored with William Rabkin)

Face of Evil
Ring of Knives (with James Daniels)
Hell in Heaven
The Dead Woman (with David McAfee)
The Blood Mesa (with James Reasoner)
Kill Them All (with Harry Shannon)
The Beast Within (with James Daniels)
Fire & Ice (with Jude Hardin)
Carnival of Death (with Bill Crider)
Freaks Must Die (with Joel Goldman)
Slaves to Evil (with Lisa Klink)
The Midnight Special (with Phoef Sutton)
The Death March (with Christa Faust)
The Black Death (with Aric Davis)
The Killing Floor (with David Tully)
Colder Than Hell (with Anthony Neil Smith)
Evil to Burn (with Lisa Klink)
Streets of Blood (with Barry Napier)
Crucible of Fire (with Mel Odom)
The Dark Need (with Stant Litore)
The Rising Dead (with Stella Green)
Reborn (with Kate Danley, Phoef Sutton, and Lisa Klink)

The Jury Series

Judgment
Adjourned
Payback
Guilty

Nonfiction

The Best TV Shows You Never Saw
Unsold Television Pilots 1955–1989
Television Fast Forward
Science Fiction Filmmaking in the 1980s (cowritten with
William Rabkin, Randy Lofficier, and Jean-Marc Lofficier)
*The Dreamweavers: Interviews with Fantasy Filmmakers of
the 1980s* (cowritten with William Rabkin, Randy Lofficier, and
Jean-Marc Lofficier)
Successful Television Writing (cowritten with William Rabkin)

MALIBU BURNING

LEE GOLDBERG

Text copyright © 2023 by Adventures in Television, Inc.
All rights reserved.

Published by Thomas & Mercer, Seattle

www.apub.com

Amazon, the Amazon logo, and Thomas & Mercer are trademarks of Amazon.com, Inc., or its affiliates.

ISBN-13: 9781662500671 (hardcover)
ISBN-13: 9781662500688 (paperback)
ISBN-13: 9781662500695 (digital)

Cover design by Christopher Lin
Cover images: © Salameh dibaei, © MCCAIG, © Terry Schmidbauer/Getty Images

Printed in the United States of America

First edition

To Valerie and Madison,
who keep the home fires burning

PART ONE
PARALLEL LINES

CHAPTER ONE

Eight Years Ago

Two federal law enforcement agents, one from the FBI and one from the DEA, were coordinating the stakeout of the Golden State Bank in Ventura, California, from a vacant third-floor office in the Erle Stanley Gardner Building across the street. The building was named after the author of the Perry Mason novels, who wrote his classic mysteries in an office on the same floor.

The agents sat on folding chairs facing a window that overlooked Main Street, the bank, and the two black SUVs that idled in front of it, so their backs were to the office door when US Marshal Andrew Walker strode in wearing a white Stetson Shasta cowboy hat and carrying a box of Krispy Kreme donuts.

"Morning, gentlemen," he said.

The men were so startled by Walker's unexpected arrival that they dropped their walkie-talkies, reached for their guns, and nearly fell out of their chairs before they realized that the only dangers they faced were from high calories and tooth decay.

"What the hell are you doing here, Walker?" asked FBI Special Agent Kent Dubrow, holstering his gun. Beads of sweat were already rising on his balding head. "You aren't assigned to this operation."

"I was in the neighborhood and thought you might be hungry," Walker said. "I always am when I'm on a stakeout."

Walker was an even six feet tall, his body linebacker thick, and he wore a loose-fitting sport coat over a JCPenney oxford shirt and Levi's 501 jeans to hide his Glock and his badge.

Ventura was a small town on the Southern California coast and had been in a slow, steady decline for decades, ever since its oil wells stopped pumping and the beach was severed from downtown by the 101 freeway. The relentless surf had eroded away much of the beach, leaving a few wet clumps of sand clinging to the long line of boulders and rubble that had been dumped along the edge of the pedestrian promenade in a desperate attempt to save it from destruction.

Business on Main Street was so bad that the few occupied storefronts were primarily filled by nonprofit thrift shops, from Goodwill to the Coalition for Family Harmony. All that downtown Ventura had going for it now was the historic San Buenaventura Mission at the northwest end of Main Street and the county fairgrounds on the rapidly eroding waterfront.

"You didn't drive all the way up from LA just to ruin my diet," Dubrow said, picking up his walkie-talkie and turning his attention back to the street.

Walker raised the lid of the Krispy Kreme box to display the wide assortment of donuts to the DEA agent. "I'm Andrew Walker, US Marshals."

"Clyde Preston, DEA," the agent said, peering into the box and sniffing the donuts like a curious beagle, which he resembled. He was short and had big ears and close-cropped brown hair. "Is that a chocolate-iced custard?"

"Help yourself." Walker had already eaten two on the drive up from the donut shop in Oxnard.

"You didn't answer my question," Dubrow said to Walker.

"I'm chasing a fugitive."

"Take a number and wait your turn to get him, which is going to be years," Dubrow said. "Diego Grillo is the American representative of the Vibora cartel, a whale. You chase minnows."

"This is a joint FBI-DEA operation," Preston added, talking with his mouth full. "We're staking out a private bank that Grillo is using to launder $1 million in marked money that he got in a drug-smuggling sting that we set up. Grillo and his bodyguards walked into the bank right before you arrived. We're taking him down and the Vibora's entire operation in America along with him. Thanks for the donuts, but whatever your interest is in him doesn't really matter."

"You can keep Grillo," Walker said. "I want the banker."

"Milburn Drysdale? The US Marshals Service doesn't enforce banking regulations," Dubrow said. "That's a job for the Treasury Department and the Federal Trade Commission. Or did Drysdale forget to pay some speeding tickets?"

"Milburn Drysdale isn't a banker and that isn't really a bank," Walker said. "You're all being conned."

Danny Cole's fake nose and mustache were itching but that didn't dim his blatantly dishonest smile. Nobody expected an honest smile from a crooked banker, least of all Diego Grillo, the drug lord from the Vibora cartel who sat on the other side of Danny's desk.

"Welcome to Golden State Bank, Mr. Grillo," Danny said. "We're honored to have the opportunity to serve your banking needs."

Grillo was known for the huge scar on his face left by a machete and the two fingers he lost blocking the blow. His mangled hand rested on the silver titanium briefcase on his lap. He was flanked by two men in dark sunglasses, who wore matching Italian suits tailored to hide the big guns in their shoulder holsters. Two more of his men were still in the SUVs outside.

Three other members of Danny's crew posing as bankers worked busily at their desks, showing no interest in the meeting. There was Kurt Sabella, who handled the staging, and Adam Horowitz, who handled the tech, and finally Tamiko Harada, who was obviously the eye candy and, less obviously, the muscle. She had two guns hidden under her desk and she knew how to use them from her days in the military, before her dishonorable discharge.

"I'd like to put some money in my children's college funds," Grillo said. "They have all recently opened accounts here."

"Yes, all one hundred of them," Danny said. "That's a lot of kids."

Grillo shrugged and stole a glance at Tamiko's bust. "I'm a virile man with many wives."

Danny said, "All of your children are studying abroad."

"They are very smart and worldly." Grillo hefted the twenty-pound briefcase onto the desk with a thud and opened it to show Danny the neat stacks of hundred-dollar bills inside. "I would like to deposit $10,000 in each of their accounts."

The deposits were just under the legal limit that would have required a reputable bank to file a report with the government. However, a reputable bank would see a hundred deposits of that amount into third-party accounts held by people residing overseas as an obvious case of money laundering. But this was not a reputable bank. It wasn't even a bank, but Grillo didn't know that.

"There's a standard 10 percent service charge for transactions of this nature," Danny said, reaching for the cash. Grillo abruptly slammed the case shut, nearly severing Danny's fingers.

"Not a penny more, Mr. Drysdale," Grillo said, "or I'll kill you and everything living that's close to you. Your employees, your wife, your mistress, your children, your dog, your goldfish, the yeast in your refrigerator. I'd kill your landscaping, too, but the drought has already done that."

"Understood," Danny said. "Perhaps we should take a moment to count the money together. I'm very attached to my goldfish."

"This is Danny Cole," Walker said, holding up his iPhone with a picture of the man. He had blue eyes, a charming smile, and relaxed, boyish charm. He looked like the stereotypical image of the fit, affable country club tennis pro who got along easily with everyone, especially the women, married and unmarried. Which, as it turned out, was exactly what he was pretending to be when the photo was taken. "He's Milburn Drysdale, your banker."

"This is Drysdale." Dubrow held up his iPhone, which displayed surveillance photos of a middle-aged man entering and leaving the bank. Drysdale had green eyes, a bulbous nose, and a thick mustache. "He doesn't look anything like Danny Cole."

It was true. He didn't look like Cole, but the mischievous sparkle in his eyes, despite the green contacts, was unmistakable to Walker.

"It's him," Walker said. "It's a disguise."

"How do you know?"

"Because I've spent three months tracking him here," Walker said. "And Milburn Drysdale is the name of the banker in an ancient sitcom called *The Beverly Hillbillies*. It's Cole's idea of a joke."

Dubrow snorted with derision. "That's all you have?"

"I can prove it," Walker said. "We can walk in there right now, arrest him, and peel that fake nose and mustache off his face."

"No, we can't," Dubrow said. "It's a private bank. The door is locked and you have to be buzzed through from inside. On top of that, it's a crowded street full of pedestrians. We can't risk provoking a shoot-out."

"Grillo has killed a dozen people and is the California head of the Vibora cartel," Preston said. "Human life means nothing to him. We won't make our move until Grillo and his motorcade are on the overpass leading to the southbound 101. We'll box him in over the freeway, where he can't escape or hurt anybody if he decides he won't go down without a fight."

"What about Cole?" Walker said. "While you're chasing Grillo, he'll get away with the money."

"Drysdale and the cash aren't going anywhere," Dubrow said. "He established this private bank to launder money for street gangs. He's not going to close up shop now that he's snagged the perfect client to whip up more business. It's a long con."

"Cole doesn't do long cons," Walker said. "This is the endgame. He's pulled a dozen heists and countless cons and always manages to slip away without getting caught. I want to end that winning streak."

"Relax, Walker," Preston said, licking some chocolate frosting off his lip. "Once Grillo is captured, we'll immediately move in on the banker and retrieve the money. We're talking a five-minute wait, tops. Then you can try to pull off Drysdale's nose."

"That will be too late." Walker dropped the box of donuts on the table and marched to the door.

"I don't see why," Dubrow said. "Whether or not Drysdale is your man Cole, he doesn't know we're here."

"Of course he does," Walker said, pausing in the doorway. "Why do you think he decided to stage his con in a bank across the street from Perry Mason's office? He's giving you the finger."

"Do not make a move until we've got Grillo," Dubrow said, "or your next job will be selling donuts."

◆　◆　◆

The instant Grillo and his men piled into their SUVs and drove off, Danny and the three other members of his crew stripped off their suits to reveal the matching bright-yellow biking jerseys they wore underneath. The jerseys were so bright they could probably glow in the dark.

"We have five minutes or less until the FBI moves in," Danny said, removing his fake nose and mustache and tossing them in the trash.

"It gives me hives knowing the FBI is right outside the door," said Tamiko as she and the others all pulled matching messenger bags from their desks and then gathered around the open case of money in front of Danny. The first things she shoved in her bag were her two guns.

"That's what makes it exciting." Danny handed them each several stacks of cash, which they stuffed into their messenger bags.

"That's what makes it suicidal," Adam said. He was short, chubby, and curly-haired. He didn't like stealing from people in person. He much preferred to commit his crimes in cyberspace, where he could hide behind a keyboard. Add to that the Feds sitting right outside and he was afraid he might have a stroke.

When Danny was done doling out cash, a stack of about $100,000 still remained on the desk. It was a vital part of the plan to make sure Grillo wouldn't be able to come after them. It was the evidence the Feds would need to put Grillo in prison.

"I hate leaving money on the table," Kurt said. He was in his forties and had the ruddy complexion and stocky build of a construction worker who'd always worked outdoors.

"Think of it as a tip to the FBI for excellent service," Danny said.

Walker sat in the front seat of his Ford F-150 pickup, which was parked on California Street, a few yards from the intersection with Main Street. The Golden State Bank was across the intersection in front of him, on the left-hand corner. The SUVs containing Grillo and his bodyguards had just left. Walker's engine was running and he drummed his fingers anxiously on the steering wheel.

On the radio, he heard the chatter as the FBI and DEA vehicles slipped into traffic, angling into position to box in Grillo on the overpass to the southbound 101 freeway. The instant that happened, Walker was going into the bank. He knew Cole was in there and it was infuriating that the only law enforcement still on the scene besides him were Dubrow and Preston, and they were up in the office, eating his donuts.

The front door of the bank opened. Three men and one woman in matching yellow jerseys, messenger bags, and helmets rode out fast on racing bikes.

What the hell?

A man and the woman peeled off and went north on Main Street. The two other men came straight at Walker, heading toward the overpass to the beach.

One of them he recognized as Danny Cole.

At least, Walker thought, Cole wouldn't be hard to spot in a crowd in that outfit. It was like he was wearing a neon sign.

Walker made a sharp, tire-squealing U-turn, nearly getting T-boned by cars traveling in both directions, and sped off westbound after the two bicyclists.

The other rider peeled off at East Thompson, the last street before the overpass that carried California Street over the 101 freeway, which cut off the city from Ventura's long beach. Walker ignored him and weaved through traffic after Cole.

California Street ended in a T intersection with Harbor Boulevard at a beachfront plaza between a parking structure and a ten-story hotel.

Danny Cole sped across the crowded plaza and veered north up the promenade, which was lined with aging beachfront condos. Walker couldn't get to the promenade without running over a lot of people, so he made a sharp right onto Harbor. He traveled parallel to Danny and the promenade, stealing glances out his driver's-side window, catching brief glimpses of the con man across parking lots and between condos in his bright-yellow jersey.

Walker knew that up ahead were the sprawling Ventura County Fairgrounds and a small Amtrak station. That's where he would cut Cole off and take him down.

Two bicyclists in yellow jerseys suddenly cut across Walker's path. He stomped on his brakes to avoid hitting them, his car coming to a rubber-burning, fishtailing, ear-ringing halt. But it wasn't the man and woman from the bank. These were two people he'd never seen before.

That's when he saw the sea of yellow jerseys and the hundreds of bicyclists that filled the fairgrounds' parking lot in front of him. A huge banner and an arch made of multicolored balloons announced that this was the starting spot for the VENTURA TO SANTA BARBARA BIKE-A-THON FOR MUSCULAR DYSTROPHY.

Shit.

◆　◆　◆

Danny rode fast along the promenade, weaving through the people strolling, roller-skating, and walking their dogs, the high tide crashing against the boulders to his left and spraying him with sea mist. To his right, behind the condo complexes he was passing, he caught flashes of the pickup truck that had started following him when he left the bank.

He had no idea who was chasing him, whether it was one of Grillo's soldiers or a cop, but he wasn't worried. He'd shake his pursuer when he reached the fairgrounds and lost himself among the hundreds of other bicyclists dressed just like him.

A dog snarled furiously as Danny passed, broke free of the woman walking him, and charged after the bike. Danny looked back at the vicious beast and, in that instant, collided with a man, who tumbled down the rocky embankment and splashed into the churning surf. Danny flipped over his handlebars and landed hard on the pavement.

The woman grabbed her dog's leash just as the beast's slavering jaws were inches from Danny's face on the ground. Danny got up and saw the man, facedown in the water, his body being smashed against the rocks.

Danny looked ahead, the fairgrounds and bicyclists only fifty yards away. He could still make it into the crowd before whoever was chasing him caught up. But what about the man in the water? How much time did he have left?

He swore to himself, slipped off his messenger bag, and hurried down the slippery rocks. He grabbed the unconscious man by his shirt, dragged him up onto the promenade, laid him on his back, and began giving him mouth-to-mouth.

◆　◆　◆

Walker braked hard, got out of his truck, and scanned the sea of yellow-clad bike riders.

Danny Cole was somewhere in that crowd. But Walker knew with crushing certainty that by the time he got reinforcements here to lock the place down, Danny and his crew would be long gone, having changed out of their jerseys and escaped any number of ways: by car, by foot, by bus, by train, perhaps even by windsurfing.

Yeah, that would be Cole's style. Just sail away, giving him the finger as he went along the water.

Walker heard sirens approaching behind him, and when he turned in the direction of the sound, he looked south down the promenade. To his astonishment, he saw Danny Cole on his knees, soaking wet, and giving a man on the ground mouth-to-mouth. The bike was on the ground, too, and a crowd was gathering, including a woman fighting to hold back her barking dog, who strained at its leash to get to Cole.

Walker hurried over just as the man on the ground began coughing up water. The man was in his fifties, also wet, blood seeping from a wound on his head. But he was breathing, and that's what mattered.

Cole leaned away from the man and reached for a messenger bag, but Walker beat him to it. He lifted it up and peered inside. It was stuffed with cash. Walker opened his coat to flash the badge and gun clipped to his belt.

"Andrew Walker, US Marshals. You're under arrest, Cole."

"What for?"

"I have no idea, but if I don't think of something, I'm sure the Feds and the DEA will. This bag is full of marked money."

Cole looked over at the fairgrounds and sighed with resignation. Walker followed his gaze and saw a paramedic unit and a fire truck arriving. Someone must have called 911. But Walker knew that wasn't what Cole was thinking about. His crew had escaped. At least the con wasn't a total disaster.

"Lie facedown, hands behind your back," Walker said.

Cole did as he was told. As Walker cuffed Cole, the dog lifted his leg, looked the con man in the eye, and peed on his bike.

"Perfect," Cole said. "Just perfect."

Walker grabbed him by the arms and pulled him up to his feet.

"Could be worse. He could have peed on you." Walker led Cole to his truck as the paramedic rushed over to help the man on the ground.

CHAPTER TWO

Seven months later, Danny Cole was back in Ventura, wearing a Tom Ford suit and sitting in the Superior Court, listening to his lawyer, Karen Tennant, present her closing argument to the stone-faced jury.

Karen was in her early thirties, poised and sharply dressed in a slim-fit, black Balenciaga hourglass jacket over a fitted Dolce & Gabbana white poplin tuxedo shirt and black, skinny leg slacks. She radiated intelligence, success, and a brutal athleticism that suggested that to stay fit, she preferred hand-to-hand combat, perhaps Krav Maga, over jogging or riding a Peloton.

"Danny Cole conned a very bad man out of a lot of money and set him up to be arrested. It worked perfectly," she said. "Mr. Cole could have fled and been rich but he didn't do that. Instead, he stopped to save a man's life. That's how he was caught and that's why he's here today. That tells you a lot about Mr. Cole's character. When it comes right down to it, he's a decent man."

She delivered that last line with absolute sincerity, which, Danny thought, either proved he'd successfully conned her or that she was a natural con artist herself. There was no question that she had her own ethical failings. He'd met her when they were both students at Stanford Law School, where he'd been accepted on the strength of a faked transcript and paid his astronomical tuition by selling stolen exams. She'd been one of his best customers. But Karen's cheating in law school didn't shake his faith today in her legal abilities. He was certain she would have graduated near the top of her class without his illicit help, though perhaps not summa cum laude, and she'd become a successful criminal defense attorney totally on her own merits.

Karen gave him an appraising look, as if judging his moral character in real time and finding it satisfactory, then returned her attention to the jury to continue her closing argument.

"Did the defendant commit a crime? Technically yes, he did. He swindled someone. Who did he con? Diego Grillo, a vicious, sadistic drug lord who ordered the torture and murders of his rivals and is responsible for the deaths of countless people who took his fentanyl-laced heroin," she said. "Do you really care if he was ripped off by Danny Cole . . . or anybody else? Of course not. Screw him. Because people like Grillo are not who the law exists to protect. It protects you, and me, and society from people like him. In fact, thanks to Mr. Cole's actions, a notorious drug lord that law enforcement has been trying, and failing, to build a case against for years is now in a federal prison for life . . . and his entire criminal operation has crumbled. The state should be grateful to Mr. Cole. They should have told him that what he did was stupid, wrong, and illegal. However, to show their gratitude for the good that came out of it, they were going to pin a medal on his chest and let him go with a warning: don't pull this crap again, or next time, you'll go to prison."

She glanced with disdain at the prosecutor, Norman Rifkin, who sat in his chair with a vaguely amused expression on his face that conveyed that he wasn't taking her argument seriously, and neither should the jury. He had the demeanor of a grade-school principal in a constant battle to control unruly students. And the yarmulke he wore, Danny thought, was a nice touch. It made him seem pious and honest. Perhaps he should have worn one, too. Or a cross around his neck.

Karen continued: "But no, they were embarrassed that he did their job for them . . . that he made them look like fools. So instead, they arrested him and he has served seven months in jail while awaiting trial on the charge of . . . *what*? Trying to cheat a horrible man out of his blood money? Come on. What kind of crime is that? How does that harm society, you, and me? It doesn't. Danny Cole has already been punished enough for what he did. More than enough. Frankly, he should never have been prosecuted."

Karen half turned toward Danny so that the jury could still see her face and her gaze of admiration tinged with a trace of sadness, an expression that said: he's a good man who's been horribly wronged. Danny tried to appear modest, humble, and a bit sad himself in response.

She faced the jury again. They didn't seem to him to be possessed by moral outrage at his unfair treatment. They looked constipated. That was never a good sign.

"It would be unjust and immoral to punish him any further," she said. "You know that in your hearts. That is what your conscience is telling you. Listen to it. Right this wrong. Find him not guilty so he can walk out that door today and begin the hard work of building on his inherent decency to become a better man. Thank you."

Karen returned to the defense table and sat down next to Danny. The jowly judge took a moment to jot down some notes or to finish the crossword puzzle he'd been surreptitiously working on. Danny rarely missed anything surreptitious, since he operated on the same wavelength.

Danny whispered in Karen's ear, "You seem pleased with yourself."

"It was a great closing statement."

"Until the end," he said. "What's wrong with the man I am already?"

"You're a crook."

"The jury hasn't decided that yet."

"Yes, they have," she said. "What they haven't decided is how hard to punish you for it."

The judge looked up and asked the prosecutor if he wanted to use his remaining time, left over from his closing statement, for a rebuttal.

Rifkin stood. "I certainly do, Your Honor."

"Proceed," the judge said with a nod that wobbled his chins.

The prosecutor stood, shaking his head and smiling as he approached the jury.

"It takes chutzpah to portray Danny Cole as a hero. But I get it. The defense can't deny the crimes Cole committed, so they are embracing them in a laughable attempt to change the narrative."

In other words, Danny thought, it's a con, and a pretty audacious one at that. What better way to defend a con man?

"Here's the truth. Cole is a professional con man and thief. He doesn't target rich drug lords like Diego Grillo because he hates what they've done. He does it because he wants their money, no matter how much blood is on it. He does it because he knows that crooks, greedy by nature, are the easiest marks of all . . . and that after he's fleeced them, they won't tell anyone, especially not the police. Cole knew we were watching and cleverly set up Grillo for capture and prosecution to prevent him from seeking retribution."

Rifkin was absolutely right, and Danny was truly proud of the scheme. It was one of his best.

"It was a brilliant con except that fate, in the form of Frank Hardison, intervened. Yes, Cole saved Mr. Hardison's life, but not out of altruistic concern for his fellow man," Rifkin said. "He did it for purely selfish reasons. He knew that if Mr. Hardison died, the police would certainly be after him this time, and not just for some swindle, but for manslaughter."

Was that why he did it? Danny didn't think so. It was the sight of the man facedown in the water, being bashed against the rocks by the surf, that had compelled him to scramble down the rocks to help. He might have done the same thing if it had been the dog instead. Nobody but Diego Grillo and his gang deserved to be hurt by Danny's actions.

Rifkin sneered at him, shaking his head in disgust.

"It was Cole's ruthless greed and avarice that put Mr. Hardison's life in danger and he knew it. You do, too. It proves that Cole's crimes, and that's *exactly* what they are, aren't isolated incidents. They can and *do* harm others."

Rifkin faced the jury and, as he spoke, made direct eye contact with every single person. His gaze was firm and authoritative.

"Don't be duped by another one of Danny Cole's cons. Don't be suckers. He needs to be punished for his crimes to the fullest extent of the law. That's the only way he'll ever change. Otherwise, he's going to walk out that door laughing at you, then meet up in Mexico with his accomplices to sip mojitos on his yacht while counting his share of Diego Grillo's drug money. That's not justice. It's an affront to decency, morality, and the law and a personal insult to each and every one of you."

Rifkin returned to his seat and the judge began giving the jury their instructions for deliberation.

Danny whispered to Karen, "I don't have a yacht. I get seasick floating on my back in a swimming pool."

She whispered back, "He's sending you a message. He's telling you it's not too late to give up your accomplices, and the money, and take their plea deal. He must be really worried about losing. I told you it was a great closing."

Danny shook his head. "No, he's sure he's won. I'm good at reading people. It's the key to my success."

"That's why you're sitting here."

Danny ignored the cheap shot. "He's thinking about his chances for promotion, which will be a lot higher if he recovers the money than if he scores a lengthy prison term for me. He's looking for a win-win situation."

"If that's what you think," Karen said, "then take the plea."

"Is that what you were signaling in your closing when you implied that I should get out for time served? That I was willing to take his offer if he sweetened it?"

She shrugged and doodled some squares within squares on her legal pad. "I may have opened the door and he stepped through it. It's called good lawyering."

"I won't betray my friends to save myself."

"Honor among thieves is such a cliché," she said. "Why bother?"

"You're the one who said I am inherently decent."

The judge finished with his instructions to the jury and sent them away to begin their deliberations over lunch. Danny was allowed to have lunch in a guarded conference room with his lawyer rather than being sent straight back to lockup, at least for the rest of the day.

In the conference room, Danny and Karen sat down at a gunmetal table, where two cold white-bread ham sandwiches waited in clear plastic containers along with two cans of Coke and two tiny bags of Fritos. The windows were barred, in case Danny was thinking about taking a flying leap to freedom five floors down.

Danny tore open the bag of Fritos. The sandwiches looked to him like they could have been stuck in a vending machine for days, weeks, or even years. It reminded him that he was facing the same fate, minus the shrink-wrap. He hoped he would emerge from his lockup looking better than the sandwiches.

He said, "I want you to start working on getting me admitted into the state's volunteer convict firefighting program."

Karen popped open a Coke and took a sip. "Don't be so negative. The jury hasn't begun their deliberations yet. Or even eaten their lunch, which has to be a lot better than ours."

"I always have a backup plan," he said. "I'm a nonviolent offender in good physical condition. That makes me the ideal candidate for the program."

She grimaced in disagreement. "Convict firefighting is slave labor, a modern-day chain gang, only worse, because instead of digging ditches or laying track, you're risking your life for nothing. You'd have to be crazy to do it."

"California prisons have twice the murder rate of all prisons in the US combined and three times the civilian rate," he said between bites of the chips. "The odds are even higher for me if there are any Viboras in my prison and they find out what I did to Grillo."

"The transcript is sealed. The prosecutors have assured me your identity is protected."

He waved that argument aside. "Okay, let's say I believe that. Even if I don't get killed, there's a high likelihood that I will be repeatedly beaten and raped in my cell just for being adorable."

"You are adorable," she said. "That's true."

"I can take my chances in prison, or I can volunteer to serve my sentence in a low-security camp in the woods, where I'll sleep safely in a bunkhouse, spend most of my time outdoors, and the only danger I will face is an occasional fire. I'd be crazy not to do it."

Karen finished her Coke, set the can down hard, like a gavel, and gave him a stern look.

"Here's what you're overlooking. The world is in a pressure cooker of greenhouse gases and, in case you haven't noticed, California is in an epic, catastrophic drought that's only going to get worse. They won't be little bonfires, Danny. They will be apocalyptic wildfires that wipe out entire communities. The wrath of God, that's what you will be facing."

Danny shrugged. "It's still safer than prison. Even the food is better."

"That's because the Department of Corrections knows that each meal could be your last."

He gave her his best smile, the one that sparked a twinkle in his eyes that weakened the resolve of his marks. "The camps are also more liberal when it comes to conjugal visits."

She arched a perfectly tweezed eyebrow. "Really? Who are you expecting to see?"

"You could visit me," he said. "Think of it as a weekend in the country."

"I don't like pine needles in my bed and I don't have sex with convicts. The only women who do are lunatics with bad hair," she said. "It would kill my career as a criminal defense attorney."

"You've slept with me many times."

"Before you were arrested. That's entirely different. But you might get lucky after the jury acquits you."

"I'd already be incredibly lucky."

"Have some faith in me," Karen said. "I'm an excellent lawyer."

The guard knocked on the door but didn't wait to be asked in.

"The jury is back," he said.

"So soon?" Karen said. "They hardly had time to eat their free lunch."

"They must have been served these." Danny nodded to the sandwiches on the table as he got up and put his hands behind his back so the guard could cuff him. "And there's an In-N-Out Burger across the street. I can smell it in here."

"The fast verdict could be good news."

It was unlikely and they both knew it. The guard cuffed Danny, grasped him firmly by the forearm, and led him to the door. Danny threw a look over his shoulder at Karen, who followed them.

"The state prisons in Jamestown and Susanville provide most of the inmates that go into the convict firefighters' program," he said. "You have to get me sentenced to one of them."

"I will," she said.

And she did.

CHAPTER THREE

Present Day
Wednesday Morning

The 710 freeway, which was completed in 1964, started at the Port of Long Beach and came to an abrupt end twenty-six miles north, on Valley Boulevard in Alhambra, five miles shy of where it was supposed to join with the southern terminus of the 210 freeway in South Pasadena. Construction of the final, short connecting piece was delayed by legal disputes, but the state went ahead and bought the hundreds of homes that it would need to demolish to build it and rented them out to people in the meantime. More than fifty years later, with the freeway project still mired in court, the state finally gave up hope, and being landlords, and sold the homes.

Los Angeles County sheriff's detective Walter Sharpe had bought one of the homes, a rambling and crumbling Craftsman that he'd been renting from the state for decades. He'd left the house at 6:30 a.m. that December morning, stopped by Randy's to pick up a few donuts and two take-out coffees, and driven south to a convenience store parking lot at the corner of Valley Boulevard and Highbury Avenue, a half block from where the 710 ended.

While Sharpe waited for his confidential informant to arrive, he listened to KNX News Radio and learned that a federal plan to connect the two freeways with a $6 billion tunnel was stalled by more legal challenges. Sharpe figured he wouldn't have to worry about any construction shaking his house for another fifty years, a problem his kids could deal with, because he'd be long dead.

At 7:15, a man in a red Jeep Cherokee pulled up beside his black county-issue Chevy Tahoe SUV and stopped driver's side to driver's side. They both had their windows rolled down. The other man, Sid Mercer, a dispatcher for the Los Angeles County Fire Department, still wore his uniform. He was on his way home after his night shift. Sid was in his fifties, like Sharpe, but he was easily thirty pounds heavier, if not more. Someday Sid would need to use the Jaws of Life just to get in and out of his car.

"Good morning," Sid said.

"You look tired. Busy night?"

"No more than usual. I was born tired."

Sharpe believed that. People often said that about him, too, because he'd never lost the baby fat on his face, which was adorable when he was a kid but, as he aged, became craggy, droopy folds of skin that made him look perpetually weary. Some people interpreted his default expression as cynicism, disapproval, or general disinterest, misconceptions about him and his attentiveness that often worked in his favor. The slight, natural slouch in his shoulders only heightened the effect and he wasn't beyond exploiting that, too. He enjoyed being underestimated.

Sid handed Sharpe a file folder in exchange for a bag of donuts and a cup of coffee.

"They were out of maple bars this morning," Sharpe said. "I got you apple fritters instead."

"It's okay. The doctor says I need more fruit in my diet."

"Maybe cut out the donut part and just go with the fruit."

"What kind of diet is that?" Sid took a big bite out of a fritter and nodded appreciatively. "It's unnatural and inhumane."

Sharpe held up the file. "Any work in here for me?"

"Nope," Sid said between chews. It's what he always said.

So that meant that he'd find at least two, maybe more arsons that some clueless firehouse captain had missed and classified as accidents or acts of nature. "We'll see. Don't fall asleep at the wheel."

Sid held up his coffee cup. "That's what this is for. See you tomorrow."

They both drove off their separate ways. Sid, to his home in West Covina and Sharpe to his office only a few blocks away, in the arson and explosives unit of the Los Angeles County Sheriff's Department.

As Sharpe carried the file, an apple fritter, and the coffee down the hallway toward his office, he passed Earl Detmer, his night-shift counterpart, who was on his way out. How Detmer managed to work an entire shift without wrinkling his crisp green tactical uniform was one mystery Sharpe had never been able to solve. The one he wore was always rumpled, even after it was cleaned and pressed.

"How was your night, Earl?"

"Eventful. A proud father up in Stevenson Ranch shot off fireworks at a gender-reveal party, sparking an out-of-control brush fire that's at a hundred acres now and zero percent contained."

"I saw that on the news last night before I went to bed," Sharpe said. "At least it happened a few days before the Santa Anas are expected to hit."

The Santa Anas were hot, dry westerly winds blasted down on drought-parched Southern California from the Sierra Nevada at more than fifty miles an hour, jacking up temperatures and sucking up all the moisture in the air, relentlessly for days at a time, creating nightmarish fire conditions.

"You're assuming the fire can be contained by then," Detmer said.

"I'm naturally optimistic," Sharpe said.

"That's what you're famous for," Detmer said. "Your cheery disposition. It's all over your face."

"Did you arrest the man who set off the fireworks?"

"Yeah, for being criminally stupid. Speaking of which, three hours after that, a woman in West Hollywood reported her car stolen. Turns out, it had been found on fire in a vacant lot in Culver City early in the evening. Imagine that."

He didn't have to. It happened all the time. "Was she underwater on her payments?"

It was a safe assumption. A burning stolen car more often than not belonged to owners who were upside down on car payments and hoping to get out from under the crushing debt. The problem with the plan was that car thieves didn't burn cars—they stripped them for parts. And people who stole cars to commit crimes would ditch them, but rarely burn them, because it would draw too much attention.

"Oh yeah," Detmer said. "Knew it the moment I saw the dealer's name on the license plate rim."

Kempton Ford. Or Kempton Toyota. Or Kempton Chevrolet.

Orville Kempton was notorious for writing long-term, high-interest car loans that saddled people with vehicles that cost more to pay off than they were worth, sometime twice as much. He had car dealerships all over Southern California.

"Kempton is the one who should be in jail," Sharpe said, "not the poor woman who got stuck with that loan."

"Nobody put a gun to her head to sign it."

"You're all heart, Earl. Any leftovers on the table for me?" Sharpe said, referring to open cases from the night before that needed additional follow-up.

"Nope, table's clean and I did all the dishes."

"Thanks," Sharpe said. Detmer was a good, dependable detective, and Sharpe respected him. But Sharpe was better.

Sharpe continued on to his office, a space prized among the detectives for having both privacy and sunlight from a window overlooking the parking lot. There was also a window out to the squad room, theoretically allowing some of his sunshine to be shared by the poor slobs in cubicles. But no light escaped from Sharpe's office because it was stuffed with . . . stuff.

He negotiated a well-worn indirect path on the linoleum between teetering stacks of papers, files, binders, and instruction manuals, then ducked past a coatrack tipping precariously from the weight of many jackets, coats, and hats, to arrive at his metal desk, where the only space not covered by books, notepads, or office equipment was a doodle-covered blotter. The layers of doodles were so thick, the white blotter was inked nearly solid black.

Sharpe sat down in his duct-taped-covered desk chair, which emitted a chorus of creaks and groans against his modest weight, and then he unfolded his napkin on the blotter like a tablecloth, smoothed it out, and set his fritter and coffee cup on it.

He was preparing to eat his breakfast and read the file his CI had given him, as a ritual he followed every morning, when there was a knock on his open door.

Andrew Walker stood in Sharpe's doorway wearing his cowboy hat, sport coat, a collared shirt, jeans, and a new pair of boots. He had a gun and his newly minted deputy's badge clipped to his belt, but it wasn't the first badge he'd ever worn, and it was far from his first day as a cop. Even so, it felt like he was a rookie again, despite all of his experience, and he didn't like it.

"Are you Sharpe?" Walker asked, pronouncing the detective's name as "Sharp-A," as if there were an accent *aigu* over the *e* at the end.

Sharpe looked up at Walker with undisguised disapproval, or perhaps that was just the permanent expression on his droopy, craggy face.

"Who told you that?" The way Sharpe spoke, like his mouth was slightly full, made Walker wonder if maybe he had some food, or a wad of chewing tobacco, tucked under his cheek. But Walker didn't see a tobacco tin or a spittoon anywhere and his fritter appeared untouched.

"The name on the door," Walker said, tapping it for emphasis.

"I mean"—Sharpe paused, as if he might spit out whatever was in his mouth—"who told you to pronounce it that way?"

"The desk officer. He said it was the French pronunciation. I'm Andrew Walker, the new deputy."

"You're early." Sharpe set down the folder he'd been about to read and picked up another one off a pile on his desk. "Do I look French to you?"

"You could be Philippe Noiret's twin brother." Walker came in, edged cautiously past the tipping coatrack, and took a seat in one of the two guest chairs. It wobbled unevenly under him, one leg shorter than the others.

Sharpe opened the file and looked down at the pages. "Who is Philippe Noiret?"

"A French actor."

Sharpe raised his eyes but not his head, which made the detective appear deeply, weepily sad. "You don't look like someone who watches French movies."

"My wife does. They put me to sleep. How can you be French and not know Philippe Noiret?"

"I'm not French."

"So why do you pronounce your name 'Sharp-A'?"

Now Sharpe lifted his head, too. "I don't."

Walker looked back at him, studying him anew, and got it. *Shar-Pei.* Like the dog with all the folds on his face. It was the detective's well-earned nickname. The desk officer had set him up. Even so, Walker grinned. "I see it now."

"See what?"

"Nothing," Walker said, not wanting to offend his new partner—and, technically, his commanding officer—in his first five minutes on the job.

Sharpe let it go. "You're an ex–US marshal. From what I've read in your file, you weren't bad at it. Why did you want to give that up to be an arson investigator?"

He didn't. But after eleven years of running all over California chasing fugitives and getting shot at, Walker's body was showing the wear and tear and so was his marriage. He had a bum knee, shotgun pellets in his back, and a wife who was eight months pregnant. It was time to slow down. Or so he'd been told.

"Chasing bad guys all over the place is hard on the body. I want a job where I mostly use my head."

"Are you smart?"

"I may still have one or two brain cells left," Walker said.

Sharpe took a sip of his coffee and seemed to regret it, setting the cup down and away from him, almost out of reach, as if it had offended him. Walker decided there wasn't anything in Sharpe's mouth. It was just how his cheeks hung. He wondered if there were cheek exercises he could do to make sure that never happened to his own face.

"What do you know about arson?" Sharpe asked.

"I once set a fugitive's Corvette on fire to draw him out of his house, but other than that, not much."

"How did you do it?"

"Simple. I broke the driver's window, dropped a Duraflame log on the front seat, squirted lighter fluid all over the interior, tossed in a match, and *whoosh*!" He used his hands to illustrate the big flames. The torching had been one of his proudest moments, though he'd nearly set his hat and eyebrows on fire.

"How did you avoid losing your badge for that?"

"The guy came out shooting and didn't survive to file a complaint." He'd shot the guy, an escaped killer, three times in the chest. He was dead before he hit the ground.

"Lucky you," Sharpe said.

"I don't know anything about fire but I know a lot about crooks, how they think, how they run, and where they hide. That's what I bring to the party."

"Pursuing fugitives is entirely different than figuring out if a fire was arson, proving who did it, and making the arrest."

"I can learn it."

"The job is mostly sitting and thinking. We rarely torch cars or shoot people. Are you going to get bored?"

"I sure hope so. I'm married with a kid on the way," Walker said. "Time to settle down and be present for my family." Carly had given him an ultimatum: spend more time at home or find a new one. She wasn't going to raise a kid on her own, which she was sure would happen if, best-case scenario, he was hardly around or, worse-case scenario, he got himself killed.

"'Be present'?" Sharpe said. "Are you in therapy?"

"My wife is a shrink."

"That must be convenient." Sharpe took a bite of his fritter and chewed it thoughtfully for a moment, studying Walker. "What's with the cowboy hat? You from Texas?"

"Burbank. I saw a cop wearing one on TV and liked the look," Walker said. "Plus it scares the fugitives. It makes them think I'm gun crazy."

"Are you?"

He honestly wasn't sure. "Maybe a little."

Sharpe glanced at the file for reference. "You've shot seventeen men."

"Is that a lot?"

"I've never shot anybody in over twenty years in the department."

That was hard for Walker to believe. "Not even a little?"

"Is it possible to shoot someone only a little?"

"I'm working on it," Walker said.

Sharpe gave him a long look, then stood up and headed for the door. "Give me a second. Don't eat my fritter."

Walker sat for a moment, pretty sure that Sharpe was going to the lieutenant to see if there was some way to get him reassigned to someone else or booted from the arson squad entirely.

He got up and browsed the piles of junk. His attention was drawn to an assortment of things on top of a teetering stack of binders. There were a few watches, a cigarette taped inside a matchbook, and several loose light bulbs filled with some kind of powder. And there was an oven timer wired to a nine-volt battery and duct-taped to a pair of road flares. That last item caught his eye.

Was that . . . *a bomb?*

Walker picked it up to study it more closely.

"Put that down before you blow up the building," Sharpe said, slouching in the doorway.

Walker carefully set the bomb back atop the unstable binder tower. "You keep explosives in your office?"

"I'm certainly not going to bring them home." Sharpe edged past him to the desk and sat down again. "We don't wear plain clothes in arson. Come in tomorrow in tactical greens."

It was the standard uniform for an LASD special weapons and tactical officer. He hadn't worn any kind of uniform in years and he wasn't looking forward to it now. But he nodded. "You went to see the lieutenant?"

"I went to another office and called him. We talked."

"You couldn't get me bounced?"

"Nope," Sharpe said.

Walker wasn't offended and had some sympathy for him. "I don't like working with a partner, either. It's going to be an adjustment for both of us. You teach me arson and I'll teach you manhunting."

Sharpe tore off a piece of his fritter and put it in his mouth. "That's what the lieutenant just told me. But I already know what I'm doing."

"Contrary to popular belief, Shar-Pei, you can teach an old dog new tricks."

Walker grinned. Sharpe didn't.

The desk phone rang. Sharpe answered it, responded affirmatively to some questions, and wrote an address down on the folder that he'd been about to read before Walker came in. Sharpe ended the call by saying he was on his way and hung up the phone.

Walker said, "You meant 'we're on the way.'"

"No, I didn't."

"I'm here and I'm getting paid to work today," Walker said. "I might as well earn it."

"Fine." Sharpe tossed him a set of keys. "You drive, Hoss."

Sharpe grabbed the folder, shoved it into a backpack he had under the desk, picked up his donut with the napkin, and they headed out.

CHAPTER FOUR

The Los Angeles County Sheriff's Department was the law in the unincorporated areas of the county and any municipalities without their own police departments. Their jurisdiction was a patchwork of places often entirely surrounded by, or butting up against, the patrol areas of other law enforcement agencies. East Pasadena, where Sharpe and Walker were now headed, was one of those places. It was a noncontiguous, unincorporated residential and industrial area encircled by the cities of Pasadena to the west and north, Arcadia to the east, and San Gabriel to the south.

But since none of those police departments, Sharpe explained to Walker, was particularly eager to investigate arsons, he didn't anticipate any conflicts over jurisdiction on this case. Sharpe wanted Walker to know what they were getting into so there wouldn't be any awkwardness at the scene.

"Those cops don't have the skills and don't like getting soot on their shoes," Sharpe said as Walker took the Rosemead Boulevard exit off eastbound Interstate 10 and headed north in Sharpe's Chevy Tahoe.

"What's the story on this one?" Walker asked, glancing at the Google Maps display on his phone, following the directions to the address that Sharpe had given him.

"A young woman supposedly tried to burn down her parents' house," Sharpe said. "The fire department quickly extinguished the blaze and a couple of deputies are holding her for us."

"Seems cut-and-dry," Walker said. "What do they need us for?"

"It's not arson until we say it is."

"Even if she was caught in the act?"

"She says she didn't do it."

"Of course she does," Walker said. "I'm sure she always carries a gasoline can and a match around the house."

Sharpe looked at him. "Who said anything about gasoline?"

"Okay, so how'd the fire start?"

"I don't know. It's our job to answer that question," Sharpe said. "It's a mistake to make any assumptions until we've actually observed the evidence at the scene."

"What do the firefighters think?"

"They don't."

The definitive nature of the statement, and the animosity behind it, surprised Walker. "Aren't firefighters the experts on fire?"

"They are the experts on water. They love the surround-and-drown method of suppression, pouring thousands of gallons of water on a fire for hours, washing away all the evidence of how the blaze was started. And if the water doesn't destroy the crime scene, all those firefighters carelessly stomping through the place and moving stuff around does. Firefighters are the best friends an arsonist can have," Sharpe said, and then added: "Firemen spray, cops think."

Walker thought the adage was a harsh appraisal, one that Sharpe had likely shared many times before. "Firefighters must love you."

"I don't want to be loved," Sharpe said. "I want to close cases."

That was the first encouraging thing Walker had heard from Sharpe so far. "Same goes for me."

Walker took a left onto East California and then a right on Vallombrosa Drive into a cul-de-sac where water was running down the street from another cul-de-sac a half block up the road. The residential neighborhood was lush and green, despite the drought, full of well-watered front lawns, tall palm trees, and overgrown pines around well-maintained 1970s-era tract homes.

"Firefighters know nothing about criminal investigation or forensics and don't care to learn," Sharpe said. "But it's the fire chiefs who decide if a blaze is suspicious or not and whether we get called in to investigate. Most of the time they're wrong. And if there's no investigation, there's no arson."

"So, what you're saying is that most arsons in Los Angeles go unnoticed and that the bad guys get away with it."

"That's what would be happening," Sharpe said, "if I played by the rules."

Walker grinned. He was beginning to like this hound dog of a guy. "That's one more thing we have in common."

Sharpe looked at him again. "You're starting to scare me."

Walker kept his grin. "Pretty soon you're going ask me where you can get a Stetson."

He turned into the cul-de-sac, where a fire truck and an LASD patrol car were parked on the damp street and a dozen residents stood on the sidewalk, looking at the two-story house at the end, where a second-floor window was scorched from the inside out. Yellow crime scene tape was strung around the house, and two deputies stood chatting with a couple of the firefighters who were packing up their stuff.

"First lesson," Sharpe said as Walker parked. "Arson is done for a purpose and it's usually for revenge, money, or hiding another crime."

"So the torch and torched will have a personal connection. That makes it easy to find the bad guy."

Sharpe grimaced at the remark. "Identifying a suspect is one thing. Proving his guilt is another, and that requires evidence, which is hard to come by in a fire."

"What about the sickos who get off on watching things burn? Those must be the really hard ones. Or do you solve them by looking in the fire crowd for a guy with a boner?"

"That kind of arsonist is like a werewolf."

Walker looked back at Sharpe. "They only come out on a full moon?"

"They only exist in fiction."

Sharpe slung his backpack over one shoulder, got out, and approached the patrol car.

Walker followed him and could see a teenage girl in the back seat of the squad car, glowering furiously at them all, her hands behind her back, presumably because she was cuffed.

A deputy marched over to meet them. He was a freckle-faced guy with a Kevlar vest under his uniform that puffed him up and seemed to give him a more aggressive gait, even standing still. He pulled back his shoulders and puffed out his chest to accentuate the effect. His name tag read Simcox. If anybody in the cul-de-sac had a woody right now, Walker thought, it was the deputy.

Sharpe introduced himself and Walker and asked the deputy for a rundown.

"The home belongs to Tyler and Skye Penfold, who are away on a Caribbean cruise," Simcox said. "Their estranged eighteen-year-old daughter, Chloe, has been squatting in the place while they're gone."

Walker had never used the word "estranged" before and it sounded odd coming out of Simcox's mouth, too, like it scratched his tongue a bit on the way out. The word hadn't been polished smooth by previous use. He'd been saving it up for the right opportunity to sound smart.

Sharpe asked, "Have you reached her parents?"

"Nope," Simcox said, his thumbs hooked on his gun belt.

"So how do you know that she's *estranged* from them and isn't house-sitting?"

Apparently, Sharpe had noticed Simcox's use of the word, too, but for a different reason.

"The window in the kitchen door out back is broken, and besides, we know her. We've been here a lot. The last time was two years ago, when she burned down the garage."

Walker asked, "How'd she start that fire?"

Sharpe glowered at him. He obviously wasn't expecting Walker to speak.

Simcox said, "She was smoking weed and hid her pipe under some paint rags. Her parents declined to press charges but they threw her out of the house. It's been quiet until now."

"What's her story this time?" Walker asked, pretending he hadn't seen Sharpe's admonishing look.

"Chloe says she was house-sitting, went to Starbucks for a coffee, came back, and was shocked to see firefighters here, battling flames upstairs."

"But you think she set the fire and, while she waited for it to get going, went out and got herself some *frappé crappé* to sip while she watched the house burn down."

"That's right," Simcox said. "She's trouble."

Walker stepped over to the car for a closer look at Chloe. Her jet-black hair was wild and her cheeks were tear streaked, but her eyes blazed with defiant fury. Walker smiled at her and turned to Sharpe and Simcox.

"She's not trouble," he said. "She's a stone-cold badass."

Sharpe sighed. "You want to be helpful, Walker? Check out the crowd for boners."

"Boners?" Simcox said.

Sharpe turned his back to them, opened the patrol car's back door, and leaned casually against it to get a look at Chloe. "I'm told you're quite a terror."

"I was," she said.

"So was I. When I was sixteen, I stole beer, hot-wired cars, and went on joyrides, until the night I slammed a Mustang into a tree and broke both of my arms. Made it hard to drink beer or drive after that."

"Bullshit," Chloe said. "There's no way a car thief can become a cop."

She had a point, Walker thought, still standing in the same spot, observing Sharpe at work, the old dog using that slouch and droopy face to his folksy advantage.

"I was a kid. My record was sealed, so my crimes were a secret," Sharpe said. "Besides, people change. They grow up."

"Or they get sent by their parents to Colorado for drug rehab and the psychiatric help they need."

Sharpe nodded. "You're telling me you didn't do this."

"I've been telling everybody. I got up. Took a shower. FaceTimed with my boyfriend. Went for coffee. Came home and the house was on fire. I have no idea how it started."

"Like the garage fire?"

She shook her head and rubbed her bare upper arm against the seat to scratch an itch. Walker noticed she had a slight rash, like sunburn or maybe poison oak, on her arm. "That was different. It was an accident, but it was my fault. This wasn't."

"How'd you get into the house?"

"With a key," she said. "I'm house-sitting."

"What about the broken window?"

"It was already broken when I got here, but that's no mystery," Chloe said. "The kids in the cul-de-sac behind us like to play baseball in the street and I found their ball in the kitchen sink."

"You didn't call the police?"

She leaned forward to show him her cuffed wrists. "Look how they are treating me. I'm not putting some poor kid through this for being a kid. It was an accident. It's not like they were shoplifting beers and stealing cars."

Sharpe smiled. "Don't tell anyone my secret while I'm away."

"It's safe with me. But what about him?"

She gestured to Walker, who thought she hadn't been paying any attention to him.

"His secrets are much worse than mine," Sharpe said.

He was probably right about that, Walker thought. Sharpe was more perceptive than he looked.

"Be right back," Sharpe said. He closed the door and walked toward the house. Walker fell into step beside him.

"I'd bet my left nut that you've never stolen a beer or anything else in your life," Walker said. "That was your interrogation technique."

"Why your *left* nut?"

"I'm pretty sure that's the one that doesn't carry its weight in the sperm department," Walker said. "I blame it for the two years of infertility shit we went through before we got lucky."

"I'm sorry I asked."

"Your interrogation technique is to say whatever you think will get the person to open up," Walker said. "I do the same thing."

They got to the front door, which had been broken open by the firefighters with an axe or crowbar. Sooty water still coursed in little streams down the steps of the soaked staircase and dripped from the second-floor landing into the entry hall. The entire house reeked of smoke.

"Is that so?" Sharpe said, stepping gingerly across the puddles, through the entry hall, toward the kitchen beyond. Walker followed him. Water dripped from the ceiling the whole way, like a light rain. He was glad to have the hat.

"For instance, depending on who I'm talking to, I've said that I'm single, married, divorced, and widowed," Walker said. "That I'm addicted to booze, drugs, day trading, porn, and gambling. That I was a foster child, an only child, a homeless child, and the eldest of six kids."

The only damage in the kitchen, besides the water running down the walls from upstairs, was the broken window, the glass on the floor, and the baseball in the sink. Sharpe used his phone to take some pictures, then returned to the stairs while Walker kept talking.

"I've said that my parents beat me, raped me, enslaved me, and sold me. That I've attempted suicide and have been diagnosed with cancer. And that I have had sex with prostitutes, children, elderly people, dead people, wild and domesticated animals, and a wide variety of pastries, meat, fruits, and vegetables."

"And that works for you?"

"Every time," Walker said. "But I have to take my hat off first so I'm not so intimidating. The action of doing it makes me seem sincere."

They went upstairs, their feet sloshing on the soaked carpet, and on to the master bedroom. Most of the damage was contained to one side of the room. The right side of the king-size bed was burned down to the box springs, the rest scorched. The fire had spread from the bed to the wall beside it, igniting the drapes and the window frame. Walker didn't have to be a seasoned arson investigator to see this wasn't an accident. Sharpe took more pictures.

Walker said, "It's obviously arson."

Sharpe examined where the headboard had been, which seemed to Walker to be the most intensely burned spot, then looked across the room to the flat-screen TV on the wall. "Why do you say that?"

"There's nothing here that would set the bed on fire. It's too warm out for an electric blanket, so it wasn't a short. Otherwise, a bed doesn't burst into flames unless my wife and I are making love on it."

"You're not seeing any accidental ignition source." Sharpe nodded. "That's a good observation." It sounded to Walker like Sharpe actually meant it. "So, how do you suppose the fire started?"

"A match and charcoal fluid? Gasoline? Paint thinner? What difference does it make? She did it. Forensics will tell you how."

"They might." Sharpe used tweezers to pick up some surviving scraps of linen, the edges scorched, and put them into an evidence baggie he took out of his backpack. Then he went to the master bathroom, which didn't make any sense to Walker, since it wasn't damaged by the fire.

There was a bath towel crumpled on the floor and a bunch of women's toiletries spread on the counter around the double sinks. Sharpe took pictures of everything, then opened a wicker hamper, looked inside, and took pictures of the clothes inside, too. Walker didn't understand why, especially since the crime was no mystery.

"The motive is clear," Walker said. "It's revenge, getting back at her parents for shipping her off to a rehab lockup in Colorado. It doesn't get more personal than torching their bed and burning down their house."

He was demonstrating that he'd listened to Sharpe's lecture about arson motives and that the crime scene ticked every box.

"That's true." Sharpe opened the shower, examined the bottles of shampoo, conditioner, and mousse, and photographed them. "How are we going to prove she did it and not someone who came in after she left?"

It's called police work, Walker thought. But what he said was: "We check every garbage can between here and Starbucks and find whatever she ditched."

"That's a lot of ground to cover."

"We'll get some deputies to help us with the legwork."

Sharpe stepped out of the shower. "Maybe we could if a person was murdered here and not a king-sized mattress."

"It's just us?"

"Afraid so."

Walker sighed. It was hard work, but at least there was no running or shooting involved, which, despite how much he complained about it, were his favorite parts.

"Fine. I'm not against dumpster diving for clues. It's good old-fashioned police work," Walker said. "But if it's just us, we'd better get started."

The two of them went outside. It was hot out, perhaps in the eighties, and that was going to make dumpster diving even more unpleasant than it already would be. In Walker's experience, hot trash smelled a lot worse than cold trash. The fire truck was gone, and so were most of the neighbors who'd been on the street. Only the patrol car remained, the two deputies sitting in the front seat, enjoying the AC. Walker realized that the other deputy hadn't said a single word to them since they'd arrived.

Sharpe stood for a minute on the sidewalk, taking in the climate. "It's going to be a scorcher today and the Santa Anas will be blowing through here this week. We're going to be busy."

"Because the wind makes people crazy."

"No," Sharpe said. "Because everything that can burn will."

Walker went toward their Tahoe, but Sharpe veered off to the patrol car instead. The rear window was rolled down in the back seat so Chloe could get some air. Sharpe leaned against the car and smiled at her.

"I like what you've done with your hair," Sharpe said. "It still looks wet."

"All I did was put mousse in it," she said.

"This morning?"

"Yeah, after my shower."

"Did you dry it?"

"No," she said. "I was going for the wet look, so what would have been the point of that?"

Walker wondered what the point was of Sharpe's question. Why was he so interested in her messy hair?

Sharpe said, "Okay, so then you laid on the bed, talked to your boyfriend for a while, and went to Starbucks."

"That's right."

"Did you turn on the AC when you left?"

"No, it wasn't this hot out yet."

Sharpe nodded, then: "How long have you had that rash?"

Now that he'd mentioned it, she noticed the itch again and rubbed the back of her shoulder against the seat. "I don't know, a few days. I think it's sunburn. Why?"

Walker had the same question for Sharpe. He'd noticed the rash before but didn't see how it mattered to the investigation.

"It makes me itch just looking at it," Sharpe said. "My daughter is your age and burns easily, too. Whenever she comes to visit us, she brings a week's worth of dirty laundry."

"Same," Chloe said. "It saves me quarters."

"Have you run a load yet?"

"As soon as I got here, but I also stripped my parents' bed and washed their sheets."

Sharpe cocked his head. "Just to be helpful?"

"Because I didn't know if they're clean or if they had some morning delight before they left. And I'm not sleeping on that," Chloe said. "It's too weird."

"Why sleep in their room at all?"

"Because I've outgrown a tiny twin bed covered with stuffed animals, which is how they've left my room, like a museum display. They have the best mattress and biggest TV in the house."

Walker couldn't see where this small talk was going, but Chloe didn't seem to mind it. She had nothing else to do and there wasn't anything confrontational or threatening about Sharpe's approach. Or, as far as Walker could see, relevant to the crime.

"Were you smoking in bed?" Sharpe asked. It was his first question with any edge to it. Maybe, Walker thought, he'd just been softening her up for this.

"I don't smoke anymore," Chloe said. "Why?"

"That's where the fire started."

"Then someone must have come in after I left and set it on fire."

"That's one possibility," Sharpe said.

An unlikely one, Walker thought.

The two deputies in the car had listened to the whole conversation in silence, but now Simcox spoke up. "Can we take her in for booking?"

"Not yet," Sharpe said. "I need you to stick around for another twenty minutes or so."

"I have to pee," the second deputy said.

"There's a bathroom in the house," Sharpe said. "It still works."

And with that, Sharpe headed back to the house. Walker trailed after him. They had work to do, and evidence to find, and none of it was in the house. It was out on the streets and there was a ticking clock.

Walker said, "We should call the garbage company, make sure they don't empty any dumpsters along the route from here to Starbucks before we can check them out. We could lose the evidence."

"You should go now and get right on that," Sharpe said without slowing. "I know that's where you shine. Follow her tracks. I'll catch up."

"What will you be doing?"

"Laundry."

Walker went back to the car and made some calls, then returned to the house, where he found Sharpe in the laundry room leaning against the dryer and reading a file. The washing machine was running, shaking and rattling as it churned the clothes inside. It sounded like a struggle. The entire room reeked of chlorine. Walker immediately felt a headache coming on and was surprised Sharpe was still conscious.

"It smells like a swimming pool in here," Walker said, taking a step out. Even the smoky air in the house was an improvement.

"Yeah. They bought cheap generic detergent from China at the dollar store." Sharpe tipped his head toward the box of detergent on top of the washer. The box read: SUPER POW DETERGENT: FORTIFIED WITH BLEACH FOR A SUPER WHITE CLEAN! "Shouldn't you be out on the mean streets following Chloe's trail?"

"I called the garbage company. We got lucky. Trash collection in the neighborhood was yesterday, so we've got the week if we need it."

"We won't," Sharpe said.

"Why are you doing her laundry?"

Sharpe looked up at Walker as if it were the dumbest question he'd ever heard. "We investigate the cause of a fire by using the scientific method. Are you familiar with it?"

"I'm a cop," Walker said, "not a scientist."

Sharpe scratched his bulbous nose. "In simple terms, it means we collect data to come up with a hypothesis, then we test that hypothesis to reach a conclusion. That's what I am doing."

"It looks to me like you're doing her laundry."

The washer stopped moving. Either the load was finished or the machine had died in the struggle.

"Look at that," Sharpe said. "The washer stopped."

"Does that mean we can leave now? Or are you going to dry and fold everything, too?"

"The machine is broken. It went straight from wash to spin." Sharpe pointed at the dial on the washer. "It skipped the rinse cycle."

"I'm sure they're clean enough."

Sharpe grabbed the box of detergent and walked past Walker, who once again had to follow him outside. Walker was already tired of feeling like he was just tagging along, even though they'd only been working together for one morning. This shit ended today.

Sharpe went straight to the patrol car and opened the back door.

"You can get out of the car now, Chloe. I apologize for your inconvenience." Sharpe looked at Simcox and his partner. "Uncuff her, Deputies. It wasn't arson."

Simcox got out and did as he was told, but he was clearly baffled. That made four of them, if Walker included himself, Chloe, and the other deputy.

"Then what started the fire?" Simcox asked.

"The washing machine," Sharpe said, then smiled at Chloe. "And your cheap parents."

Chloe rubbed her uncuffed wrists. "What did my parents do?"

"They bought cut-rate detergent." Sharpe held up the box of Super Pow to illustrate his point.

Walker didn't see the fault in that. "Why pay more for a name brand? Soap is soap."

"No, it's not," Sharpe replied. "The reason the laundry room smells like a swimming pool is because there's way too much chlorine in this fortified detergent. On top of that, the broken washing machine skips the rinse cycle, so the chlorine stays in the sheets, building up wash after wash after wash." Sharpe shifted his attention to Chloe and pointed to her arm. "That's why you got a rash sleeping in their bed."

Chloe scratched at her arm again. Just mentioning the rash made it itch. "But I don't get what started the fire. What was the spark?"

"You were," Sharpe said. "The mousse in your wet hair reacted with the chlorine in the sheets to create an exothermic chemical reaction."

Simcox said, "What's that?"

"Fire," Sharpe said.

Chloe thought about that for a moment, then asked, "So why wasn't I burned?"

"Because your hair got the pillowcase wet," Sharpe said, "but once you left the house, the mixture dried, it heated up, and that started the chemical reaction. We'll have to test the detergent and the sheets to be sure, but I'm certain of my conclusion."

"Thank you." Chloe gave Sharpe a hug, which he warmly accepted, giving her a fatherly pat on the back.

"I'm just doing my job."

Sharpe left his card with Chloe, bagged the detergent, and went back into the house, where Walker silently helped him bag the wet laundry and bottle of mousse and collect more samples of the sheets for the lab to analyze. Walker spent the time mentally reviewing everything they'd seen and that he'd missed. He wasn't too hard on himself. He lacked the technical knowledge to actually determine the cause of the fire, but he could appreciate the keen observation that was involved in Sharpe's conclusion.

When they got back in the Tahoe, Walker started up the engine and rolled down the window a crack to get the hot air out, and they idled while the air conditioner got the interior cool. He turned in his seat to face Sharpe. "I've got to hand it to you. That was some real impressive Sherlock Holmes stuff you did."

"No, it wasn't. It was simply the scientific method," Sharpe said. "Observe the evidence, develop a hypothesis, and then test it."

"Had you ever heard of wet hair starting a house fire before?"

"Nope."

"Then how did you know to look for it?"

"I didn't," Sharpe said. "But if Chloe was telling the truth, the fire had to start somehow. I simply followed the evidence."

The air was getting cool. Walker rolled up his window to keep the air in. "What if she was lying?"

"The evidence would have revealed it," Sharpe said. "Just like it revealed this solution."

"Maybe to you," Walker said. "Nobody else would've seen it."

"Then there would have been no evidence to charge her. She still would have walked away from this."

"Maybe from the law, but she'd have been convicted by her family," Walker said. "That court doesn't need evidence."

"Neither did you," Sharpe said.

Walker held up his hands in surrender. "Lesson learned. Are we going back to HQ? Or do you want to grab lunch first?"

"I want to see what's left of a West Hollywood apartment building that was blown up in a gas leak last night."

He gave Walker the address, and Walker typed it into the Google Maps app on his phone. "Did I miss the call from the dispatcher or the lieutenant sending us out there?"

"Nope."

Walker was confused. "I thought you had to wait for a heads-up from the fire department that something doesn't smell right before you can roll to a scene."

"If I always waited for that, half the arsons in this county would go undetected." Sharpe held up the file he'd brought with him from the office, which he'd been reading in the laundry room. "I start each day by reviewing the reports of all the fires in the county that the department responded to the previous night."

"So that's what you meant by not following the rules. How do you get your hands on those reports?"

The wily bastard.

"I have a CI inside the fire department."

The Google Maps lady gave them some directions. Walker pulled out and steered the Tahoe back to Rosemead Boulevard and then north toward the westbound 134 freeway.

"How does the fire department feel when you start poking around the ashes of fires they think don't need to be investigated?"

"They're usually long gone by then, so they don't know I'm doing it until I've caught the arsonist," Sharpe said. "Complaining about it then would only shine a big fat spotlight on their mistake."

"Yeah, but what happens when you show up uninvited and the firemen aren't gone yet?"

"Last time, they were hosing down a few hot spots and accidentally doused me right off my feet. Broke my wrist in three places." Sharpe pulled up his left sleeve to show some tiny scars, presumably from setting his bones with pins and screws. "Now it's screwed together like an IKEA coffee table."

Walker had only known Sharpe for a few hours, but he was still mad about what had been done to him. It wouldn't be happening again, that was for damn sure. "They won't pull that shit with me around or someone's likely to get shot."

"I don't think the lieutenant would appreciate that."

"Don't be so sure. Maybe it's why he paired us up. The more cases you solve, the better he looks."

Sharpe gave him a look that Walker read as a thoughtful reappraisal.

"You may have a point," he said.

CHAPTER FIVE

Six Years Ago

It was early afternoon in Montecito, California, but thick smoke blotted out the sun, making the flaming crowns of the burning trees on the ridges and down in the canyons look like giant sparklers against the roiling, dark clouds.

Danny Cole dangled over a ravine that was churning with flames. He slashed away with a roaring chain saw at the brush on the steep hillside around him while Arnie Soloway, his newbie "bucker," held him by the belt so he wouldn't plunge to his death.

The two men led a line of fourteen convict firefighters in face shields, safety goggles, and bright-orange Nomex suits who were now cutting a swath of dry, naked earth in an attempt to deprive the voracious blaze below of the fuel it would need to rampage up the hill to a neighborhood of multimillion-dollar homes.

Danny was a "sawyer," hacking everything in their path, while their buckers watched their backs and tossed the cuttings down the hillside. Behind them, other convicts scraped the earth raw with hand tools. They took their orders from Hanrahan, the "swamper," an experienced convict firefighter who was in constant radio contact with the professional firefighters in charge of battling the wildfire.

There wasn't a single armed guard watching over the convicts and the only walls imprisoning them were made of flame. What set them clearly apart from other firefighters was the color of their Nomex uniforms and the letters CDCR on the back, which stood for California Department of Corrections and Rehabilitation. Professional firefighters wore yellow Nomex suits with their agency letters—LAFD, SBFD, and so on—emblazoned on the back.

Danny had never been so lean and ripped—with real muscle, not prison-yard weight-lifting muscle—a body shaped by the grueling daily hikes through the rocky Santa Monica Mountains carrying a twenty-pound chain saw and a fifty-pound pack of tools, food, and water. His once-smooth card-dealer's hands were calloused from months of cutting brush and digging fire road, and his fingernails were perpetually char-blackened from clawing through the smoking dirt of the after-blaze to grind out the remaining embers.

And now, Danny boiled in his own sweat inside the Nomex, sawing at the thick tangle of dry, sharp brush, moving with practiced, mechanical determination, the straining muscles in his arms, back, and legs throbbing with pain. He sucked scorching air into his soot-clogged throat and nostrils and down into his tight chest, searing his lungs.

It was miserable work, nothing he'd ever imagined himself doing.

But he had no regrets about choosing this over prison. Because most of his days were spent at a minimum-security firefighting camp in the Santa Monica Mountains, living out in the open air, the salty sea breezes wafting through the oaks against blue, perpetually sunny skies. A typical dinner was barbecue spareribs cooked on an outdoor grill and served at picnic tables under the stars.

Sure, each morning began with rigorous exercise—planks, step-ups, lunges, push-ups, crunches, and five-mile runs through the mountains—followed by a long day of carving fire roads out of the rugged hillside and clearing thick brush to prevent fires. But it made the days pass quickly. And he only occasionally had to risk his life.

Like he was right now, on an "out of country" job helping to fight a massive wildfire in Santa Barbara County, ninety-five miles north of Los Angeles. It was Danny's third field trip, but it was the first for Arnie, his new bucker. They'd worked together for a few months on smaller, less intense fires close to home, and the enormity and unfamiliar environment of this one were distracting him.

Arnie was a fast-talking, gregarious guy in his early thirties who ran a car-leasing scam. He'd find desperate people who couldn't afford their luxury car leases anymore and offer them a fast, simple way out—he'd take the cars and make a deal with their lenders to assume the remaining payments. The lessees would be out free and clear, no strings attached or dings on their credit rating. Of course, he never made any payments and either leased the cars to other suckers or sold them for cash. It was a doomed scheme, but it was lucrative for the few years it lasted, setting up him, his wife, and their two kids comfortably in a 4,500-square-foot house in Porter Ranch.

Bobby Logan, the bucker for Sam Mertz, the sawyer working alongside Danny, was distracted, too. Logan was a reedy, acne-scarred junkie in his twenties who'd stolen cars to feed his drug habit. He'd fought an out-of-country wildfire before in San Diego, but he wanted to be down in the flames, right in the heart of it, where the real risk was, not holding on to Mertz's belt with one hand and chucking the cut bushes and branches into the blazing chasm with the other.

Mertz was a barrel-shaped man in his forties with big cartoon-character hands that belied the extraordinary delicacy he used to crack safes, pick locks, or set explosives to get a vault open. But his expertise, from what Danny had gleaned from the anecdotes Mertz shared, was undermined by poor planning. Mertz needed someone like Danny to plot his heists if he wanted to stay out of prison.

Arnie Soloway clapped Danny twice on the shoulder, the signal to pause. Word had come down the line from Hanrahan. They were being swapped out for a while by a fresh convict crew, just arrived from

Yosemite. Everybody but Logan was glad to hear it. Logan loved it out here. He was bored and miserable during their downtime.

They trooped single file back to the road, passing the new crew as they came in, and took a school bus back to base camp, an evacuated high school in town. The parking lot was filled with tents, firefighting vehicles from all over the state, and several food trucks. The caterers had multiple huge barbecue grills going, cooking hamburgers, steaks, and chicken, and a buffet line with pizzas and pastas, fresh fruit and vegetables, and an array of desserts.

Danny's crew didn't stop to clean up. They dropped their tools and went straight to the buffet, grabbed trays, and heaped food onto their plates, then carried their meals to a picnic table in the schoolyard. All of the men were ravenous.

Arnie had a mountain of food in front of him that included two rib-eye steaks and a pile of macaroni and cheese on one plate, a huge slice of chocolate cake on another plate, a big bowl of melting ice cream, and two Cokes to wash it all down with. He sat at one end of a long picnic table with Mertz, Danny, and Logan.

"This is fucking great," Arnie said as he dug into his food.

Danny said, "I ache everywhere. I am drenched with sweat and black with soot. What am I missing?"

Arnie ate a mouthful of steak before answering. "I'm supposed to be doing five years in prison. Instead, I'm in Montecito eating dinner at Ruth's Chris."

Mertz regarded the morsel of rare steak on his fork. "Is that what I'm eating? Because all I'm tasting is smoke. I've got it everywhere. In my mouth, nose, even my ass."

"Don't try to eat your food through your ass and it will taste a lot better," Arnie said. "This is the best rib-eye steak I've ever had. And I'll tell you what it tastes like: freedom."

Arnie wolfed down more of it.

Logan ate slowly, his attention on a nearby table full of yellow-suited Santa Barbara County firefighters, the men laughing and smiling in easy camaraderie, despite their shared grime and weariness. The firefighters seemed like a family to Danny, not a group of coworkers stuck doing a miserable job or a bunch of convicted criminals thrown together by their shared willingness to face fire rather than live in cells.

Danny said to Arnie, "You know why they feed us like this, right?"

Arnie's mouth was full, but he answered anyway. "To show their appreciation for our dedication and hard work out there."

"Because it's ten thousand calories so we'll have the energy we need to hack away at brush for hours while facing a tsunami of fire."

"Just like those guys." Arnie pointed a fork at the table of firefighters. "We're all doing the same job. Nobody is treating us like criminals."

Mertz said, "Except those guys are getting paid sixty grand a year plus benefits to risk their lives. We're getting two bucks a day and no benefits."

"I'm not in a cell. I'm outside," Arnie said. "And do you see any guards here? Any razor-wire fences? I don't. Those are the benefits."

Nobody at the table was going to argue that with Arnie. It was why they were all there. But Danny thought Arnie was not seeing the big picture.

"I can think of only one other situation when convicts get fed this well."

"I can't think of any," Arnie said.

"Their last meal on death row," Danny said. "Right before they get a lethal injection or a whiff of poison gas."

Arnie laughed. "Good one. Let me ask you a question, Danny. If it's so bad, why are you here and not inside?"

A fire department helicopter, launching from the parking lot, streaked over their heads, carrying a hotshot team of firefighters out toward the smoke-shrouded hills where the fire was making its relentless advance toward the sea, heading right through some of the priciest homes in Santa Barbara County. Logan watched the chopper longingly.

"I didn't say this isn't better than prison," Danny said, when the sound of the chopper wouldn't drown out his voice, "but I'm also not drinking the Kool-Aid."

"It's Coca-Cola." Arnie held up one of his two cans. "Try getting that inside. Or chocolate cake."

Mertz shook his head and looked at Danny. "Give it up. It's like talking to a child."

Logan said, "You guys are missing the best part."

Arnie forked off a chunk of his chocolate cake, even though he'd just swallowed a mouthful of steak. "The desserts?"

"How good it feels to be doing something meaningful," Logan said. "I feel like a hero instead of a fuckup. When I get out, I'll be wearing yellow."

Mertz followed Logan's gaze to the professional firefighters at the next table and shook his head. "You think the fire department is going to hire an ex-con who stole cars to support his crack habit?"

"Why not? I'll already have the same skills and years of experience as the pros," Logan said. "And my criminal record will be expunged."

That last comment bothered Danny. "Who told you that?"

"The prison counselor who recruited me for the conservation program. Said it was a chance to turn incarceration into career training."

I thought I was the con man, Danny thought. But he kept it to himself.

Arnie pointed a fork at Logan. "You really want to do this when you get out?"

"Hell yes."

Mertz shook his head again. "Perfect choice of words."

"I love everything about it," Logan said.

Arnie asked, "Even the fire?"

"Especially the fire. The high when you're fighting it is better than crack, only legal. I can't support a family smoking crack." Logan had a pregnant girlfriend on the outside.

Danny said, "There's only one lasting benefit from this experience: a permanent get out of jail free card."

That got Arnie's full attention. "We'll never get arrested?"

"No. It means the next time you're convicted of a crime"—Danny shifted his gaze to Logan—"and most addicts are recidivists, you'll never see the inside of a prison cell again. You'll be sent straight back here and rise up the ranks." Danny nodded toward Hanrahan, who sat at the end of the table, his radio beside his plate. He was nearing fifty years old, had a construction worker or contractor vibe, but his skill was breaking into homes, not building them. "This is Hanrahan's third go-round and now he's the swamper."

Hanrahan didn't do grunt work anymore. He trained and supervised. In the field, he was responsible for the crew, giving them orders and keeping them safe, watching the weather, brush, and fire for any signs of danger.

"I'm not Hanrahan," Logan said. "I'm staying clean."

Mertz nodded. "That's exactly what Hanrahan used to say."

"How would you know?" Arnie asked.

"This is my second tour."

While they were all watching Hanrahan, he took a call on his radio and abruptly stood up to address the table. "Chow time is over. We're moving out."

Arnie protested. "I haven't even finished my first rib-eye yet."

"The fire has changed directions," Hanrahan said. "They need us to create a containment line fast."

The crew was bused to a neighborhood of huge evacuated mansions built on staggered pads, like steps on a staircase, up a densely wooded hillside. There were several fire trucks parked on the street, the firefighters unfurling hoses, ready to douse any embers before they could ignite anything. The wind was blowing the smoke their way, but it was only dropping ash now, not embers.

The crew spilled out of the bus and took in the scene while Hanrahan met with one of the firefighters to discuss their deployment. Danny estimated the unoccupied mansions on the street represented at least a half a billion dollars in real estate, not counting the cash, jewelry, artwork, and vehicles they contained.

Arnie admired the nearest estate, which had a six-car garage and more columns than the Parthenon, maybe four of which were structurally necessary. "They ran off and left all this? How many doors do you figure are unlocked?"

"It doesn't matter," Danny said. "They all have incredible state-of-the-art alarm systems. Motion detectors, heat sensors, lasers, pressure pads, cameras everywhere."

"All worthless now," Arnie said. "If an alarm goes off, nobody is going to respond."

Logan pointed to a patrol car parked at the top of the street. "There's a cop right there."

"He'll leave at the first sign of fire," Arnie said. "He's itching for an excuse to go."

Danny said, "Even if you could get in there and pillage the homes, how would you get away with what you stole? All the roads are closed and there's fire everywhere."

Arnie shrugged. "I don't know, but there's got to be a way."

Hanrahan came over to them, gripping his walkie-talkie like it might try to escape. "Come on. We've got a containment line to cut. Our way down is through this yard."

He led them into the backyard of the Parthenon house, past a huge pool with a grotto and swim-up bar, and on to the edge of the property, where the fire department had already cut an opening down onto the ridge in the wrought-iron fence.

Danny could see the fire advancing like a wave over the next ridge, down the ravine toward their hillside. Helicopters dive-bombed the blaze with water and retardant, trying to slow its relentless march, buying the convict crew time to hack and clear.

The crew trudged down the slope, which was overgrown with bone-dry bushes and trees. But at least it had been terraced at some point to prevent landslides, giving them a ledge to work on instead of clinging to the steep ridge.

They spent the next few hours hacking out a containment line, pushing through the brush and hard soil and their own exhaustion. They cleared their line, but when they felt the lick of flames below, they retreated uphill and into a backyard with a large, green, well-watered lawn and a pool that resembled a lazy river around a rocky waterfall.

Hanrahan told them that another convict crew on the opposite side of the street had also cut a containment line, so the plan was for everybody to stay put in the neighborhood and hope the fire didn't break through. There was no backup plan. Their lives were in the hands of the firefighters now.

Danny, Arnie, and Mertz walked back toward the mansion itself, a contemporary glass-and-steel structure that looked more like an art museum than a home. The first floor was filled with modern art, classic paintings, and all kinds of sculptures.

Arnie pressed his face up to the glass, though it wasn't necessary to see what was inside. "Imagine what these people would think knowing a bunch of burglars, thieves, and drug addicts were lounging around their property."

Danny said, "They'll never know. We all look like firemen to them." He smiled and waved at one of the many security cameras on the house and around the property. "And the fire department certainly isn't going to say anything about us."

Mertz pointed to one of the paintings, a portrait of a young ballet dancer in front of a mirror. "Is that a Degas?"

"I think so," Danny said, and noticed two contemporary paintings of backyard pools outside sunny California homes. "And two Hockneys."

"I'm not a Hockney fan," Mertz said.

"Me neither," Arnie said, "but I like it when they get into fights on the ice. You got a roll?"

He tapped Danny's backpack. Arnie was asking for a roll of toilet paper, an essential resource to carry. There weren't any outhouses or porta-potties in fire-choked mountains.

"Here? Now?" Danny asked.

Arnie shrugged. "I had a big lunch."

Danny dropped his pack. Arnie unzipped it, pulled out a roll of toilet paper, and headed for the well-manicured shrubs that surrounded the property. They'd all had to pee and shit in the wild before. It came with the job, but they rarely did it in people's yards, and certainly not when there were cameras around.

Mertz watched Archie disappear into the greenery. "Do you think he really has to take a shit or is he making a statement?"

"Maybe both."

The two men went back to the pool and sat on two chaise longues nice enough to be living room furniture. The other six chaise longues were already occupied by their fellow convicts, most of whom were fast asleep. But Logan stood, watching the firefighters douse a line of blazing trees at the edge of another property. The wind had picked up and embers were flying through the air, most of them landing harmlessly on the patio and well-watered grass or in the pool.

"I wish I was in the fight," Logan said.

Danny knew that all it would take was a big gust of wind for the fire to leap over their hastily cut containment lines and turn the neighborhood into an inferno, but he was too tired and comfortable now to be worried. "What do you think we've been doing?"

"Scut work," Logan said. "It's different when it's you against the flames."

"It certainly is." Mertz stretched out with a yawn, smearing dark soot on the overstuffed white cushions. "You can be burned alive in seconds."

That's why Danny was glad they were here, watching the show, and not in it. He didn't want to be anywhere near a thirty-foot-tall wave of flame moving at them at thirty miles per hour.

He didn't get a thrill from facing death. He got it from taking a huge gamble against impossible odds and insurmountable obstacles to win a pot of gold. There was no profit in firefighting.

And yet today, there was an ember, metaphorically speaking, that managed to get past the containment lines of logic and reason into Danny's mind and ignite the dry kindling at the edge of his imagination . . .

The ember was something Arnie said to Danny when they'd first arrived in the neighborhood and seen a half billion dollars in vacated real estate and all that treasure for the taking.

There's got to be a way . . .

CHAPTER SIX

Present Day
Wednesday Evening

It took Walker almost ninety minutes in heavy rush-hour traffic to get from East Los Angeles to his ranch-style home in Reseda, and that didn't count the two stops he had to make on the way.

He parked his truck beside his wife's BMW in their attached garage and went inside the house through the laundry room, carrying a grocery bag and a take-out bucket from KFC.

"Is that you, Andy?" Carly called out from somewhere deeper inside the house.

He stopped at the washing machine, picked up the half-empty carton of Super Pow on top of it, tossed it in the trash, and replaced it with the new box of Tide he had in the grocery bag.

"No, it's Colonel Sanders," he yelled back.

He walked into the unoccupied kitchen and set the KFC bucket on the table.

"Thank God," Carly said. "I've been fantasizing about you all day. I can't take it any longer."

"You're that horny?"

Walker found her in the family room sitting in his La-Z-Boy recliner, the leg rest fully extended, her hands resting on her huge belly.

The weight gain had been a radical change for Carly, who'd been effortlessly thin her entire life. Even her freckled face had become fuller with pregnancy. She wore a bathrobe, a tank top, and baggy sweatpants, going for comfort over style since she was only dealing with patients on the phone these days. Her obstetrician had told her to take it easy the last few weeks of her final trimester and she obeyed him.

"I'm that hungry," Carly said, a playful smile on her face that made her green eyes shine. "Where's the chicken?"

"In the kitchen," he said, taking her by the arms and gently lifting her up out of the recliner. The chair had once been his exclusive domain, but that was over now. She'd made it her own.

"You should have brought the bucket out here with you."

"We can have a proper dinner."

"Why? Are you expecting a royal visit?"

They walked down the short hall to the kitchen. He pulled out a chair for her and she eased into the seat, her legs spread to comfortably accommodate her belly. "I'll get us some plates and silverware."

"That's not necessary." Carly tore the lid from the bucket and frisbee'd it into the kitchen sink, then snatched out a greasy thigh and took a big bite out of it with a satisfied moan.

"Yikes. You're scaring me."

"Just keep your hands away from the bucket and you'll be fine."

Walker quickly snatched a drumstick and sat down before she could strike. "How are you feeling today?"

"I've got more gas than the *Hindenburg*," Carly said, her mouth full. "Don't light a match near me or I'll explode."

"You've pretty much summarized my day, too."

"Your new partner must have been thrilled. I told you not to have that breakfast burrito."

"Different kind of gas," Walker said, then told her about his first two arson-investigation cases in detail, starting with the second one, the gas explosion at the apartment building. Sharpe immediately deduced, from a smudge of melted wax in a kitchen cupboard, that it wasn't an accident. Someone had loosened a gas line to the oven in an empty apartment and left a lit candle in the cupboard to spark the explosion. Sharpe and Walker arrested the former tenant of the apartment, who'd staged the arson because he was enraged about being evicted so the landlord could gentrify the building.

She ate four more pieces of chicken and the two buttermilk biscuits while he talked. "I feel like I'm playing Dr. Watson to Sharpe's Sherlock Holmes."

"That's good," Carly said, wiping the grease off her face with her napkin. "Dr. Watson never tore his right meniscus kicking down a door or his left one tackling a fugitive pedophile."

"That's true. But he got hemorrhoids from sitting on his ass all day." He was happy about becoming a father, but at the same time, he was already resenting the child for forcing him into what felt like an early retirement. He hated himself for feeling that way, and when that happened, he found himself blaming Carly instead. And he hated himself for that, too.

"Don't you dare complain to me about hemorrhoids." Carly stabbed her finger at his face. "It feels like I've got a second baby growing in my ass. One more unexpected joy of impending motherhood that nobody warned me about."

Walker wasn't the only one in the marriage making a big sacrifice for parenthood and he felt an immediate stab of guilt for being so selfish. He grinned at her. "God, you're sexy when you talk like that."

"Too bad for you, because I'm never having sex again."

Walker offered her the empty bucket. "You want to pick out the crumbs of batter? It's original recipe, your favorite."

"No, I'm not an animal," she said. "You haven't finished putting together the crib."

It was an abrupt and unexpected change of subject and not one that he liked. He set the bucket down between them. "It's a more complicated task than it looks. I'm doing it in stages."

"Or the changing table."

"The instructions are in Chinese," Walker said. "I need to find a translator."

"Or the rocking chair."

"It didn't come with the little tool thingy for the special screws. I need to write the manufacturer a stern letter."

"Then you've got nothing else to do but rub my feet while I eat the batter crumbs." Carly reached for the bucket and swung her feet onto Walker's lap.

"Sounds like the perfect evening to me."

"Smart man," she said.

CHAPTER SEVEN

Five Years Ago

The massive Crags Fire started when a weed-abatement crew hired to cut a Malibou Lake hillside covered with tall, hay-dry mustard grass accidentally set it aflame when one of their old gas-powered Weedwackers overheated, spitting out sparks.

The blaze, fed by the brush and driven by high winds, quickly roared uphill in minutes, furiously growing in speed, size, and intensity before the first firefighters even arrived.

Soon the inferno was rampaging southwest, forcing the evacuations of residential neighborhoods and the isolated homes and horse ranches scattered atop the hills and down in the canyons throughout the Santa Monica Mountains all the way to the Pacific Coast Highway.

The California Department of Corrections and Rehabilitation Conservation Camp was located in the middle of the evacuation area. That wasn't fate—it was by design so the convict firefighters stationed there could be immediately deployed to protect homes unwisely built on land that had been consistently ravaged by wildfires since the dawn of time.

As the blaze roared implacably toward them from the northeast, Danny and his crew rushed in Jeeps to nearby Wishbone Canyon, where a ridgeline split in two, both ends buttressed by cascading hills that spilled into the gulch that divided them. One of the hills, against the west-facing slopes on the eastern ridge of the wishbone, was graded for homes, but so far only one had been built, a massive mansion encircled by palm trees and backed up against a ragged slope of dense, tangled chaparral.

The blaze was already climbing up the other side of the Wishbone's eastern rim and would soon top it and rage down through the brush toward the house unless Danny's crew succeeded in cutting enough of it away to create a containment line.

Danny could hear the crunch and snap of the hungry inferno devouring brush, huffing plumes of dark smoke and hot embers that blew over the top of the ridge and down into their shielded faces. Arnie was Danny's bucker again and Mertz and Logan worked nearby. Hanrahan stood between the crew and the house, where he could keep an eye on everything and stay in verbal contact with everyone.

Down at the house, two fire trucks and eight firefighters were preparing to defend the isolated property. Beyond them all, and down to the south, Danny could see a small hamlet of mobile homes left abandoned to fate in the lower hills.

Logan said, "There's one house here and six mobile homes down there. Why aren't we protecting them?"

Mertz snorted, though not loud enough to be heard over his chain saw, pausing the work for a moment to say, "Because all those mobile homes combined aren't worth as much as the master bedroom closet in this house."

"But we can make a real stand down there," Logan said. "This house should be sacrificed to save the others."

Arnie laughed. "What planet are you living on? The world doesn't work that way."

"It should," Logan said.

"And I should own that house instead of that asshole," Arnie said, pointing at Roland Slezak, the homeowner who'd refused to obey the mandatory evacuation order and had stayed behind, phone in hand, to boss around the firefighters.

Danny had overheard the argument between Slezak and the fire captain when they'd first arrived and as they were trooping up the hill.

"You shouldn't be here," the captain said. "You were told to evacuate."

Slezak was a short, manic man in a Japanese silk T-shirt, Italian cashmere sweatpants, and a pair of Air Jordans that gave him a few extra inches in height.

"Everybody in Malibu who evacuated to the Peninsula Hotel on blind faith that firefighters would protect their homes is going to come back to ruins," Slezak said in a nasally voice that made his nostrils sound like twin kazoos. Or, Danny thought, a pair of duck whistles. "If I wasn't here, you wouldn't be either. I told the governor I wasn't leaving until I was looking a firefighter in the face."

"Here I am," the captain said. "Now you can go."

"I'm staying to make sure you do your job." Slezak spotted a firefighter with a chain saw approaching one of the palm trees and he yelled out, "What the fuck do you think you're doing?"

The firefighter said, "It's too close to the house. I'm cutting it down."

"The hell you are," Slezak said. "That's a $10,000 tree."

"It's a $10,000 torch," the fire captain said. "It will only take a few embers to ignite it, and then it will spew fire on your house."

Slezak turned to him. "Then don't let embers get here. Douse that fucking fire." He pointed to the hill behind them for emphasis, and the giant, roiling cloud of smoke and flame on the other side. "Or do I need to call the governor again?"

Danny didn't hear what was said after that because they were out of earshot by then, and the roar and wailing of the approaching firestorm was much louder that Slezak's temper tantrum.

But Logan said, "Putting those palm trees around the house was like building a moat full of gasoline."

Logan had become a self-taught expert on firefighting since joining the volunteer crew, but Danny knew he was right. Building isolated houses in the middle of the mountains was dumb enough. It was pure arrogance adding to the risk for the aesthetics.

Now, about twenty minutes after Danny had overheard that exchange, flames were dancing on the hill above them and raining down embers, Satan's version of a snowstorm.

Danny and the rest of the convicts had made progress on cutting a containment line across the slope, but he knew it wasn't good enough. They'd have to clear the entire hill of brush to make a difference, and that wasn't going to happen in time. The firestorm had become too fierce, too strong, spewing embers that would just blow right over the naked earth.

A succession of helicopters flew eastward over their heads, dropping water scooped up in buckets from Malibou Lake onto the other side of the hill. But on this pass, some of a chopper's water slopped onto their slope, sending down a cascade of surface mud and pebbles that made Danny slip off balance as he was cutting.

"Careful, man," Arnie said, grabbing him and keeping him upright. "One slip of that chain saw and it's your leg that gets cut, not the brush."

"Tell them that," Danny said, gesturing up at the chopper. Arnie gave the pilot the finger instead, though it was unlikely anybody up there saw it.

The crew resumed their work slashing at the brush for a few more minutes, embers swirling all round them, when another helicopter dumped a thousand gallons of water, some of it slopping over on their side again. Water sluiced down the slope, washing away another layer of soil, undermining their footing, and freeing rocks that pelted them like an attack from an angry mob. It was a struggle just to remain standing. Danny couldn't saw at the same time, so he shut the machine down.

At the house below, embers ignited one of the palm trees, and the firefighters converged on it, watering it down to prevent it from generating embers of its own. Slezak furiously screamed something at them that Danny couldn't hear. He was busy trying not to fall. He grabbed on to a spindly little oak sapling for balance and called out to Hanrahan.

"This is a lost cause. We have to go."

Hanrahan pointed to the fire captain. "Not until he says it is."

Just then, another helicopter dive-bombed the ridge with water, but way too soon, most of his load falling on their side of the slope, creating a small avalanche of mud, rocks, and brush.

Hanrahan saw it and he yelled, "Watch out!"

The warning wasn't enough. The mudslide knocked Mertz and Logan off their feet and they tumbled down, losing their tools in the fall. Danny managed to hold firm to his sapling but saw a rock the size of a football smack into Arnie's helmet with a loud metallic bang and a gruesome crunch.

Arnie dropped and Danny reached out for him, grabbing his arm, his deadweight pulling him down, too.

Both men rolled, slid, and cartwheeled in the mud, rocks, and weeds down the hill, landing on the hard graded dirt below.

Danny immediately crawled to Arnie, who was motionless, and saw blood seeping from under his smashed helmet, his open eyes unseeing, his pupils wide.

Hanrahan hurried over, saw the situation, and called out, "We need a medic."

Logan came over, too, his entire body covered in mud, and looked down in horror at Arnie. "What the hell were they thinking dropping that water on top of us?"

"They were thinking about saving the house," Danny said, then moved aside as a firefighter rushed up.

"I'm a medic," the firefighter said. He checked Arnie's pupils and breathing, swore to himself, and then began CPR.

"We've got to get him out of here," Danny said, feeling helpless.

Hanrahan hurriedly conferred with the fire captain, exchanged a few words, then rushed back to the circle of men around Arnie. "We have to put him in a buggy and take him to the next ridge for evac. They can't bring a chopper in here."

That was unacceptable to Danny. "Bullshit. If they can fly choppers in to dump water, they can do it to save a firefighter's life."

"They can't," Hanrahan said. "There's no safe place to land here and it's too dangerous a spot to hover and lower a rescue basket."

Danny looked at the house. Two of the palms were aflame now. He knew why there wouldn't be a medical evac here: Slezak didn't want those embers whipped up onto his house by a low-flying helicopter.

"It's him, isn't it?" Danny said to Hanrahan. "He's the one choosing his house over Arnie. He's the one who called some politician to order that water drop."

"Let it go," Hanrahan said.

It filled Danny with rage. He started for that selfish asshole, but Mertz blocked him, holding him back.

"Do you really want to add more years on to your sentence?" Mertz said. "Do you want to spend those years in a prison cell? Because that's what will happen if you assault a civilian, especially one with big friends in city hall and Sacramento."

Danny knew Mertz was right and nodded to show it.

Mertz let him go.

Danny wouldn't get the satisfaction now of hitting Slezak in the face. But he would get him someday, and when he did, Slezak wouldn't know who or what had hit him, only that it was devastating.

Danny, Mertz, and Logan carefully lifted Arnie and carried him to a Jeep. They all climbed in and the firefighter continued to apply CPR.

Mertz drove, speeding the Jeep down the two-lane road, across to the Wishbone's western ridge, and up to its highest point, which had also been graded for future development.

A Los Angeles County Fire Department helicopter hovered overhead and lowered a rescue basket for Arnie. The men placed him into the basket and strapped him in, and then he was hoisted up to the helicopter, which immediately swooped northwest, away from the wildfire and to the nearest hospital.

Logan turned to the firefighter. "Is he gonna make it?"

The firefighter was spared having to answer when his radio crackled. He was needed back right away and so were the convicts.

Danny looked to the east, back the way they'd come, and saw the tsunami of flames cascading down the southern end of the ridge into the lowlands, smashing into the community of mobile homes, incinerating them all.

Logan was right before, Danny thought—that's where they should have been, not up on that graded hill, where Slezak's house stood unscathed, protected by firefighters and saved by the water drops that had injured Arnie.

But Danny didn't have time to worry about Arnie's fate. The crew was quickly dispatched to dig away at the scorched earth the fire had left behind to make sure it wouldn't rise again like the walking dead.

Ten hours later, bone tired and caked with mud and soot, Danny and the other convict firefighters returned to their camp, which had miraculously survived the flames, and lined up to undergo a routine security check by the guards before being allowed back into their barracks to eat, shower, and sleep.

The guards looked through their packs and patted them down, making sure they'd brought nothing back besides bruises, blisters, and burns. None of the convicts ever admitted to an injury or ailment worse than that—short of something as obvious as a compound fracture, missing eyeball, or amputated thumb—because they didn't want to be sent away to the prison doctors.

The medical wards in California's prisons were repeatedly and consistently cited by federal authorities for rampant malpractice, negligence, and incompetence that bordered on depravity. The convicts knew that border had been crossed long ago. It was worse than the Dark Ages. It was surprising that the doctors weren't using leeches and bloodletting as their primary treatments.

So, the convicts preferred to soothe their pain with booze made from the rubbing alcohol in first-aid kits or wrung from sanitary hand wipes. That's also what they did that night, back in their barracks, to unwind and to ease their worry about Arnie.

They didn't know that he'd already been declared brain-dead and was being kept clinically alive only long enough to salvage his organs.

Over the following days, the Department of Corrections and fire officials buried the report of his accident and subsequent death and refused to let inmates talk to the press.

Arnie Soloway's organs, bones, and tissues were sold for $40,000, but the money didn't go to his wife and two kids. It was deducted from the $100,000 in medical bills his widow was saddled with for his care (including $2,000 for the helicopter evac from the fire zone) but was unable to pay.

Months later, a *Los Angeles Times* investigation into the Crags Fire revealed that some state and local politicians, pressured by unnamed "rich and famous" contributors to their election campaigns, had allegedly ordered the fire department to prioritize certain homes and neighborhoods for protection over others. Nobody was disciplined as a result of the embarrassing revelations, but county fire officials promised that "substantial changes" would be made in the procedures for allocating manpower and resources.

From that moment on, Danny had two goals he couldn't stop thinking about: how to get vengeance from everyone responsible for

Arnie's death and the cover-up . . . and how to get away with pillaging the mansions that were left uninhabited and unprotected during a wildfire. Both of those challenges, posed in some way by Arnie, shared the same mantra.

There must be a way.

By the time Danny Cole was released from prison four years later, he knew exactly how to do it all.

CHAPTER EIGHT

Walker sat on a bench in the empty locker room at headquarters and pulled a nylon compression sleeve up his right leg and over his throbbing knee, which was aching because he'd spent a few hours last night on the floor, trying in vain to assemble the damn changing table. He was tempted to shoot it.

He put on his shoes, stood up with a wince, tucked in his shirt, buckled his belt, and looked at himself in the mirror.

It felt like a step backward to be in uniform again, even if it was tactical greens, favored by SWAT, rather than a patrol deputy's khaki shirt, dark-green slacks, and gold-buckled heavy utility belt.

He wore a dark-green shirt with hidden buttons over a black tee and matching slacks with a black nylon utility belt for his gun, two ammo magazines, a set of cuffs, and a small Maglite. No Taser, baton, or all the other stuff a patrol deputy would have to lug around.

He picked up his Stetson from the bench and put it on. Now he didn't look so bad. In fact, he looked great, radiating confidence, authority, and all-around badassery. It was amazing the difference the right hat could make.

"If you're done admiring yourself," Sharpe said, appearing out of nowhere behind him, "we've got to go."

"What's up?"

"There's a fire in the Sepulveda Pass, close to the Getty Museum. It's zero percent contained and growing exponentially every minute, thanks to the wind."

"How'd it start?"

"That's what we're supposed to figure out," Sharpe said. "I'm not sure, but I think that may be why they call us arson investigators."

And with that, Sharpe walked out.

Walker holstered his gun, closed his locker, and followed Sharpe out to the parking lot.

Sharpe tossed him the keys to the Tahoe. "You drive. Use the siren."

Gladly, Walker thought. It was why he'd become a cop in the first place.

◆ ◆ ◆

They took the 101 freeway north, then the Ventura Freeway west, toward Interstate 405 South, which cut through the Sepulveda Pass, where the fire raged along the eastern rim.

Sharpe told Walker to take that route because the wildfire was moving southwest, driven by thirty-mile-an-hour winds, and he wanted to come at it from behind, to the ground it had already burned, to find its likely origin point.

Walker primarily used the carpool lanes. But when they were too congested, he sped along the tight shoulder between the carpool lane and the median's K-rails instead, nearly shearing off the driver's side mirror or sideswiping the stalled traffic on the passenger side on countless occasions.

Sharpe turned on the AM radio just loud enough so they could hear the news from KNX 1070 but not so loud that it drowned out the LASD dispatcher's voice.

The news reports were all about the surprising intensity and speed of the fire, the shutdown of both directions of the 405 through the Sepulveda Pass, the just-ordered evacuation of the surrounding neighborhoods, and the closure of the Getty Museum, which was atop the western rim, directly in the path of the blaze if it jumped the freeway.

"This is the worst kind of fire," Sharpe said.

"Fire is fire, isn't it?" Walker asked, enjoying the high-speed drive in the tight lane. It felt like he was piloting an X-wing down the Death Star's exterior trench to shoot a missile into its thermal exhaust port, saving the Rebel Alliance. All that was missing was incoming laser fire, but he heard it in his mind.

"This one is a fast-moving, wind-driven firestorm moving southwest along the busiest freeway in California and it could torch the edge of Bel Air on its way into Brentwood, two of the wealthiest neighborhoods in Los Angeles," Sharpe said. "Oh, and it might also take out the Getty Museum, which is full of priceless art. On top of that, shutting down the freeway will create a traffic nightmare in a city where even on a good day a tennis shoe in the fast lane is enough to create total gridlock."

"It will be Carmageddon II," Walker said, a reference to what the media called the weekend, a few years back, when the 405 through the Sepulveda Pass was shut down for a key step in the construction of the new Mulholland overpass to replace the old one.

"There was advance warning for that," Sharpe said. "Now all those diverted cars are going to hit the surrounding streets and canyon passes at the same time hundreds of homes are being evacuated, clogging roads just when fire trucks are trying to get to a raging fire that's roaring through ravines and up the dry hillsides faster than Superman with dysentery looking for a bathroom."

Ahead and off to his left, Walker could see the thick, churning column of brown smoke rising from the mountains and tilting southwest against the backdrop of an otherwise cloudless, bright blue sky. Using his siren, his horn, and aggressive tailgating, he forced aside other cars and edged their Tahoe across five lanes of traffic as they approached the intersection with the 405.

The exit to the southbound 405 was closed to civilian traffic, two California Highway Patrol cars forming a loose barricade at the off-ramp, but Walker's Chevy Tahoe, siren wailing, was waved right through.

He followed the ramp, which curled around and under the Ventura Freeway onto the eerily empty 405, then he floored it up into the Sepulveda Pass.

"Keep your eyes open," Sharpe said. "There's an unmarked fire road exit coming up on your right. It's where the sound wall tapers off."

Walker found it and peeled off the freeway onto a single-lane asphalt road that was usually blocked by a locked gate but was open now and manned by another CHP officer. The road ran uphill, then cut across the slope, between the freeway below and a residential neighborhood and a private school above, before hitting Mulholland, where the ridgetop road met the enormous landmark overpass that caused the last Carmageddon.

Now, high above the pass, Walker could see the enormity of the blaze that was marching across the opposite ridge, in the thick, brush-filled hill and crevices between the freeway and the exclusive $100 million homes above, leaving naked, blackened, smoking ground in its wake. The Getty Museum, atop the western side of the pass, was almost completely obscured by the thick smoke from across the 405.

Sharpe pointed to the other side of the overpass. "That's where we're going."

Walker took Mulholland east across the overpass, but before the road curved north and up onto the ridge, Sharpe told him to pull over at a turnout where several LAFD and LACFD vehicles were already parked.

They got out and Sharpe headed for a dirt footpath that led up toward the burned hillside, perhaps two hundred yards away, where Walker could make out the tips of several power poles.

Walker followed him up the trail, which wound through thick, prickly weeds and a smattering of boulders. The sky here was clear, and the ground untouched by flame, but everything smelled of freshly burned wood anyway, even though the smoke wasn't blowing in their direction.

"The fire started somewhere up there," Sharpe said.

"How do you know that?"

"Because brush fires can't burn against the wind. So logically, if you go upwind, you'll locate the origin point on the edge of the burn pattern. Then you have to find what sparked the fire and what fed it."

They passed a ragged makeshift tent strung between two bushes, a bedroll and trash bags full of something, perhaps clothes, underneath it. The tent was surrounded by trash, mostly take-out containers from KFC and other big fast-food chains, but also an empty carton of Reynolds Wrap and dozens of water bottles, some filled with what looked like urine. Yet the garbage was strangely neat and organized, separated by restaurant brand, and then by type of food waste. There were individual piles of chicken bones, apple cores, spareribs bones, banana peels, and other produce waste. Walker was surprised that wild animals hadn't already scattered it all into one big mess. Perhaps they had, and whoever lived there just kept obsessively separating everything again.

As the ground got steeper, and rockier, and harder to climb, Walker's right knee began to ache. "Isn't it unusual for an arson to happen in broad daylight?"

"Not when the target is in brush or in a wilderness area," Sharpe said. "Then it's almost always done in daylight."

"Why is that?"

"Because there's nobody around, so there's no need to hide," Sharpe said as Walker stumbled on a rock but caught his balance before he fell. "And so the arsonist can see where he's going."

"Isn't that what flashlights are for?"

"It's pitch-black out here at night. Using a flashlight would be like firing up the Bat-Signal," Sharpe said. "Everybody would see it in the homes across the pass, maybe even some of the drivers on the freeway."

"But if you set the fire in daylight, it's the same problem. People are going to see the smoke right away and call 911. The firefighters could show up before you're gone."

"You're right," Sharpe said. "That's why in this situation an arsonist is more likely to use some kind of a time-delay device so he can get out safely before the flames start, which is good for us."

"Why's it good?"

"Because most of the devices are improvised, badly designed, and don't entirely work and what's left of them can tell you a lot about the arsonist," Sharpe said. "The conception of the device, the materials used to build it, and how it was assembled can reveal his education, his thinking, his financial status, his age, his cultural background, his dexterity, his occupation, and even his location. If he wasn't extremely careful, it might even give you his DNA and his fingerprints. It's almost like a written confession with a driver's license stapled to it."

Walker nodded. It made sense.

The two men reached a blackened slope where a line of power poles stretched across the base of the hill and Walker saw a dozen orange-suited firefighters attacking the charred dirt with pickaxes, rakes, and shovels, presumably to snuff out anything hot that might rekindle a fire.

Walker spotted some gang tattoos on the neck of one of the orange-suited firefighters. The man made no attempt to hide his Rolling 60s Crip ink as he clawed at a burned, but still smoking, tree stump with his pickax.

Sharpe stopped to survey the scene and sniff the air. Walker stepped up beside him and asked, "Are gang members allowed to become firefighters?"

"Nope."

"So, why's that guy got gang tats on his neck?" Walker gestured to the firefighter taking apart the tree stump.

Sharpe followed his gaze, then replied, "Because he's a convicted felon. Everyone in an orange suit is doing prison time."

"You're shitting me," Walker said, looking at the crew again. "They are all criminals?"

"They are part of the California Department of Corrections volunteer firefighter program."

"But they're just walking around free, carrying pickaxes," Walker said. "And I don't see any armed guards."

"They're under the supervision of the Los Angeles Fire Department." Sharpe gestured to two yellow-suited, unarmed firemen that Walker hadn't spotted before. They didn't seem to be paying too much attention to the prisoners.

"That's it?" Walker nodded toward the gang member again. "What's to stop that Rolling 60s Crip over there from clobbering those two with a shovel and just walking off back to the hood?"

"Nothing," Sharpe said. "They are pretty much on the honor system."

"If they had any honor," Walker said, "they wouldn't be in prison."

"Maybe so, but only five people have run off in the sixty-year history of the program. But this is only a field trip. When they are done here, they'll go back to a camp in the Santa Monica Mountains that's essentially a low-security prison."

Walker met the eye of the Rolling 60s Crip, who rested the pickax on his shoulder and glared back at him.

This is a disaster waiting to happen, Walker thought.

Sharpe continued walking along the line of power poles, Walker at his side, until they came upon two men in blue windbreakers with ARSON INVESTIGATORS written in yellow on the back, crouching beside a fire-blackened metal power pole.

"Terrific." Sharpe stopped walking. "I was hoping they wouldn't be here yet."

And that's when Walker realized something that should have been obvious to him before they left office. The Sepulveda Pass wasn't in the Los Angeles County Sheriff's jurisdiction. It was LAPD country. "Those guys are with the Los Angeles Fire Department and we aren't supposed to be here."

"There's nothing wrong with a little emergency tourism."

"Yes, there is. It's like when the Feds show up at a crime scene where they have no jurisdiction, just so they can walk around modeling their stylish FBI windbreakers for the TV cameras," Walker said. "I hate that shit and now we're doing it."

"Do you see any TV cameras here?"

"So you came just to be an asshole?"

"I came to be helpful," Sharpe said, and started walking toward the investigators.

"It's the same thing," Walker said, joining him.

One of the LAFD agents spotted them and scowled. "What are you doing here, Shar-Pei? This is a private party and I'm sure that nobody sent you an invitation."

Sharpe held up his hands in surrender. "I was in the neighborhood, Scruggs, and I'm breaking in a new investigator." He cocked his head at Walker. "He's totally green. I thought a visit to a fire of this magnitude was a rare opportunity that would be a master class for him."

The body language of the two LAFD detectives seemed to Walker to change into something more welcoming, but not by much. Apparently, Sharpe had given an acceptable excuse for invading their turf.

Sharpe said, "Andrew Walker, meet Al Scruggs and Pete Caffrey, LAFD's top two arson investigators. Watch and learn."

Walker shook hands with the two men. Scruggs had a pug nose that was so out of place on his big, hard-featured face that it looked to Walker like it might have been transplanted from an organ donor. Caffrey's most notable features were his shoulders, which slanted at thirty-degree angles from his neck. If Caffrey lowered his arms to his side, Walker thought, his unbuttoned windbreaker would slide right off.

Caffrey said to Sharpe, "There's a lot of smoke around, but I can still tell when it's being blown up my ass."

Sharpe pointed at Caffrey. "There you go, Walker. First important lesson: study the smoke. I told you every word they said would be gold. School him, boys."

And with that, Sharpe wandered off, leaving Walker with them.

Scruggs nodded at Walker's Stetson. "Nice hat. Where'd you transfer from? Texas Rangers?"

Walker got that question a lot, given how similar his name was to the character Chuck Norris had played on TV. "US Marshals Service."

Caffrey said, "That's a strange career move."

"I've got a pregnant wife who wants more we time and less me time."

Scruggs nodded. "I've been there."

"How'd it turn out for you?" Walker asked, genuinely interested in the answer.

"I ignored her complaints and stayed in firefighting, meaning ten days at the firehouse, twenty days off. I discovered later that during the ten days I was gone, there was another guy in my bed," Scruggs said. "Now two-thirds of my salary goes to my first wife in alimony and child support. I wasn't going to make that same mistake with wife number two, so here I am. I'm home just about every night. Of course, that doesn't mean she's not screwing the pool guy right now."

"You don't have a pool." Caffrey sighed. It seemed to Walker that this was a story Caffrey had heard before and didn't want to hear again. "It's no big mystery what happened here. Wind damaged this power line, sending out sparks that ignited the dry mustard grass."

Got it, Walker thought. Ignition source: power line. First fuels, the weeds. Case closed.

"How can you tell that's what happened?"

"The story is at your feet. The fire ran with the wind," Caffrey said. "The ground is black southwest of the power poles, the same direction the wind is blowing and the wildfire is still advancing."

Scruggs added, "And there are no traces of any incendiary devices or accelerants."

It was dry, parched dirt under Walker's feet, but black on the hill. The only thing missing was a circle and a big, fat arrow marking the spot where the fire began. He could see already that determining the origin of a fire out here was a lot easier than on the streets or in a building. The crime scene told the story. Then again, it always did, though not as clearly as it did here. Here the fire wrote the story in black that couldn't be missed.

Scruggs kept talking, enjoying his role as teacher.

"My educated guess is that a cable failed after years, maybe decades, of wear and tear and arced against the steel tower, shooting off a spray of hot sparks, up and down the line. You can see where the sparks flew from the poles, igniting this field of weeds, blowing a ton of embers into those parched trees only a few yards away. That's what quickly turned a small brush fire into a major catastrophe."

As Scruggs talked, Walker noticed Sharpe examining things, the way he had in the apartment building, and realized that his new partner wanted him to keep these two occupied while he snooped. That was fine with Walker. He had plenty of dumb questions he could ask.

"Wouldn't the burning brush alone have been enough to start and feed a wildfire?"

Caffrey shared a look with Scruggs, then: "Hasn't Shar-Pei talked to you about mass dynamics?"

"All he's talked about is why he prefers Fatburger over In-N-Out." That was true. It was the topic of conversation after their unsatisfying lunch at McDonald's on La Brea yesterday.

Now they all glanced at Sharpe, who was walking along the fire line, sometimes going in circles or doubling back, like a dog sniffing around for the right place to pee.

"That's because the old dog doesn't want anyone below him to succeed," Scruggs said. "He's afraid if you learn anything, you'll take his job."

"So why is he letting me talk to you?" Walker asked, to shift their attention away from Sharpe and back to him.

Caffrey said, "Because he thinks we don't know shit because our background is in firefighting, not police work. But he's never faced flames. We know fire a lot better than he does."

"We also know In-N-Out is far better than Fatburger," Scruggs said.

"No contest," Walker said.

"Here's what you need to know about wind-driven wildfires," Caffrey said. "For an ember to start a blaze, it has to have enough mass to sustain heat over the duration of the distance it travels in the air and not be blown out by the wind that's carrying it. If it burns out midway, it lands as ash, and it won't ignite anything."

Walker glanced past the detectives at Sharpe, who was taking a picture with his phone of something on a boulder. Sharpe had placed a measured strip, similar to a small ruler, beside whatever he was photographing for scale.

Scruggs pointed to the thicket of charred tree trunks up the hill. "That was a dense stand of trees. That's a lot of fuel. The heavier the fuel load, the larger and more powerful the heat plume becomes, lifting the firebrands into the air and out in front of the main fire."

"What's a firebrand?"

"Essentially a big ember," Caffrey said. "Trees have more mass than weeds. Their embers are dense—think bits of bark versus leaves—and hold their flame. The firebrands are lifted up in the heat plume and, in a strong wind, can travel half a mile or more, spreading the blaze wherever they land, which is exactly what's happening now."

Scruggs scratched his pug nose, which was so bizarrely small compared to the rest of his features, Walker thought it was possible he might accidentally flick it right off his face. "If those trees had been just a little further away from this brush, and less densely packed, and there was no wind, this wildfire might have been contained before it spread."

Walker nodded toward the trail. "I saw a homeless person's shelter back there. Couldn't he have tossed a cigarette or something into the brush?"

"Same story," Caffrey said. "Not enough mass. The wind would've blown out a tossed cigarette or a pack of matches before it landed and we'd have found evidence of them. The fire clearly spread laterally, directly from this line of power poles. It's a no-brainer."

"Thanks, guys," Walker said. "I've learned a lot."

Scruggs said, "Don't tell Shar-Pei that. We want him to keep underestimating us."

"Deal. One night you'll have to let me buy you two some beers." Walker shook hands with them again and went back to Sharpe, who was still studying the boulder he'd photographed. "I kept them distracted so you could poke around and find something they missed that you can humiliate them with later."

"What makes you think that's what I wanted?"

"I'm a trained detective," Walker said.

"I thought you were a manhunter."

"Same thing."

"I'm not convinced," Sharpe said. "Let me guess what Beavis and Butt-Head said caused this fire. Since it's windy, and there's been no lightning, and nobody left a gasoline can or unexploded time bombs around, and the only conceivable accidental source of fire out here, so far from roads, homes, and anything else that might create sparks, is the power line, then it must be the culprit."

"Well, when you put it like that, it does seem obvious."

"Those two are exceptional at discovering the obvious," Sharpe said. "And if they make a quick determination, that gets the pressure off of them and satisfies everyone, except maybe the electric company. What else did you learn from them?"

"A few things about mass dynamics."

"Good, so you'll understand why this is strange." He pointed to a burn mark on the boulder that he'd photographed.

The mark didn't seem that strange to Walker. "It looks to me like an ember landed on it and burned out because it was close enough to the origin to still be carrying heat, but landed on a nonflammable object, so it burned itself out."

"Two minutes with Dumb and Dumber and you're talking about origin and heat load. Impressive," Sharpe said, clearly unimpressed. "Except the wind is blowing in the opposite direction, so how did the ember land here?"

"Maybe there was a lull."

"A lull?"

"In the wind," Walker said. "It happens."

"Really?" Sharpe asked. "Is meteorology a hobby of yours?"

"I flew kites when I was a kid," Walker lied, then theorized: "It would only take a couple of seconds for the ember to travel this short distance."

"And now you're an expert on ember velocity, too. Wow. You forgot to mention that you have a degree in thermodynamics."

Walker took a closer look at the burn. It looked like someone had mashed a cigarette out on the boulder. Sometimes the simple, obvious solution was the best, so he said, "Or maybe someone just snubbed out a cigarette on the rock."

"Like who?"

"Whoever lives in that makeshift shelter back there. We should ask him," Walker said. "At the very least, maybe he saw what happened."

"He's gone and I don't think he left a forwarding address."

Now Walker felt better. They'd just stepped into his comfort zone.

"I know where he is."

CHAPTER NINE

Four Months Ago

Prior to his release from the penal system, Danny Cole was transported from the conservation camp in the Santa Monica Mountains to the California State Prison in Lancaster for processing, which meant he had to spend his last few days as a convict in one of the cells he'd literally walked through fire to avoid. Those were the longest two days of his sentence. His fear was that he'd be shanked in the prison yard or showers. But nobody paid any attention to him.

He stepped out into the hot desert air wearing the same Tom Ford suit he'd worn at trial. Although the suit was wrinkled, rumpled, and a bit tight on his now-bulkier frame, it turned out to be the appropriate dress for the occasion, considering there was a Rolls-Royce Cullinan limousine waiting for him outside the gates. A uniformed chauffeur stood in front of the half-million-dollar SUV holding an iPad with Danny's name on the screen, a bizarre sight against the bleak, parched backdrop of endless sandy flatlands dotted with cactus.

"To whom do I owe the pleasure?" Danny asked the chauffeur, who held open the back door for him.

"The Law Firm of Rosetti, Ryan, and Petrocelli."

Danny smiled. That was where Karen Tennant, his defense attorney, worked as a senior partner. Danny climbed in and found a bottle of champagne waiting for him. He didn't open it, for fear he'd finish the bottle and arrive wherever they were going totally plastered. The destination turned out to be Shutters, a Cape Cod–style luxury hotel right on Santa Monica Beach in Santa Monica. When they arrived, the chauffeur handed him a card-key to one of the oceanfront suites.

Karen greeted Danny at the door of the suite in a negligee and he was glad he'd resisted the bottle. He wanted to be completely sober for this.

◆ ◆ ◆

Hours later, they lay naked in the four-poster bed together, the sea breeze from the half-open white-shuttered balcony doors cooling their hot, sweat-dappled skin.

Karen rested her head on his muscled chest and absently stroked his flat stomach. "You're a much harder man than you were before."

"I haven't had sex in eight years."

"I'm not talking about that . . . well, not entirely. You've got pecs and a six-pack. But it's not a prison-yard body."

"What kind of body is it?"

"The kind you see in firefighter calendars," she said.

"I've never seen a firefighter calendar." He gently disentangled himself from her, reached across the bed, lifted the bottle of Dom Pérignon from the ice bucket, and refilled their glasses on the nightstand.

"It's suburban-housewife porn."

"You aren't a suburban housewife." Danny offered her a glass and she sat up in bed to take it from him.

"Doesn't mean I don't enjoy their porn," Karen said, taking a big sip. "I didn't think I'd ever get to live the fantasy."

Danny sipped his champagne, got up, and carried his glass with him across the room to the table, where some beluga caviar and toast still remained from their first postcoital snack. "I thought you didn't sleep with convicts."

"You aren't a convict anymore. You've paid your debt to society, though you still have one with me."

"I didn't just pay that off?" He spread the caviar on the toast and ate it.

"You aren't that good in bed," she said. "But I am forgiving the interest."

"Thank you," he said, eating some more and washing it down with the champagne. "You'll have your money soon."

"Is it derived from ill-gotten gains?"

Danny came back to the bed with his champagne. "Are we still bound by lawyer-client confidentiality?"

"Yes."

"Of course it's ill-gotten. I'm a criminal."

"A hardened criminal," she said, glancing below his waist. "Your share of the Golden State Bank swindle?"

"That's right." He set his glass down on the nightstand and got back onto the bed beside her.

"What makes you think it hasn't been spent by your accomplices?"

"Because I trust them," he said. "And I earned it."

"By not giving them up to save yourself."

"I would have lost myself if I did that." Danny took her empty glass from her and set it on the nightstand. "I am nothing without my integrity."

"Funny word coming from a self-avowed criminal. But I suppose that's what makes you such a good con man. Your integrity."

Danny turned on his side and began lightly tracing her body with his fingertips. "What happened to my inherent decency?"

"You tell me," Karen said. "What are you going to do now that you're out?"

"Put what I learned over the last seven years to good use."

Her breathing was beginning to quicken. "Don't tell me you want to be a fireman."

"No, but what I do next will be about more than enriching myself," he said. "I'm going to right some wrongs."

"You're going to do some good." She arched her back, her body expressing the direction she wanted his fingers to travel. He was good at following direction.

"While being very, very bad," Danny said.

"So, my closing argument wasn't a total lie."

"The most convincing lies are based on some truth."

She drew him on top of her. "Is that the secret to your success?"

Danny brushed her cheek with his lips. "Why? Do you want to become a con artist?"

"I already am. And I've got the law degree to prove it," she said, running her hands down his back. "What have you got?"

"A prison record and a drug lord's money."

"You win." Karen grabbed him by the ass and kissed him.

The next morning, Karen gave Danny the new credit cards and driver's license he'd asked her to arrange for him some months back, as well as a sheet of paper containing the home addresses and current employers of two women he'd never met but who shared something in common.

"Thank you for this," he said, slipping the envelope into the inside pocket of his Tom Ford jacket. While they'd been asleep, he'd had the hotel clean and press his clothes, which were delivered first thing in the morning. "Though I never expected you to deliver them to me in quite this way."

"I can't imagine why you wanted to know about those women," she said, dressed for work and presenting a far more professional attitude than she had during their night together. "But I'm sure I don't want you to tell me."

"I don't intend to fleece them," he said, "if that's what you are worried about."

"I know you don't," Karen said. "They aren't wealthy or craven enough to be one of your targets. Even so, I hope the next time I see you won't be behind bars."

"It won't be." He kissed her. "This was a sweet and thoughtful way to ease me back into civilian life. I'm touched."

"You were more than touched," she said. "I'm afraid I may have bruised you."

They kissed again and he promised to see her soon, someplace where the only bar she'd see would be serving them martinis.

Danny walked a half block up Ocean Avenue to the Avis Rent A Car located in the Loews Hotel, where he broke in his credit card on a week's rental of a sensible and anonymous Toyota Camry. He drove another half block up to the Nordstrom department store at Santa Monica Place and emerged an hour later wearing a polo shirt, khaki slacks, and new Nikes, carrying his Tom Ford suit in a garment bag and the rest of his new clothes, shoes, and toiletries in a new rolling suitcase.

From there, he drove 116 miles north to Bakersfield, California.

From 8:00 a.m. to 5:00 p.m., Diane Krepps-Soloway worked as a cashier at the WinCo Foods on Coffee Road, conveniently located a few blocks from her parents' run-down 1980s tract home, where she lived with her two kids, one in sixth grade, the other in junior high. That meant she could have breakfast with her kids before they went to school and be home in time to help her elderly parents with dinner before rushing to her second job waitressing at a diner called Coffee on Coffee. She got about five hours of sleep a night and looked it.

But that's what Diane had to do to survive since her husband, Arnie, went to prison and they lost everything—their Porter Ranch home, their matching BMWs, and their savings. And then they lost him. In desperation, she'd moved in with her parents, her kids sharing the guest room while she put a window air conditioner, a dresser, and a futon in the garage and called that her bedroom (though her father still had his tools, a workbench, and the 1966 Impala he'd been "restoring" for decades in there).

The stigma of what Arnie had done, even though she'd known nothing about her late husband's car-leasing swindle before his arrest, had tarnished her, too, as if she'd committed the crimes with him merely because she'd enjoyed the spoils. And there was no hiding from it, not as long as Google stayed in business. So the two dead-end jobs were about the best she could do, though often she lay on her futon, fantasizing about abandoning her family, changing her identity, and starting life over in Paris.

Danny knew all of that, though her fantasies were just a guess, before he walked into the WinCo, a brightly lit twenty-four-hour warehouse supermarket that looked like the bastard child of a one-night stand between a horny Costco and a drunken 99 Cents Only Store. He picked up a six-pack of Coke and a box of granola bars and stood in line at her register to pay for them just so he could get a look at her.

Diane was only in her early thirties but looked closer to fifty to him. She had permanent dark circles around her eyes and sickly pale skin. Her brown hair was tied back in a bun so tight, it seemed like some kind of ritual self-flagellation. She was heavyset, her shoulders hunched forward as if she were trying to stand straight while carrying a backpack stuffed with bricks. It was depressing. She'd done nothing to deserve this.

Danny wordlessly paid cash for his purchases, went to his car, and drove a few blocks south to the Residence Inn on Espresso Road, where he checked in and took a long nap. Karen hadn't let him get much sleep the night before and the three-hour drive up to Bakersfield had exhausted him. And after years of sleeping on a bunk, the comfort of a hotel bed was impossible to resist.

At 8:00 p.m., Danny got a booth at Coffee on Coffee, a diner that had once been a Sambo's, and many other restaurants since then, but through it all, had remained a monument to linoleum, Formica, and vinyl.

Diane approached his table, pulled an order pad from her apron, and held a ballpoint pen to the page. She showed no indication that she recognized him from their brief encounter a few hours earlier in her checkout aisle.

"What'll it be, sir?"

He looked up from his laminated menu, which not only listed the food they served but had pictures of everything, too. "Why is everything around here named for coffee?"

"What do you mean?"

"Well, there's Coffee Road, Espresso Road, Latte Lane, Cappuccino Way," Danny said. "Were Folgers Crystals created in Bakersfield or something?"

That brought a brief smile to her face and when it did, for a split second, he caught a glimpse of how she looked before she was hit by a freight train carrying a mile-long load of bad luck. "Besides Coffee Road, which has been here forever, it's only those new streets around the new hotels that continue the theme. So I guess you're from out of town and got a room over there."

"You should be a detective," he said, and immediately regretted it. The remnants of her smile disappeared, along with any lightening of her mood, at the mention of something related to law enforcement.

"What'll it be?" she said again.

He ordered a cheeseburger and a chocolate milkshake. When Diane delivered his meal, she told him that she hoped he enjoyed it, set his check on the table, and walked away.

They didn't share any more words after that, but he left her a twenty-dollar tip in the hope that maybe it would bring some of her smile back, if only briefly. He intended to make a better effort at it soon, one that would make her smile last for a lifetime.

◆ ◆ ◆

Danny left Bakersfield early the next morning and returned to Los Angeles, stopping in Simi Valley on his way back to take a slow drive around the cyclone-fenced perimeter of Picture Car City, a vast parking lot filled with all kinds of vehicles.

Behind the fence were taxis, police cars, ice cream trucks, sports cars, cable cars, school buses, motor homes, armored cars, limousines, tanks, fire trucks, armored tactical vehicles, ambulances, vintage cars, gasoline tankers, racing cars, motorcycles, and examples of just about any other vehicle on wheels. And just about all of the vehicles were fakes, rented to the studios for use in movies and TV shows.

The only security at the lot that he could see was the barbed wire atop the fence and a couple of ancient security cameras on posts, and based on the dog crap everywhere, some Dobermans were lurking around. In other words, no security at all, at least not from a professional like Danny Cole.

It was good to know.

◆ ◆ ◆

The eighty-foot yacht docked in Marina del Rey looked less like a boat than a starship that had landed on the water and floated into a slip. It was sleek and aerodynamic and yet without any sharp corners, as if it were designed to be undetectable by radar. It seemed to be in motion, even when it was standing still.

Danny walked up the gangway onto the yacht, where Tamiko Harada and Kurt Sabella were waiting to greet him. He hadn't seen them since their escape on bicycles from the fake bank in Ventura. The years had been good to them. They were tan and fit and dressed casually—Tamiko in a low-cut sundress and Kurt in a loud Hawaiian shirt and shorts. After getting hugs from both of them, Danny was led back to the bow, where there was a banquette table with a deli platter and three tall glasses filled with some kind of iced tropical drink.

Tamiko offered him one of the glasses. "Would you like a mojito?"

Danny accepted the glass with a smile that acknowledged he understood the reference to his trial. "Very funny. I didn't see you in the courtroom when the prosecutor gave his closing statement."

Kurt raised a glass of his own to Danny. "We got the transcript. Made for good beach reading when we were on the Riviera."

Danny sipped his drink. It was delicious. "The transcript was supposed to be sealed."

"Nothing is sealed from Adam Horowitz," Kurt said.

Danny was lucky that Diego Grillo's cartel didn't have anyone as deft at hacking as Adam or the drug lord's killers would have found a way to take him out in prison. But Danny would start looking over his shoulder, just in case he was wrong about that.

Tamiko gave him a once-over and seemed to like what she saw. "You look buff."

"I did my time as a convict firefighter," Danny said, taking a seat on the plush banquette. "They make you exercise."

"I thought the only exercise you liked was sex." She took a seat next to him, close enough that he could feel her breast pressed against his shoulder. He wondered if the loose, low-cut neckline of her dress was for his benefit, an invitation of sorts, not that he'd even consider taking advantage of it if it was. Mixing sex and business on a con was never good.

"I didn't have any opportunity for that."

Kurt said, "At least not the kind you wanted."

"'Gay for the stay' is what I call it," Tamiko said.

"Not an issue you've had to deal with lately," Danny said. "I see you've done well for yourselves and stayed out of trouble while I was gone."

Kurt gestured to the yacht around them with a sweep of his arm. "This isn't my boat."

"Or mine." Tamiko explained to Danny that she and Kurt crewed on the yacht for the owner, a big-time Hollywood agent. He used the yacht as a weekend getaway from the stress of living in his Bel Air home, and had it sent to Cannes during the film markets there as a place to stay, cut deals, and make a big impression. Kurt handled maintenance, as an engineer and all-around fix-it man, while she handled hospitality and, when necessary, security. Tamiko and Kurt basically lived on the yacht, even when it was in port, which was most of the time. Although they appeared to be a couple, Danny knew Tamiko and Kurt were just friends-with-occasional-benefits, no strings attached.

Kurt made himself a fresh drink. "The fact is, we're broke."

"And bored out of our minds," Tamiko said. "A half a million dollars doesn't go as far as it used to eight years ago."

"We would have gotten into trouble while you were away," Kurt said, "if we knew someone smart enough to get us into it without us all being caught."

"I got caught," Danny reminded them.

"Not because you weren't smart," Kurt said.

"Do I have any money left?"

"Actually," Tamiko said, "you're the only one of us who came out of that scheme ahead."

"I spent eight years in prison."

"Where you couldn't spend your money," she said. "We lost ours."

Danny wasn't surprised. The two of them were both precise, dependable, and focused on a job, but when it was over, life was a constant party. They didn't invest in anything tangible like real estate because the life of a career criminal was, by nature, a nomadic one. Buying material goods (and a place to put them) meant making yourself a stationary target. Plus, staying still was dull. Life was in the living, in the excitement, the risk, and the pursuit of pleasure. Their money was spent on experiences, not invested for something as vague as the future.

Kurt spoke up. "But you lucked out. Adam shrewdly invested your money. The value has quadrupled."

He took a piece of paper out of his shirt pocket and handed it to Danny. There was a figure written on it. Seven of them, to be exact. Danny was impressed by the appreciation in value and that neither Kurt, Tamiko, nor Adam had been tempted to pocket the profits and just leave his principal intact. Thieves who didn't steal from other thieves, even when nobody would notice, were a rarity. He'd lucked out when he'd chosen this crew. He hoped that luck would hold.

Danny folded and pocketed the piece of paper in his pants as if it were a cashier's check. "Where is Adam?"

"Up in San Francisco. He started a security firm," Kurt said. "Companies actually pay him to break into their systems and steal shit and it's entirely legal."

Tamiko added, "He's 'testing their vulnerabilities.'"

She said it using air quotes, which made Danny smile.

"The morons," Kurt said. "It's like inviting a wolf into the henhouse, then giving him the key so he can come back again whenever he likes to have another meal."

"At least Adam hasn't gone entirely straight."

"What about you?" Tamiko patted Danny's pocket, the one with the slip of paper in it. But she left her hand on his thigh. Definitely an invitation. "That's enough money to retire on."

"I have something else in mind for it."

Tamiko gave his thigh a squeeze. "A scam?"

"A heist?" Kurt asked.

"Equal measures of both. With some retribution thrown in. I've been planning it for years. It's going to cost me every penny."

"I'm on board," Tamiko said, bouncing with excitement.

"So am I," Kurt said.

"Don't be so quick to agree. I have to warn you, it's the most ambitious and dangerous scheme I've ever attempted. You won't just be risking your freedom. You'll be risking your lives. That's not hype," Danny said. "It's the truth. And while you're thinking about that, remember all of my careful planning was undone last time by a dog. There are even more variables I can't control or foresee this time."

Kurt nodded, warning understood. "How lucrative is it?"

The money was always the only thing that mattered to Kurt. Yet, Danny knew, as important as it was to him, he was terrible at holding on to it. "Millions of dollars for each of us."

Tamiko bounced again. "How much fun will it be?"

Danny grinned. "It will be epic."

CHAPTER TEN

Present Day
Thursday

Walker and Sharpe sat in the Chevy Tahoe, which was parked in a red zone on a Sherman Oaks side street south of Ventura Boulevard that gave them a view of the Kentucky Fried Chicken on the next corner, where they were waiting to spot the homeless resident of the encampment they'd seen near the flashpoint of the wildfire raging in the Sepulveda Pass.

They passed the time listening to news reports about the ever-growing blaze that had been christened the Skirball Fire and that was 0 percent contained. Sixteen homes had already been destroyed. Celebrities were tweeting about their harrowing escapes, their Oscars and Emmys clutched to their breasts. And the Getty was preparing for the worst, securing all of their masterpieces in what they hoped were fireproof rooms.

Sharpe tapped his foot nervously on the floor mat. "What makes you think he's going to show up here?"

"This is the only KFC near his place," Walker said.

"How do you know that?"

"My wife craves KFC lately, so I know where all of them are."

"It doesn't mean he'll show up here today."

"He had more trash from KFC than anywhere else. I think some-body in there slips him a leg and thigh to make him go away. It's a small price to pay to keep him from lingering outside and scaring off custom-ers," Walker said, then changed the subject, because he was beginning to worry that he was wrong. "Do you believe the Skirball Fire is arson?"

"It was probably caused by failed power lines."

"What about that burn spot on the boulder?"

"A lull in the wind," Sharpe said. "It's not the first time I've seen a burn spot where there shouldn't be one."

Walker almost asked, "Then why were you trashing the two LAFD investigators and giving me shit?" But that would have sounded too whiny—plus another, more productive line of inquiry occurred to him. "But you want to be sure."

"I wouldn't be sitting here if I didn't."

"If it was arson," Walker said, "how does setting a fire out there help someone get revenge or make a buck?"

"It doesn't. The motives for arson are entirely different when the fire is set in the wilderness."

"The fire is in the middle of Los Angeles, the second biggest city in America, burning a path between hundreds of mansions in Bel Air and twelve lanes of freeway," Walker said. "That's hardly the wilderness."

"Where it started is," Sharpe said. "A wilderness arsonist is likely to be an educated man with a car, a decent job, and a connection of some kind to first responders, or have a hero complex, or both. He wants to be the one to show up and save everybody. But no caped crusaders have appeared, so we can scratch that motive off the list."

"You really think a cop or firefighter could have set the Skirball Fire?"

"I'll tell you a dirty little secret. Nationwide, about a hundred fire-fighters a year are arrested for arson, and that number has been consis-tent for decades. Nobody talks about that."

"Except you, of course," Walker said. "It's another reason why fire-fighters adore you."

Sharpe turned in his seat to face him. "I knew an arson investigator who started fires just for the glory of solving them. He figured out how they were done, though somehow the culprits always eluded him. He didn't elude me. I put him in prison. It's his desk you'll be sitting in, if you manage to stay on."

"Thanks for the vote of confidence," Walker said.

"We could be here all day." Sharpe turned back to face the KFC. "This is getting us nowhere."

"You'd be surprised how far you can get on a case while sitting on your ass doing nothing. It's counterintuitive but true."

As if on cue, a woman wearing several layers of filthy clothes emerged from an alley down the street from the KFC and ambled up toward the restaurant. Her face was deeply tanned and her head was wrapped in a turban of aluminum foil. The *he* they were looking for was actually a *she*.

"Voilà," Walker said.

"There are a lot of transients around here," Sharpe said. "How do you know she's the one?"

"I saw an empty Reynolds Wrap carton outside her shelter but nothing wrapped in foil in her shelter," Walker said, then added with a grin: "You have to be more observant."

Sharpe ignored the good-natured dig.

They got out of the car, managed to catch a green light, and crossed the street to the restaurant.

"I was observing the fire scene," Sharpe said. "You know, as in the things that matter."

"Big mistake. That's like going into a house where someone has been killed and only looking at the blood spatter on the walls and the corpse on the floor and not what's in the refrigerator."

"Why would I look in there?"

"You can learn a lot about the people from what's in their fridge," Walker said. "You might also find another body, chopped up into little pieces and put in ziplock baggies."

That had happened to Walker once. Now he always checked the fridge—or in this case, the metaphorical fridge.

They reached the woman just as she was about to open the door to the KFC. She glared at them with green eyes fogged with cataracts.

"I wondered when you'd show up," she said. "Can you tell me what I'm thinking?"

Walker answered, "I wish that big, handsome hunk of a man would get out of my way so I can get my chicken?"

She grinned, revealing a lot of missing teeth. "Not knowing what's going on in my mind must be driving you crazy."

"Us crazy?" Sharpe said. "We're not the ones with foil around our heads."

She wagged a dirty, bony finger at him, the curled nail long enough to be registered as a lethal weapon. "Because you're already under remote control. That's not going to happen to me."

"Why would anyone care what you're thinking?"

She cackled, then said, "You tell me. You're the ones so desperate to know what's on my mind that when you couldn't get into my skull with your satellites, helicopters, drones, and so-called UPS trucks, you finally showed up to face me. I'm sure you're trying to penetrate my brain right now with your so-called cell phones. It won't happen. None of your signals are getting through my force field. I've got magnets in every pocket."

She reached into one pocket and pulled out a handful of kitchen magnets of different shapes and sizes to prove it. One of the magnets was SpongeBob SquarePants.

"Nice collection," Walker said. "I'm Andrew Walker, and this is Walter Sharpe. We're arson detectives with the Los Angeles County Sheriff's Department. What's your name?"

"Margaret. As if you didn't know."

"We're investigating the cause of that fire." Walker gestured behind him to the massive plume of smoke over the Sepulveda Pass. "We could use your help, Margaret. Can we buy you lunch?"

"So you can drug me, throw me in the back of a so-called Amazon truck, and take me to thought police headquarters and put your implant back in my brain again?" She shook her head. "No way."

Back in her brain? Walker wondered how it had been removed the first time and hoped she hadn't done it herself.

Sharpe looked at Walker. "This is a waste of time."

Walker ignored him and held up his hands to Margaret in a gesture of surrender.

"All we're interested in is the fire, Margaret. We know you live up there. Did you see or hear anything before it happened?"

She narrowed her eyes at him. "Did you?"

"I wasn't there," Walker said.

"Your mind-raking drones were, like they always are, but this time one of them crashed."

"Why do you say that?"

"Because I crashed it." Margaret grinned proudly at him. "I closed my eyes and hit it with a thought bomb. When I stepped out of my tent a few minutes later, the hill was on fire. And now, here you are, afraid I might bring down one of your helicopters or satellites next time."

Sharpe sighed. "With another thought bomb."

Margaret looked at him. "I've been practicing."

"What exactly is a thought bomb?"

She pointed to a piece of foil over her forehead. "I peel this up for one second and unleash a concentrated, powerful thought."

"Like what?" Sharpe asked.

"Oh, wouldn't you like to know. Do you think I'm insane?"

"Yes," he said, then shifted his gaze to Walker. "We're done."

Sharpe walked away, but Walker stayed. He had the car keys anyway. "We didn't find any wreckage on the hillside."

"Of course you didn't," Margaret said. "And you'll make sure nobody else does, either. I have no evidence, if that's what you're worried about." She leaned close to him, sharing a secret and a lot of body odor. "But we both know the truth."

"Did you see or hear anything out of the ordinary this morning?"

"Not until now. It's ironic that I am on your mind because you can't get into mine. See? I don't need any of your devices to know what you're thinking." She smiled and went into the KFC. The interview was over.

Sharpe was right, Walker thought. Waste of time.

He walked back to the Tahoe, where Sharpe was waiting, leaning against the front grille.

Walker asked, "How's that lull theory looking to you now?"

"Much more likely."

Walker unlocked the car. "Unless Scruggs and Caffrey are really with the thought police."

"I doubt it," Sharpe said, opening his door. "They can barely read their own minds."

When Walker got home that night, he found Carly in the kitchen cooking, pots and pans everywhere, along with bags of flour, sugar, and chocolate chips, cartons of eggs, and sticks of butter. She wore an apron and was stirring something in a bowl.

"It smells great in here," he said. "What are you making?"

"Chocolate cake and brownies."

"Yum. What's for dinner?"

She took a chocolate-covered spatula out of the bowl and licked it. "Chocolate cake and brownies."

He gave her a kiss on the cheek. "What's for dessert?"

Carly tossed the spatula in the sink and poured the batter into a brownie pan.

"Bacon and eggs or one of the chicken pot pies in the freezer."

"Mind if I eat dessert for dinner?"

"Sure, but I'll be skipping dessert," Carly said. "I don't want to overindulge."

"Wise move." Walker took a bottle of beer out of the refrigerator, popped the top off, and sat down at the kitchen table.

"You can relax tonight. I hired a handyman and he stayed all day. The changing table, rocking chair, and crib are all finished, the loose electric socket in the hall is fixed, the barstools aren't wobbly, and the toilet doesn't make that wheezing sound anymore."

"Sounds like you kept him busy."

"He took care of all your husbandly duties."

"All?"

"I lost track of how many orgasms I had today." She put the brownie pan in the oven and set the timer.

"Because he made love to you," Walker said, "or because you get off on watching a man do chores?"

"The chores, of course." She came over to the table, took off his hat, and kissed him on the cheek. "What kind of wife do you think I am?"

"A very pregnant one."

Carly put his hat on her head and sat down sideways on his lap. She weighed two tons, and it felt like his right knee might snap. But he tried not to show the pain.

She asked, "And how was your day?"

"I didn't have a single orgasm."

"But you weren't shot or stabbed and you're home for dinner, so it's a win," she said. "At least for me."

"Me too. But at work, all I do is follow Sharpe around while he lectures me."

"That makes sense. You still have a lot to learn," Carly said. "Things will change once you know what you're doing and can start being more active in the investigations."

"I don't like not knowing what I'm doing."

"Nobody does. It takes time." Carly got up from his lap and waddled back to the kitchen. She opened the freezer and took out a carton containing a frozen chicken pot pie. "You can't expect to become a genius like him overnight."

"I never said he's a genius."

Carly unwrapped the pie, put it in the microwave, and set the timer. "You said he's Sherlock Holmes, which is saying the same thing." She opened the fridge, took out a bowl of frosting, and stuck her finger in it. "What matters now is that you find a way to work together until you can carry your own weight." She licked the chocolate off her finger and came back to the table with the bowl, sitting down on his lap again. He tried not to wince. "Until then, look at the bright side."

"What's that?"

"You're keeping regular, predictable working hours and you haven't touched your medical deductible. You get to be here for me and, soon, for your son. It's what we wanted."

It's what *she* wanted, Walker thought. But what he said was, "It's just that I'm a man of action who is sitting on his ass."

"Don't worry. Once the baby is here, you'll have plenty of action in your life again." She stuck her finger back in the bowl and swept up another glob of chocolate frosting. "You'll be changing diapers and we'll be taking turns at night doing the feedings."

"It's not the same kind of action."

Carly offered him her frosting-covered finger. "Thank God for that."

Walker licked her finger clean.

CHAPTER ELEVEN

Four Months Ago

The Dollar Tree was in a run-down cinder-block shopping center in Carson, California, a South Bay city where the outside air quality was about the same as breathing directly from the exhaust pipe of a big rig truck, which is what happens when you're surrounded by oil refineries and freeways. But that was clean, fresh air compared to being stuck inside a Dollar Tree that reeked of cleansers, cheese, plastic, spoiled milk, potato chips, and grease. The disgusting scent was just one of the many reasons Bobby Logan missed prison or, more precisely, living in the Santa Monica Mountains, breathing air rich with the scents of the sea and the pines.

Now, Logan was in aisle three, unloading bags of pork rinds from a cart onto the shelves, working for a woman who, as it happened, lived on pork rinds and Cheetos, was a devoted Trekkie, and thought of the store as her starship. It was a shit job, but the only one he could get with his résumé. No fire department would hire him.

He spent his days making minimum wage loading and unloading stock, sweeping aisles, and cleaning the store and his nights in a dreary studio apartment that made his bunk in the conservation camp seem like the Four Seasons Hotel by comparison.

All he thought about was fire. Lately, he'd been thinking about watching this place burn. But that wouldn't be satisfying. He didn't want to watch flames—he wanted to charge right into them, to battle them. He wanted it as much as he once wanted crack.

Logan thought about fire and prison so much that he was tempted to rob the damn store just so he could be sent back. He was entertaining that fantasy when someone asked: "Excuse me, can you tell me where I can find the Grey Poupon?"

Logan knew the voice. He looked up to see Danny Cole standing there in a loose-necked short-sleeve shirt, khaki slacks, and loafers, the picture of a well-off businessman slumming at the Dollar Tree. "How did you find me?"

"I followed a fire engine," Danny said.

That stung. "If you've come to humiliate me, you're too late. This place has already crushed my spirit. It's worse than prison."

"So escape. I don't see any bars."

Logan continued stuffing bags of pork rinds onto the shelf. "It doesn't mean they aren't there. If I walk out, where do I go? How do I make money? Nobody except a place like this will hire a junkie ex-con."

"Are you using again?"

"Nope," Logan said.

"Then you're an ex-junkie ex-con."

"I'm always gonna be a junkie, just one who isn't using," Logan said. "At least for now." Because this job, and the miserable life he had now, could certainly drive him to it. Maybe even tonight. "Why are you here, Danny?"

"To ask you a question. How badly do you want to fight fires again?"

"More than I've ever wanted anything."

Sheila, the manager, appeared at the opposite end of the aisle, her hair in a tall basket-weave bouffant that hadn't been stylish since the original *Star Trek* in the 1960s, which was where she copied it from, showing the stylist at Supercuts pictures of Lieutenant Uhura, Nurse Chapel, and Yeoman Rand for reference.

"We have an emergency in aisle three that demands your immediate attention, Ensign."

"What is it?" Logan asked.

Sheila put her hands on her hips and glowered at him. "What is it, *Captain*."

Logan thought it was impossible to feel more humiliated, more pitiful, than he already did, but this moment, in front of Danny, proved him wrong.

"What is it, Captain," Logan repeated by rote, his back to Danny.

"A woman brought her dog into the store and he urinated on the floor," Sheila said. "Clean it up."

"Shouldn't she do it? It's her dog."

"You have a lot to learn about customer service. Get to it. Every second is critical," Sheila said, then marched away. Logan reluctantly turned back to Danny, who pretended to find a canister of Pringles endlessly fascinating.

Danny said, "We need to talk, Bobby."

"I've got a break in a few minutes," Logan said. "I'll meet you at El Pollo Loco, across the parking lot."

And with that, he went to get a bucket and a mop.

Danny watched Logan go, then took the canister of Pringles up to the checkout line, where Sheila was working the cash register. He handed her the Pringles and she rang him up.

"That will be $1.07."

He gave her the money and spoke in a low voice, bordering on a whisper. "Hey, have you ever seen that show *Undercover Boss*? The one where CEOs pretend to be new workers in their own store?"

"Once or twice. I prefer *Star Trek*. Any *Star Trek*. Original, Next Gen, Kelvin timeline, whatever."

"That's a shame."

"Why?"

Danny gestured to the back room as Logan emerged with the mop and bucket. "You'd have recognized him, too. He was on the show last season."

"Who is he?"

"The CEO of Dollar Tree, of course."

Sheila looked back, but Logan had already disappeared behind the aisles. *"Him?"*

"On the episode I saw, he promoted a manager who treated him nicely to vice president and gave her a $50,000 gift to pay off her student loans," Danny said. "But another manager, who treated him badly, he decimated, ridiculed, and humiliated before firing her on national television. She's a pariah now. Even her husband divorced her."

The manager looked at the back of the store again, but she still couldn't see him. "You must be mistaken. He was in prison. He's lucky to have this job."

"It's his cover. Do you think a hardened criminal would take orders from you? He'd slit your throat, empty the register, and head straight for Mexico," Danny said. "That man is the CEO. He's worth millions. I'm sure there are cameras hidden all over this store. If he takes a break, then comes back afterwards and quits, you'll know you're on the show. That's what they always do on the last day of the charade. And then the next time you'll see him will be when a TV crew shows up at your door. It will either be your lucky day . . . or the worst moment of your life."

"Thanks for the heads-up," Sheila said.

"See you on TV." Danny took his Pringles and walked out. Once he was out of her sight, he dropped the canister, which was two months past its expiration date, into a trash can, then crossed the parking lot to the El Pollo Loco. He ordered a Coke, sat down at a table, and waited. A few minutes later, Logan came in, looking a bit dazed.

Danny asked, "What's wrong?"

Logan sat down across from him. "The strangest thing just happened. The manager handed me a twenty-dollar bill, said lunch was on her, and promoted me to chief engineer."

"Chief engineer?"

"I have no idea what it means, either. She's a Trekkie and likes to think of the store as her starship," Logan said. "I call it the USS *Soulcrusher*."

"Catchy."

"You were right when you told me in prison that I was being conned, that I'd never get hired as a firefighter when I got out."

Danny shrugged. "I'm a professional con man. I know a con when I see one."

"What they don't tell you when they talk you into the volunteer program is that to be a firefighter on the outside, you are required to be certified as an emergency medical technician," Logan said. "That's something they are never going to do for a junkie or an ex-con. I'm both. You also need to have an official completion certificate for every stage of firefighter training you've done and those bastards in the prison system didn't give us those, either."

"You could sue them," Danny said.

"What lawyer would be crazy enough to take the case on contingency? Besides, it would drag on for years and we'd lose."

"There's another way to get back at them for what they've done to you," Danny said, leaning forward, his arms on the table. "And, at the same time, avenge Arnie Soloway's death, make a ton of money, and be a firefighter again."

Logan studied him, leaned close, and lowered his voice. "You're planning a job?"

"A heist during a wildfire . . . and I'd like to survive it with everything we're going to steal," Danny said. "To do that, I need criminals with firefighting experience. Do you know any?"

Logan smiled. "Maybe one or two."

◆ ◆ ◆

Adam Horowitz was occasionally approached by people who mistook him for the actor Jonah Hill and asked if they could take a selfie beside him. He was always glad to oblige, especially when the request came from a woman. It was amazing to Adam how many of those women would sleep with him, too. That's what could happen when you closely resembled an unattractive character actor and not one of the Hemsworths, because the mistaken identity didn't become obvious to the women once his clothes came off. But tonight he hadn't gotten lucky and brought any Jonah Hill groupies back to his apartment.

He sat at a horseshoe-shaped desk in front of picture windows that offered him a spectacular thirty-story-high view of the San Francisco skyline and the bay beyond it . . . if there weren't six flat-screen monitors in the way. He ate sushi with his left hand while he typed with his right on one of the three computer keyboards in front of him, his eyes flicking between the lines of code scrolling by on the six screens. The only other furniture in the apartment was a king-size bed, a couch, and two barstools at an island in the kitchen.

Danny Cole stood behind him, looking out the window at the Transamerica Pyramid, appreciating the enduring audacity of the design. Adam was the only thief he knew who actually kept his money, finding all kinds of ways to store it or invest it, but not because he coveted wealth or needed the financial security. Money didn't matter to him, beyond simply assuring that his creature comforts and technological needs were met. Adam was terrified of boredom and craved challenge.

"You have an incredible view from up here," Danny said.

"I like to look down on people," Adam said, continuing to eat and type. "It makes me feel superior."

"I thought hacking into computer networks and destroying the lives of anyone who annoys you by maxing out their credit cards with drug purchases, or putting them on sex offender watchlists, or sending offensive texts under their names to their loved ones made you feel superior."

"That too."

Danny glanced at all the code flitting by on the screens. It might as well have been Sanskrit to him. "What are you doing?"

"Breaching an insurance company to see if I can download the medical records of 1.2 million clients," he said. "And hacking into a special effects house in India to steal the rough cut of the latest Marvel movie."

"They are paying you to do that?"

"The insurance company is."

"And Marvel?"

"I don't want to wait until summer to see the movie," Adam said. "Could you please grab me a Monster from the fridge?"

Danny went to the refrigerator, which was filled with cans of Monster, Red Bull, and Hi-Tiger energy drinks. He took a Monster, popped the top, and brought it to Adam, who grabbed it with his left hand without pausing the frantic typing he was doing with his right.

"You seem to be doing really well for yourself, Adam. Going straight obviously agrees with you."

"I haven't exactly gone straight. I've just found a way to monetize my villainy."

"By getting paid to break into companies and download sensitive material instead of doing it without asking."

"It's not nearly as exciting without the risk," Adam said.

"But this way," Danny said, "you won't end up in prison."

"'Prison' is a relative term."

"Not to me."

"Jesus." Adam stopped typing and turned to face him. "How many different ways do I have to imply that I'm dying to work on another big scam? Are you going to recruit me or not?"

"I was, but you're way too eager," Danny said. "It makes me nervous."

"You are never nervous."

"You don't know how dangerous this heist is."

Adam set down his can and pushed his rolling chair away from the desk, giving Danny his full attention. "Let me guess: if it goes wrong, instead of going to prison, I could get killed."

"You've been talking to Tamiko and Kurt."

"No, but that's the warning you gave me when you recruited me for the banking scam that fleeced Diego Grillo and his cartel. How is this any different?"

"We could all burn to death," Danny said.

"You said if we screwed up the banking scam, Grillo would amputate, emasculate, and disembowel us before stuffing our body parts in barrels of lye and dumping them into the sea."

"That was true."

"But here I am," Adam said. "I had a lot of fun and made a fortune off that scam while you went to prison. So, I owe you one."

"You don't owe me anything."

"Okay, then you owe *me* for not taking your share of the loot. So, I want in."

Danny couldn't argue and didn't intend to. It was better if Adam felt like he forcing his way in instead of being coerced.

Adam said, "What will I be doing for you on this heist?"

"For starters, creating a fake identity for me as a British tech investor with verifiable liquid cash resources of at least $150 million and a bank letter to prove it."

"Any reasonably intelligent eight-year-old with an internet connection could do that for you." Adam gave an overly theatrical yawn. "Come on, Danny. Give me a challenge."

"You will have to take full, simultaneous control of the highly sophisticated, top-of-the-line security systems for three individual Malibu estates and disable all communications—cellular, cable, internet, radio, and otherwise—indoors and out, in the entire neighborhood."

Adam thought about that a moment. "I assume I'll also be monitoring all the police bands while you burgle those houses."

"That's right."

"It's a good thing I can do two things at once with these hands," Adam said. "But I do that every day."

"You might need your toes, too, for this," Danny said. He'd saved the best for last. "We'll be pulling off this heist in the middle of a wildfire. So you'll also be tracking the inferno that'll be blazing towards us all. When that happens, you might find yourself wishing for a tidal wave."

Adam smiled. "*Now* we're talking."

CHAPTER TWELVE

Present Day
Friday Morning

Walker had barely stepped out of his truck in the LASD parking lot on that fatefully hot, arid, and very windy morning when Sharpe intercepted him.

"We have to go," Sharpe said. "I'll drive."

"Where are we headed?" Walker fell into step beside him and they walked across the lot to where the official vehicles were parked.

"Another brush fire broke out an hour ago in the Santa Susana Pass, just south of the Simi Valley Freeway."

That was in Chatsworth, which, as far as Walker could tell, wasn't in the LASD's jurisdiction. He'd checked the maps when they got back to the office yesterday. "More emergency tourism for your idle amusement?"

"We've been assigned to investigate." They got into the Tahoe. Sharpe put on the siren and peeled out of the parking lot, tires squealing. "The fire broke out in the hills between Chatsworth Park and Santa Susana Pass State Park. That's Hellmouth."

"Hellmouth?"

"The Capital of Clusterfuck." Sharpe sped onto the freeway on-ramp to the 10 west, taking the curve so fast it felt like the SUV might roll over.

"You'll have to be more specific."

"Santa Susana Pass Park is state land that straddles the City of Los Angeles and, a mile or so to the west, Ventura County," Sharpe said. "Chatsworth is city land, but Bell Canyon, Oak Park, and Agoura, the open space a few miles southwest, where the fire is now heading, are Los Angeles County territory. A fire anywhere in that area poses an immediate threat to all those jurisdictions. So, the Los Angeles Fire Department, the Ventura County Fire Department, the Los Angeles County Fire Department, and the California Department of Forestry and Fire Protection agreed decades ago to provide mutual aid whenever a blaze breaks out there."

"Sounds like NATO for wildfires." Walker grabbed hold of the "oh shit" handle above his door as Sharpe snaked around cars at high speed. The old dog's recklessness behind the wheel both surprised and impressed him.

"That's a generous way of looking at it." Sharpe swerved around a big rig and nearly sideswiped a Prius. "But yeah, that's right. There are other Hellmouths around the county. Malibu Creek State Park, up in the Santa Monica Mountains, is another one."

"It seems to me that's a good thing. It means massive resources will be brought in to put the fire down."

"Yes, it does, and that means a world of shit for us."

Sharpe explained that an Incident Command Center would be established, run by a fire chief who'd act like General Patton, directing every aspect of the battle to defeat the wildfire. All of the fire agencies involved, regardless of whether they were local, county, or state, and all of their manpower and resources would be under the chief's command.

"We're going to be horseflies buzzing around their heads while they are trying to fight a war. They don't want law enforcement involved until it's all over. They don't care how it was started, only how it ends," Sharpe said. "I can understand that. But by then, if it was an arson, the evidence is gone, too."

"Is it always that way?" Walker asked.

"No," Sharpe said. "Sometimes it's worse."

"What could be worse?"

"When they want us involved from the start."

Walker was confused by Sharpe's rant. "You're never happy, are you?"

"What happens then is that some old-fart fire suppression chief from Incident Command, instead of a law enforcement official, will try to tell us how to run our criminal investigation, something he knows jack shit about," Sharpe said. "We'll end up trapped in a conference room with investigators from the LAFD, LAPD, ATF, CHP, CAL FIRE, all the way down to the Girl Scouts of America. And the result will be a press release that says nothing and that nobody will read."

"If it's all a pointless waste of time, just a conspiracy of bureaucracy and incompetence designed to aggravate, delay, and sabotage your arson investigation, what do you suggest we do?"

"Isn't it obvious?" Sharpe gave him an angry look, though Walker wished he'd just keep his eyes on the road. "Our jobs. On our own. Any way we can. Are you up for that?"

Going rogue? Rules be damned? Do whatever it takes to get his man? Finally, Sharpe was speaking Walker's language. "It's my specialty."

"I figured that."

"What gave me away?"

"The cowboy hat was a subtle clue," Sharpe said.

❖ ❖ ❖

Walker had never been to Santa Susana Pass State Park, but he recognized the huge boulders, sandstone outcroppings, and dramatic rock formations from the many alien worlds and western badlands he'd seen on TV. That was because, as Sharpe had told him as they drove up the fire road through the crags, there used to be several full-time "movie ranches" here. But all of those western sets and studio facilities were destroyed decades ago by the many catastrophic wildfires that regularly swept through the area, which was a natural highway for fire.

That historical, geographical, meteorological, and cataclysmic fact was being proved once again today as they reached a rocky peak overlooking a line of huge power lines and the flatlands beyond it, where a windblown surge of fire marched ever southward to the sea. A waterdropping helicopter swept over the blaze, spilling its load on the flames, but to little noticeable effect.

On the eastern fringe of the fire, a scattering of palm trees in a tightly packed neighborhood of two-story condos was ablaze and spraying embers into the wind, alighting rooftops that dozens of firefighters were desperately dousing with their hoses to keep the buildings from burning.

Walker noticed that one of the power-line towers was badly scorched, a severed cable dangling from the top, and that the land downwind was blackened, as if the structure were casting a massive shadow far wider than itself. He assumed the tower was where the fire began, as it had in the Sepulveda Pass.

Sharpe parked their Tahoe behind a red LAFD-badged SUV, where a lone firefighter stood surveying the scene, a walkie-talkie in his hand. The firefighter was suited up in the usual reflective Nomex turnout gear and wore a white helmet that identified him as a fire chief.

As Walker got out, he noticed a few of those errant burn spots, like the one Sharpe found in the Sepulveda Pass, dotting a couple of the large boulders upwind from the singed tower.

The fire chief, an African American man with a gray-flecked mustache, didn't appear pleased to see them. "I asked the county to send me another fire battalion and I get you instead, Shar-Pei. You could have at least brought a water bucket."

"I'm sure the cavalry is right behind me," Sharpe said.

The chief looked past Sharpe to Walker. "Looks like one of them came with you, but without his horse."

Sharpe smiled at that. "This is Andrew Walker. He's new to the arson unit. Walker, this is LAFD Battalion Chief Roy Tighe, the man in charge."

They shook hands, and Tighe said, "That implies I have some control over what is happening here and I don't. I feel more like an observer."

Walker said, "What do you see?"

"The future and it's ugly. This fire was five acres when I got here thirty minutes ago. It's at about forty acres now. It's only going to get worse."

Sharpe nodded. "Because the wind is building and you're shorthanded."

"Under the mutual aid pact, Ventura County was supposed to send a full brush fire response team, but they're battling to keep a hundred-acre brush fire from reaching downtown Ventura."

"I didn't know there was a fire up there," Sharpe said.

"It broke out last night, so all they could spare now is two engines and twelve firefighters, and they just got here," Tighe said. "LA County has their hands full with that fire up in Stevenson Ranch, which is heading this way, so they didn't give me even half of what I was expecting. And LAFD is fully engaged on that fire in the Sepulveda Pass."

"Leaving you to do the best you can with maybe a third of the manpower and equipment you need," Sharpe said.

"We got some county Firehawks"—Tighe gestured to the choppers dropping water on the fire—"but with these winds, they aren't very effective. They'll be grounded soon because the winds will make it too dangerous to fly."

Walker asked, "Are more ground reinforcements on the way?"

"Eventually," Tighe said. "But this blaze is moving into open space and not threatening many structures yet, except for a few outliers we can cover . . ." He gestured to the condos, where firefighters were making progress putting out the tree fires and keeping the rooftops from burning. "So we're third or fourth in line for resources right now. It was the worst possible timing for a fire to happen right here."

"I wouldn't want to be in your shoes, Roy," Sharpe said. "What are you going to do?"

"Kick it upstairs. I'm waiting for the assistant chief to arrive and take charge. He's got bigger balls, bureaucratically speaking, than I have," Tighe said. "Besides, I've got a bad feeling they are going to need me in the field. If the wind picks up, and forecasts say it will, this fire could have Bell Canyon for lunch and Calabasas for dinner."

Sharpe mulled that for a moment. "You going to make a stand on the 101 freeway to try and keep the fire from jumping?"

"If they'll let me." His radio squawked with a call from one of his units, and he moved away to respond.

Walker waved Sharpe to follow him over toward a cluster of boulders. "I've noticed some things about this fire."

Sharpe regarded him dubiously. "Do tell."

"To my totally untrained eye, it looks like the power line caused this one, too. But I am seeing more of those burn spots on boulders upwind from the fire than we did in the Sepulveda Pass." Walker pointed out one of the spots on a boulder.

"It's different geography here. The wind whips and whirls through these hills and ravines. It's not uncommon or surprising to see some burns outside the line in a situation like this." But even as Sharpe was saying that, he took out his phone and snapped a photo of the burn spot on the boulder.

"I was also thinking about mass theory and fire plumes."

"Is that so?" Sharpe took a knife and an evidence baggie out of his pocket, bent down, and scraped the soot from the spot on the boulder into the baggie.

"It's all dry brush out here, but not many trees," Walker said. "So what set those palms on fire way over there, to the southeast?"

"Good question." Sharpe straightened up and shoved the baggie into his pocket. "Let's go take a look."

They got in the Tahoe and Sharpe drove up the wrought-iron fence line between the condos and the open space of the park. They got out and walked up to the fence.

Walker peered into a tiny backyard near one of the charred palm trees. The small concrete patio around a small kidney-shaped pool was dotted with scorch marks from falling embers.

Sharpe walked along the fence line, looking into each yard, then stopped suddenly, took out his phone, and snapped a picture of something.

When Walker came up beside him, Sharpe pointed at the backyard pool. "What's that?"

Walker saw something white and rounded floating in the pool amid the bits of charred palm frond. "It looks like a burned eggshell."

"I'd like a closer look," Sharpe said.

In other words, Walker thought, *go get it for me*. He sighed, checked quickly for any signs of a vicious guard dog, and then scaled the chest-high wrought-iron fence, careful to drop gently onto the patio, sparing his still-sore right knee any extra stress. He picked up the pool net pole, reached it out over the water, and scooped the white thing into the net along with some of the burned palm frond bits.

Walker brought the net close and examined his catch. "It's a scorched Ping-Pong ball."

"Do you see a Ping-Pong table or any paddles or balls around here?"

Walker glanced around the yard. "Nope."

"Let me have that ball," Sharpe said.

Walker held the net out over the fence for Sharpe, who plucked out the burned ball and dropped it into an evidence bag. "Do you think it means something?"

"I think it's weird." Sharpe wrote something on the bag with a pen and stuffed it into his pocket.

"Yeah, but when has a Ping-Pong ball ever started a fire?"

Sharpe got a strange look on his face and cocked his head like a dog hearing an unusual noise he didn't recognize. "Let's go."

Walker dropped the pole, climbed the fence, and landed on his feet on the other side. "We're done already?"

"We're just getting started." Sharpe tossed Walker the car keys. "You drive. Go back down the fire road, then head south on Topanga Canyon Boulevard."

"Where are we going?"

"Shopping," Sharpe said.

CHAPTER THIRTEEN

Three Weeks Ago

The blue Ferrari 488 Spider was the perfect car for taking the hairpin turns on Latigo Canyon Road, heading south into the Santa Monica Mountains toward the sea. But the Beverly Hills rental car company wouldn't have been pleased knowing how fast and dangerously Danny Cole was driving on the two-lane ridgeline road, where one tiny miscalculation could send him plunging off a cliff.

Then again, Danny thought, they could hardly be surprised. Who rented a Ferrari with any intention of driving slowly? Nobody. The point of a Ferrari was to drive fast and be seen doing it, to express your daring, your virility, and your wealth, which was exactly why he chose the car for the character he was playing today.

He was on his way to see Levi Brisker, a real estate developer. Brisker had used the money he'd inherited from his father, who'd owned a carpet-cleaning business, to buy and flip homes, fast and on the cheap. He became so successful at it that he sold his father's business and invested all of his profits from the sale, and his flipping, into building a multimillion-dollar spec mansion in Beverly Hills. It was a huge gamble, but it paid off—he sold the luxurious new home for three times what it cost him to build.

That sealed his doom.

Each spec house Brisker built after that was bigger and more extravagant than the last, each profitable sale emboldening him to add more square footage and more outrageous, attention-grabbing luxuries to the next house, spiking his construction costs into the tens of millions of dollars, eventually narrowing his pool of potential buyers to billionaires.

But the homes became a reflection of Brisker's aspirations and desires, which he wrongly assumed were shared by the top 1 percent he was trying to wow. To Danny, that was like assuming that every emperor or king had the same tastes as Caligula. The billionaires Brisker courted had their own ideas of luxury, extravagance, and decadence and didn't want to buy into someone else's.

He'd invested everything he had, and borrowed even more, to build a ridiculously opulent 21,000-square-foot home that stood alone on the eastern ridge of Wishbone Canyon. But his luck had run out. Nobody wanted the house, even after he'd lowered the price from $100 million to $75 million, nearly what it had cost him to build, and his impatient lenders and furious unpaid contractors were on the verge of forcing him into bankruptcy.

Now Levi Brisker's last hope was about to arrive in a blue Ferrari.

Danny took a left onto Wishbone Road and followed it as it wound up the unpopulated hills of oaks and dry brush that buttressed the western slope of Wishbone Canyon's eastern ridge. The road doubled back to the north, and shortly after that, he made a right onto the unmarked driveway leading to Brisker's spec house. But Danny paused for a moment to look down the road and visualize what lay ahead. He knew the road forked a quarter mile farther up, one road continuing north, the other crossing the fusion point of the imaginary wishbone to reach the opposite western ridge. He knew because he'd studied the map very closely, even though he'd traveled the road before, a journey he'd never forget.

He drove on. The driveway led to a sleek steel-and-glass bridge over a moat to a circular travertine-tiled motor court and the white-marble two-story modernist house that curved around it. In the center of the motor court was a marble reproduction of Michelangelo's *David* sculpture in a fountain of "dancing water" spouting in an ever-changing variety of arches, geysers, and sprays. Danny wondered if Brisker also had a copy of the *Mona Lisa* inside, hanging above the mantelpiece.

Danny parked at the front door and got out of the Ferrari, and Levi Brisker bounded out of the house to meet him.

Brisker wore a red T-shirt under an unbuttoned, dip-dyed white linen shirt, the lower half looking as if it had been dunked in a can of blue paint. The shirttails hung over a pair of green faded-linen drawstring pants and orange calf-leather loafers without socks. He looked like a walking pile of M&M's.

He offered his hand to Danny. "Mr. Templar, it's a pleasure to meet you. I trust you had a good flight."

They shook hands, and when Danny spoke, it was with a refined British accent, perhaps with a touch of an Irish lilt, since he'd honed it by studying Pierce Brosnan. "When you own the jet, Mr. Brisker, it's always a good flight. Otherwise, what would be the point?"

"So true. That's why I never fly commercial. Please call me Levi. Welcome to the Epitome." He spread out his arms in an expansive gesture that invited Danny to take it all in, as if he were presenting one of the natural wonders of the world.

"Which begs the question . . . epitome of what?"

"Everything anyone would ever want in a home: opulence, beauty, grandeur, space, comfort, privacy, safety, views. We have it all in twenty bedrooms, forty baths, and two chef's kitchens, but I'd rather show you than tell you. The house sells itself."

"If that were true," Danny said, "it would have sold months ago."

"Ah, but only a few people on earth have the financial resources and the grand vision to occupy this rarified property, much like the pantheon of gods who resided upon Mount Olympus."

"But they were all content to sit on clouds hurling lightning bolts at mortals. They had no use for showy extravagances like a moat or a marble driveway."

Levi smiled, exposing two impossibly perfect rows of teeth that were as white as the marble on the house. Perhaps, Danny thought, they *were* marble.

"Everything you see here does more than merely dazzle the senses, stimulate the imagination, or soothe the soul, Mr. Templar. The moat is an eye-popping indulgence that deters invaders, but it's also a relaxing lazy river that wraps around the house for your guests to enjoy and supplies the water for a fire-retardant sprinkler system. And this marble motor court isn't just breathtaking grandeur but a buffer that will keep the flames of a wildfire from ever touching the house."

"I'm impressed," Danny said, and he actually meant it.

"It's only the beginning. The Epitome has its own independent, solar-based power supply and is designed to be a home, an office, a showplace, a resort, and a fortress."

Levi led him into the grand two-story oval foyer, where dual sweeping staircases encircled the space and an elaborate mosaic in the center of the marble floor. Beyond it was the great room, its floor-to-ceiling windows offering an IMAX view of Malibu and the Pacific.

"Directly below us, two floors down and carved out of the bedrock, is an impregnable panic room and the underground garage, which can hold fifty vehicles and has a rotating car elevator."

"Where does it elevate cars to?"

"Right here." Levi hit a button on the wall. The mosaic on the floor slid away, a protective railing popped up to encircle the open space, and a chrome-plated Lamborghini Aventador rose up from below, spinning slowly on a circular platform that was lifted nearly to the domed skylight above by a Swarovski-crystal-entwined black-marble pillar. Pinpoint halogen lights lit up from strategic points on the walls, making the Lamborghini glow and the crystals sparkle. "Your vehicles are expensive works of art and now they can be displayed like it. The Lamborghini, and an Aston Martin in the garage, are included in the purchase price, of course."

"Of course," Danny said. "But I wouldn't want to be standing under that car when the big one hits."

"The Lambo is secured to the base. The entire display can withstand a magnitude eight earthquake, just like the house itself, which is secured to the bedrock and rests on dampeners to absorb the shock waves."

"So that crystal elevator tower isn't just a feat of engineering or even a work of art—it's a metaphor for the house itself, one that also sends a constant subliminal message that you are safe here."

Levi practically danced with delight. "Amazing! You're truly the first person to feel the essence of this special place as I do, to appreciate its beauty, its complexity, its unique duality, on an emotional and, dare I say it, spiritual level."

Danny had to choke back a laugh. The ass-kissing was almost as over the top as the house itself. Levi's poor salesmanship might be another reason why the house had failed to sell. Billionaires enjoyed respect and supplication, but not groveling.

The tour continued through the home's bedrooms, bathrooms, and kitchens, with a visit to the bar (a four-hundred-year-old Scottish pub that he'd had dismantled, brick by brick, shipped to Malibu, and rebuilt downstairs), bowling alley, movie theater, and candy room, which was obviously inspired by Willy Wonka's chocolate factory. Instrumental versions of "The Candy Man" and "Pure Imagination" played in a loop on speakers hidden within a garden of buttercups that squirted butterscotch syrup with a swipe of the hand. All that was missing was a river of chocolate and the singing Oompa Loompas, but Danny assumed that was only because Brisker had run out of money.

Although the house appeared from the outside to be two stories, there were actually two more floors underground. The first subterranean level held the home theater, bowling alley, and pub. Below it were the garage, a safe room, and a wine cellar. The ground-level floor was where the foyer, great room, main kitchen, formal dining room, library, another home theater, and several bedrooms were located. The top floor was mostly bedrooms and baths, and another safe room. All four floors were connected by various staircases and a single glass elevator.

They returned to the great room, where the two-story floor-to-ceiling windows provided spectacular unobstructed views of the mountains and the Pacific, clear out to Catalina Island. But the view Danny was most interested in was directly across the ravine, on the shelflike pads graded into the westside slope of Wishbone Canyon's eastern ridge. That's where Roland Slezak's mansion still stood, along with the two other estates that had been built in the years since Arnie Soloway's life was needlessly lost in the Crags Fire. There was also a water tank on the ridge above the homes, a smart move by the three homeowners to protect themselves from another wildfire.

"You mentioned earlier that the house can withstand an earthquake," Danny said. "But what about wildfires? What if the winds blow the flames past the moat and the motor court?"

"The roof is stone aggregate," Levi said, wiping butterscotch off his palm with a napkin embossed with the words THE EPITOME. "The walls are built of steel and reinforced concrete. The underground garage is carved into solid bedrock and can be sealed off for use as a fallout shelter. This house is fireproof."

"All of that might keep out the flames . . . but what about the heat and smoke?"

"The Epitome has a computerized, carbon-filtered airflow and conditioning system that controls the temperature and automatically adjusts the environmental pressurization inside the home to prevent contaminants outside from entering, whether it's from smoke, smog, or a flatulent guest letting one rip on the driveway."

"I'm sold."

Levi looked a bit dazed. He hadn't been expecting that. At least not now, or that directly. "You're going to make an offer on the house?"

"I'm going to do better than that, Levi," Danny said, speaking with his natural voice. "I'm going to save your life. And I know what you're thinking: 'Buying the house is what will save my life . . . and hey, where did his cool British accent go?'"

Levi reached out a hand to the wall to steady himself, as if the house, despite resting on dampeners designed to keep it level, were swaying anyway. "I don't understand."

"Your big problem is that you're a con man who has suckered himself, which is a professional hazard. Believe me, I know."

"You're a con man?"

"All salesmen are. Like you, I sell dreams. But you're so bedazzled by your vision of this house that you can't stop putting money into it, getting deeper and deeper into debt. You're the Cadillac salesman who buys a top-of-the-line Coupe deVille that he can't possibly afford, because he actually believes his pitch about the status, power, and sex that owning the car bestows upon the buyer. So, when he's faced with the reality of losing the Cadillac, his job, his house, his wife, and worst of all, his dignity, he jumps off a bridge."

"I lease a Bentley."

"You're missing the point, Levi."

"You're not buying the house from me."

"No, I'm not. Nobody ever will. It's the epitome of self-delusion. You listed it a year ago for $100 million and haven't had a single offer. You've spent $70 million and counting on construction costs . . . and it's still not finished. Work has stopped, and the city hasn't signed off on the key permits, so it's unsafe to occupy."

He waved away the problems. "That's just red tape."

"You've also run out of cash and have defaulted on your loan," Danny said. "So, here's what's going to happen. Within weeks, if not days, your creditors will foreclose on you, forcing you into bankruptcy.

The court will put the house up for auction and sell it fast, and nowhere near what the house has cost to build. The losses will be in the tens of millions of dollars. Dozens of lawsuits will be filed against you, perhaps even criminal charges, but you don't have to worry, because you'll be dead long before any of that happens."

"I'm not jumping off a bridge," Levi said, but he did sit down on a couch.

"Of course not, because you won't get the chance. The instant this house goes into receivership, the Mexican cartel I know you convinced to launder their drug money by investing in this house will dismember you with a chain saw, stuff your cock in your mouth, and FedEx your head to your family in Tel Aviv. But I can save you from that."

Levi looked up at him, and it was clear from the hopeless expression on his face that the reality of his dire situation had hit home, which Danny knew from experience happened quickly when envisioning your genitals being hacked off.

"How can I be saved if you're not going to buy my house?"

Danny stepped up to the window and gestured to the three huge homes across the ravine. "What would happen if all the houses around here burned . . . and the Epitome was the only one left standing?"

"A picture of it, pristine and white, surrounded by nothing but black, scorched earth, would be published all over the world. It would become famous for being impervious to fire."

"Wrong answer. What you'd have is the only premium property available for sale to all those wealthy, powerful people who just lost their homes to the flames . . . people who demand immediate gratification . . . but who know it will take years to rebuild. What do you think will happen?"

Levi thought about it for a moment and smiled, showing off those whiter-than-white teeth. "There will be a bidding war to end all bidding wars to purchase this place. I'll be able to pay off my debts and walk away with a substantial profit."

"And all of your appendages. That's what I'm offering you."

Levi stood up and joined Danny at the window. "Anybody can set these hills on fire. I don't need you for that."

"I'm not just lighting a fire. I'm directing the blaze, making it go where I want it to, when I want it to, before the fire department can put it out. How many people do you know who can do that?" Danny tipped his head toward the opposite ridge. "You need me to make sure those houses burn."

Levi's gaze drifted over to the three homes, alone on the hillside, and Danny knew he was imagining them gone, just blackened, naked earth where they once stood. "What will you get out of it? A cut of the money from selling the Epitome?"

"Nope. That's all yours. What I want has nothing to do with you or the sale. So, you have nothing to lose . . . and your life to gain."

Levi met Danny's gaze. "I don't have much time before my creditors take the house."

"How many weeks?"

"Three. At most."

"No problem. We can move in today and make that deadline." It coincided perfectly with Santa Ana season. Give or take a few days.

"We?"

Danny slipped an arm around Levi's shoulders and led him to a floating glass staircase that wrapped like a vine around a transparent tube containing an elevator platform. The two men continued talking as they went down the steps to the lower floor. "My crew and I will need to stay here until the fire passes through this canyon and those houses are ash. But we'll be gone before the smoke clears and nobody will ever know we were here."

"I still don't see the profit in this for you."

"It will become clear to you over the next three weeks because you'll be here, keeping up appearances, until the big day." They walked down a hallway to the facade of the Scottish pub, the actual four-hundred-year-old bricks, storm-weathered sign, and heavy wooden door rebuilt in front of them. The Ye Old Highwayman, resurrected in Malibu. "But everything depends on this house being as fireproof as you say it is. Because if it's not, if this is just $70 million of drywall and bullshit, then we're all going to die . . . me and my crew in the fire, and you to the cartel butchers."

The paneling, stone floors, and original bar reeked of decades of beer, cigarette smoke, fried food, and just a hint of puke. Danny went behind the bar, where he found two coasters embossed with THE EPITOME and two glasses with the name etched onto them. He set them all in front of the jittery builder, who clearly needed a drink.

Levi sat on one of the barstools. "You're asking me to gamble my life on you, and let you use this house, based on what? That you were able to trick me into believing you're rich?"

"Wrong question, again. What you should be asking me is how did I know about your secret deal with the cartel?"

"Because you're an undercover FBI agent and this is a ridiculous attempt to entrap me in a sting."

"Close." Danny took an unopened bottle of Macallan Rare Cask, cracked the seal, and poured healthy portions into the two glasses. He needed the drink because he was about to take a huge risk to seal this deal. "I know about it because I'm financing this scheme with the money I swindled from Diego Grillo. Cheers."

He raised his glass and so did Levi. They both took a sip. "You set up that fake bank scam? I thought it was an FBI operation."

Danny took another sip to fortify himself for something he rarely did in a con: telling the truth.

"They took credit for my scam because otherwise they'd have to admit I played them. Not only did I take Grillo's money, I got the FBI to send him to prison so he couldn't come after me, destroying his cartel, which created the opening for his rivals to grab his business and make the mountains of cash they tried to launder through this house.

If I could do that, what do you think my chances are of getting you out of your mess and saving your life in three weeks compared to the odds of you succeeding on your own?"

Danny could tell by the look in Levi's eyes that he'd made his point, that he'd manipulated the FBI and a drug cartel and gotten away alive. That took brains and balls, two parts of Levi Brisker that would soon be in uncomfortably and unnaturally close proximity if he didn't take this opportunity. Of course, Danny also went to prison, but there was no reason to share that inconvenient fact.

Levi knocked back the rest of his Scotch and held out his hand. "Don't worry. It's fireproof."

Danny shook it. They had a deal.

CHAPTER FOURTEEN

Present Day
Friday

Sharpe had Walker stop at Pep Boys, where he bought antifreeze, and at Leslie's Pool Supply, where he bought "pool shock" granules to clean water, and at Ace Hardware, where he bought a PVC pipe–cutting garrote, and at Dick's Sporting Goods, where he bought a bag of Ping-Pong balls.

Sharpe did not explain why he was doing all this shopping, so Walker didn't announce that he was driving through McDonald's on the way back, either. He ordered a Big Mac, fries, and a Coke, but Sharpe didn't get anything. Walker ate his lunch while he drove, finishing it by the time they reached LASD headquarters.

They went straight to Sharpe's office. Sharpe spread a newspaper out on his desktop and started unpacking his purchases. He tore open the bag of Ping-Pong balls first and took one out, offering it to Walker.

"I need you to hold the ball between your thumb and forefinger, like so," Sharpe said, demonstrating by showing Walker how he held the ball himself.

"Got it." Walker took the ball and held it as instructed. Sharpe took out the garrote, which had a looped, rubber-wrapped handle on each end, and wrapped the wire around the middle of the ball. "You want to strangle a Ping-Pong ball?"

"I want to cut the ball in half." Sharpe began sawing the wire through the ball. "Maintain pressure, but be careful not to crush it."

"Are we doing laundry again?"

"If you mean conducting a test to confirm a hypothesis, then yes." The hollow ball separated. Sharpe set aside the garrote, took the two halves from Walker, and set them on the newspaper.

"What's your hypothesis?"

Sharpe opened up the bag of pool shock. "Actually, it's yours."

"I don't remember offering one."

"You asked if a Ping-Pong ball could start a fire. The answer is yes, it can." Sharpe took a spoon out of a nearby coffee cup and used it to measure some granules from the bag, which he carefully poured into one half of the Ping-Pong ball. "It used to be that just a vigorous game of table tennis could spark an inferno."

Walker plucked another ball from the bag of them and examined it between his thumb and forefinger. "They seem pretty harmless to me."

"They are now. But they used to be made out of nitrocellulose, which is highly flammable." Sharpe opened his desk drawer and began searching through the junk for something. "Just the friction of the ball hitting the table at high speed could send a fireball at your opponent. Or the ball might burst into flame when you smacked it with your paddle."

"You've got to be kidding."

Sharpe sorted through paper clips, business cards, nails, plastic cutlery, wire cutters, tiny screwdrivers, broken sunglasses, old mints, receipts, thumb drives, wads of Kleenex, electric wire, tweezers, and curled-up tubes of what appeared to be various ointments, creams, or toothpastes. Walker didn't see the full labels on the tubes, though one looked like Preparation H.

"It was a serious problem," Sharpe said, "particularly in competition play. Now the balls are made of ABS plastic, so they don't ignite anymore."

"That's a shame, because the possibility of seeing an explosion had to be the only reason anybody watched a Ping-Pong game." Walker tossed the ball against the wall. It bounced back in his direction but out of reach for him to catch without taking a dive. It bounced around the room before falling irretrievably behind a file cabinet. Sharpe didn't notice—he was still occupied searching his drawer.

"But there's still a way Ping-Pong balls can cause a fire." Sharpe found what he was looking for: a tiny tube of Super Glue.

"Let me guess. Beer pong."

"Firefighting." Sharpe forced the drawer closed.

"That sounds like a contradiction."

Sharpe uncapped the Super Glue tube and carefully ran the wet tip along the edge of one half of the severed Ping-Pong ball, then put the two halves back together and presented the restored ball to Walker. "Hold this for a minute or two until the glue dries."

He opened another desk drawer and began searching for something else. While he did, he continued talking to Walker.

"You've heard the phrase 'fighting fire with fire.' The way it's done is by creating backfires, controlled burns to remove the brush that could fuel a wildfire. That isn't easy to do over a wide area in a short amount of time, especially in rough terrain, because firefighters have to walk along the line using drip torches." Sharpe pulled a package of syringes from the drawer, set them on the desk, shook out one syringe, then tore off the plastic wrapping that contained it. "But now that's changed. Some twisted genius, probably a crazed table tennis star, came up with the idea of weaponizing Ping-Pong balls and dropping them from helicopters instead."

"How do you turn a Ping-Pong ball into a firebomb?" Walker asked.

"I'm going to show you." Sharpe opened the bottle of antifreeze and collected some of the fluid with the syringe. "But let's make a couple more of those balls first."

◆ ◆ ◆

Sharpe and Walker went out to a corner of the asphalt parking lot where there weren't any cars. Walker carried a bag full of Ping-Pong balls that had been sliced open, half filled with pool shock granules, and glued back together. Sharpe had one strap of his investigation backpack slung over his shoulder and held an aluminum baking pan in his hands, which were covered in thick fireproof gloves.

"The Ping-Pong balls in your bag are filled with potassium permanganate, a widely available disinfectant with a variety of uses, like cleaning swimming pools," Sharpe said, setting the pan down on the ground. "If you inject the balls with ethylene glycol, which is commonly used as antifreeze, it creates a self-igniting chemical reaction within about thirty seconds."

"You mean an explosion."

"I mean a fireball." Sharpe removed a ball from Walker's bag, set it in the tin pan, then reached into his backpack for a syringe filled with antifreeze. He pulled off the needle guard, crouched beside the pan, and injected the ball with the syringe.

Within two seconds, the ball burst into an intense ball of flame that was quickly reduced to nothing but a black spot, very much like the ones Walker saw on the rocks in the Sepulveda Pass and that morning in Chatsworth.

"They toss these balls out of helicopters?"

"They have a device that injects the balls and immediately shoots them out," Sharpe said. "It can release dozens of them a minute."

"What happens if one of these balls gets stuck in the machine after it's been injected?"

"Disaster." Sharpe bent down and collected the char left over by the Ping-Pong ball into an evidence baggie and then wrote some information on it with a Sharpie, which Walker thought was the perfect, and ridiculously obvious, writing instrument for the investigator. "Not only that, but dense smoke, high wind, and mountainous terrain makes it extremely dangerous to fly a helicopter into a fire zone even when the aircraft isn't loaded with thousands of tiny bombs. But now the Forest Service is using a new method for deploying these fireballs."

Walker heard people talk about religious epiphanies. Being an atheist, he'd never had one of those, but he wondered if the feeling was similar to what he experienced in the instant when all the puzzle pieces fit together in whatever mystery he was trying to solve. He had that feeling now, though in a different way than ever before, because he hadn't even been aware that there was a mystery, or that he was trying to solve it, until the epiphany itself.

But it all fit. Everything they'd seen the last two days, and even the crazy stuff that Margaret, the transient with her head wrapped in foil, had told them. Walker knew what the Forest Service's new method of deploying Ping-Pong ball bombs was.

"Mind-reading drones, only without the mind-reading equipment."

"That's right. It's called the Icarus." Sharpe took a bottle of water out of his bag, unscrewed the top, then set it aside. He took another ball from Walker's bag, placed it in the tin, and injected it with antifreeze, only this time, once it started to burn, he doused it with water.

What was left of the Ping-Pong ball looked to Walker exactly like what they'd recovered from the pool in Chatsworth. "You're going to have the lab compare the scorched Ping-Pong ball and ash you recovered in the field with the ash left behind by this experiment."

"Yes, I will, except it will take days, if not weeks, for the lab to give us the results. We won't have them in time." Sharpe collected the scorched remains of the Ping-Pong ball and bagged it.

"In time for what?"

"To prove the wildfires in the Sepulveda Pass and the one in Chatsworth were intentionally set by the same man."

Walker felt a charge of pure happiness. Now he didn't feel like a tagalong. Now he saw his purpose in this investigation, his chance to step up and do what he did best. "It's proof enough for me."

"What good does that do us?"

"Because now I've got someone to hunt," Walker said. "And I always get my man."

◆ ◆ ◆

They took the samples they collected in Chatsworth and from their parking lot experiments to the crime lab, but they didn't have to go far to do it. The Hertzberg-Davis Forensic Science Center was located on the California State University, Los Angeles, campus, only two miles north of LASD headquarters, right across the I-10 overpass.

Afterward, they went back to Sharpe's office, where he pulled a crumpled brown paper bag from the bottom drawer of his desk and said, "We need to go back out to Chatsworth and collect more evidence. Map the scene, photograph the upwind burns to establish the drop pattern, and search every backyard pool, dog bowl, bird feeder, and fountain to see if we can find another unburned ball to confirm our hypothesis."

Walker waved all that away. "That will take too much time."

"It's standard investigative procedure." Sharpe took a plastic-wrapped white-bread sandwich out of the bag. It was peanut butter and jelly. "We'll need that evidence to make a case in court."

It was a lunch a mother would give a kindergartener. Walker wondered if maybe Sharpe had a box of animal crackers in the brown bag, too.

"Fine, assign some grunts to do that," Walker said. "You and I need to narrow in on the Burner."

"The burner?"

"The Torcher."

"Are you referring to the arsonist?" Sharpe asked, eating his sandwich.

"We can do better than that," Walker said. "How about the Incinerator?"

"How about the arsonist, as in someone who commits arson."

"We can circle back to that. You told me that the time-delay device was like a confession." Walker picked up one of the Ping-Pong balls on Sharpe's desk. "So, what does this tell you about him?"

"That we are dealing with a highly intelligent, financially well-off man with fire experience and technical expertise," Sharpe said. "He knew about Icarus drones, how to create his own fireballs, and how to stage the arsons to look like power-line failures."

"Which points to a firefighter or an arson investigator."

"A very rich one with engineering skills, because he bought an expensive industrial drone and retrofitted it to inject and deploy the fireballs."

"Or he did it the easy way and stole an Icarus."

"That's only easy if you're an experienced thief."

"Or if you're already working at a fire station that has an Icarus or for the company that makes them."

Sharpe considered that possibility for a moment as he finished his sandwich. "We can call the Icarus manufacturer first, ask if any of their drone inventory is missing, and while they're checking, we'll get a list of their customers and reach out to each one of them."

"Before we do that, I want to get a sense of the firebug we're chasing," Walker said. "Let's talk motive. For an urban fire, it's got to be revenge, money, or hiding another crime, right?"

"Yes, but these fires are in the wilderness, what we call 'wildland fires,' so it's likely a first responder, or someone who makes a living off them, trying to whip up work."

"But this isn't the wilderness. We're right in the middle of the city, so it could also be about making money, getting revenge, or covering up another crime."

Sharpe shook his head. "Someone might torch a stolen car used in a drive-by shooting or a bank robbery, or set fire to a house where they've killed someone, or burn an office to destroy incriminating files, but only weeds and trees have burned so far. It's not about money or covering up a crime."

"So maybe it's revenge," Walker said.

Sharpe reached into his bag, but instead of pulling out a box of animal crackers, he held a two-cookie lunch packet of Oreos. "The locations of the fires are on public land, miles apart. Who does that hurt?"

"He made it look like the wildfires were sparked by power-line failures. Maybe his grudge is against Edison," Walker said, referring to the local electricity provider. "If hundreds of homes are destroyed, and some lives lost, and if Edison appears responsible because of their negligence, they would be prosecuted and sued for hundreds of millions of dollars. Maybe the Incinerator is a lawyer. It fits the whipping-up-business motive for wildland fires."

Sharpe frowned and Walker couldn't blame him. The scenario didn't feel right to Walker, either. "Scratch the lawyer scenario. It's too much trouble for a lawyer to go to for the chance at a possible big payoff that's years down the line."

"Maybe embarrassing Edison is all the arsonist is after," Sharpe said, nibbling on a cookie.

"I don't buy it," Walker said. "There's got to be a much bigger, immediate benefit. Why set the fires now?"

"That's easy," Sharpe said. "Because he needed the Santa Ana winds to make it instantly believable that the fires were caused by failed power lines."

"Yeah, but why in those two places?"

"That's where power lines run across remote open space and where he could pilot a drone from a safe distance away without being seen."

"That's not what I meant," Walker said. "There are lots of places like that in LA. Why pick those two specific places? And where's the money in it for him *today*, not years from now?"

"I don't know," Sharpe said.

"We're missing something."

"We're missing everything."

"No, it's right in front of us," Walker said. "We just don't see it yet and we're going to feel really stupid when we do."

"Let's start by finding out where he got the Icarus drone." Sharpe wrote something down on a piece of paper and slid it across the desk to Walker. "This is the name of the manufacturer. Start with them. While you do that, I'll call the lieutenant and brief him on what we know, or *think* we do, and ask him to send some investigators out to Chatsworth and the Sepulveda Pass to gather evidence while we chase the drone angle."

Walker left Sharpe's office, went to the nearest desk, and called the manufacturer of the Icarus. He reached a helpful manager who said he'd check their stock to see if they were missing drones but that it was highly unlikely they were. But in the meantime, he would immediately email Walker a list of all their customers. That said, the manager hadn't heard about any Icarus drones being stolen . . . and the firefighting community was a very small world.

The call ended just as Sharpe emerged from his office and approached the desk where Walker was sitting. "The lieutenant thinks our theory is weak, but he'll let us run with it for the rest of the day."

It was already late afternoon. "The day is almost over."

"That should tell you how seriously he takes our theory. We'd better hope the crew he's sending to Chatsworth finds another Ping-Pong ball in a fountain or something."

"That's not how we're going to close this case." Walker's phone pinged, indicating the arrival of an email. He checked it out. It was from the drone manufacturer. "I just got the list of Icarus customers. You call half and I'll call half. Maybe one of them is missing a drone."

CHAPTER FIFTEEN

Two and a Half Weeks Ago

It wasn't until Alison Grayle reached out to open the door to Dorothy's Chuck Wagon diner in the small community of Garner's Crossing in the San Bernardino National Forest that she noticed the dirt under her fingernails from burying another damn medical bill at her husband's grave.

She probably should have waited to file the bill until after her interview with the *New York Times* reporter, but the cemetery was on the way to the diner and she was angry. She didn't want the bill waiting for her at home, as welcome as a pile of shit left by the dog, if she'd even had a dog, or to feel it in her purse, like a boat anchor weighing her down to the bottom of Misery Lake.

Maybe that was a bad decision. Maybe carrying that pain and anger would have been a good thing for the reporter to see on her face. Instead, he'd just notice her wrinkled blouse, the dark roots in her bottle-blonde hair, and her dirt-caked fingernails and decide that she'd given up on personal hygiene, that she'd gone crazy, and dismiss her story as baseless ranting.

All of this crossed Alison's mind in the seconds it took to walk the few feet of scuffed linoleum from the diner's front door to the window booth where the reporter sat waiting for her.

Ed Murrow slid out of the booth and rose when he saw her approach. He looked just like she'd pictured a *New York Times* reporter would—thirtyish, wearing glasses, a corduroy jacket, a collared shirt, a loosely knotted tie, and khaki pants. There was a notebook, a pen, and an iPhone on the table beside his empty mug of coffee and a pie plate scattered with crumbs.

"Sorry I'm late," Alison said.

She assumed that he'd come all the way from New York City, then driven three hours east from Los Angeles and on up to the San Bernardino Mountains, where tiny Garner's Crossing, established in the 1800s as a stagecoach station and trading post, was nestled in a national forest, midway between Lake Arrowhead and Big Bear Lake. They had a population of just under five thousand people, though it often seemed like it was closer to fifty and the other zeros were a typo made by some bored typist at the Census Bureau.

Murrow offered her his hand. "I was beginning to worry that you'd stood me up."

"Why would I do that?" Alison shook his hand and felt an instant, almost shocking sense of familiarity and comfort in his grip. It was something about where his hand was calloused, and where it was soft, but also the strength and firmness.

It felt like she was holding John's hand again.

She didn't want to let go.

"Lots of reasons," Murrow said. "For instance, you could have been frightened about what might happen if you went public with your story. Or maybe somebody intimidated you into keeping quiet and not seeing me."

That was a joke, though she knew he didn't intend it to be. "The scariest thing that could happen to me already did, Mr. Murrow. I'm broke and my husband is dead. So nobody can scare or intimidate me. I have nothing left to lose."

"That's very sad."

Alison realized that she was still holding his hand. Embarrassed, she quickly let go, too quickly, and slid into the booth, thinking, *What is wrong with me?* She set her phone and car keys on the table and dropped her purse next to her on the bench seat.

"You didn't come all this way to hear a story with a happy ending." Murrow slid back into his seat. "The ending hasn't been written yet."

"It has for me."

He smiled, and when he did, she actually felt some hope. "Maybe I can change that. You must think so, too, or you wouldn't have agreed to meet me."

"I want to shame them, Mr. Murrow, that's why I'm here. The problem is, I don't think they have any."

"That's because the US Forest Service and the Office of Workers' Compensation are government bureaucracies. They are designed to be unfeeling. That's how they sap people of all hope and make them quit."

"I thought reporters are supposed to be objective."

"It's a fact, not an opinion or a bias. The key to change isn't making them feel something, it's touching the hearts and minds of the people out there." He pointed out the window, not to anyone specific, just to the world at large. "Make them cry. Make them angry. Make them think. That's when change will happen. Sharing your pain with me can do that."

It was definitely a mistake burying the medical bill, she thought. It would have explained so much to him.

The waitress came by with a coffeepot, refilled Murrow's mug, and, because she knew Alison, brought her a mug, filled it, and left behind two little canisters of creamer. She was Dorothy's daughter Dot, who was twenty-two going on forty, and seemed to have been born in a waitress' uniform.

"How are you doing, honey?" Dot asked Alison, but she cast a warm smile at Murrow while doing it. Dot was notoriously man-hungry but found few in Garner's Crossing to her liking.

"I'm surviving, Dot, thanks for asking," Alison said.

"Shoot up a flare if you'd like some pie."

Once Dot left, Alison turned to Murrow. "Let me tell you what I mean by surviving."

"Okay," he said, setting his iPhone on record and sliding it into the center of the table between them.

She supposed he did it less to make sure he got good sound than to let her know he was recording their conversation. Alison poured the creamer into her coffee, took a sip, then told him about her morning.

"I got a hospital bill today for $1,700 for miscellaneous care, whatever the fuck that is, for my husband, a man who has been dead for two years. I called the hospital to ask what it's for, but the agent said the only person she could talk to about it is him. But he's dead, I told her. She said, 'Then I can't help you.' So I buried the bill at his grave, along with all the others I've been sent and can't pay." She held up her hand to show him the dirt under her fingernails.

He gently held her right hand and examined her nails and she was jarred again by the familiarity of his touch. Why did a reporter have hands like that? Like a firefighter's? But he didn't, of course. He was probably an avid gardener when he wasn't interviewing crazy, bitter widows.

"It would be funny if it wasn't so tragic," he said, letting go.

"Do you want to hear a funny story?"

He leaned back in his seat. "I have a bad feeling that it's not going to be funny at all."

"It begins with a boy named John Grayle. He loved the outdoors. He was a Cub Scout, a Boy Scout, and Park Service volunteer before joining the Forest Service, where his father worked as a park ranger. But John wanted more adventure than being a forest cop."

"So, he became a wilderness firefighter."

She nodded. "His dream was to be a smoke jumper, to parachute into the heart of a fire zone and try to stop the flames from advancing. It finally came true for him when he was accepted by the Thunderbird Hotshots."

"They are the elite of the elite," Murrow said. "The Navy SEALs of firefighters."

"That's their reputation, but it's not matched by the pay: $25,000 a year. Who can support themselves on that? Rent alone is going to be $1,200 a month, minimum."

"How do they do it?"

"By living on the overtime and hazard pay they get during wildfire season," Alison said. "But even then, what they earn is barely above the poverty line. Maybe another ten grand. Now here comes the funny part. John was deeply and genuinely devoted to protecting the forest from fire, but if it wasn't for the lightning strikes, or idiots who don't snuff out their campfires, or even the occasional arsonist, he'd starve to death or die of boredom. He was constantly wishing that the forest would burn."

She laughed ruefully, more for effect than anything else.

Murrow wasn't laughing at all. "It must have torn him up with guilt."

"Which is also why he had a drinking problem," she said. "Hilarious, isn't it?"

It was a vicious circle that couldn't be broken. She felt something on her cheek, and when she went to wipe it away, she realized it was a tear. How long had she been crying? She dabbed her eyes with a napkin.

Murrow pretended not to notice by taking some notes. "It explains why so many wilderness fires are started by first responders, or someone else who depends on them for their livelihood."

"That's everyone. Up here in Garner's Crossing, the definition of 'fire' is 'money'—not just for the firefighters, but also for restaurants, hotels, heavy equipment operators, even the hookers. Then there's all the people who make a living cleaning up and rebuilding after a blaze."

"But at the same time, the idea of an uncontrollable fire destroying the forest and their town must terrify them."

"Not as much as poverty does," Alison said. "We aren't Lake Arrowhead or Big Bear. We don't have ski resorts or a lake or any industry of our own besides first responders. We had a string of wildfires up here that were sparked by a firefighter's ex-wife who wanted to be sure he could keep up with his child support and alimony payments. But at least if you understand fire and are familiar with the land here, there's a strong chance you can set a blaze that won't endanger people or homes . . . but it's not an exact science."

"You should know," he said. "Wasn't that your job as a meteorologist for CAL FIRE?"

Yes, it was. She'd wanted to use her meteorology degree to get a job in TV, but she didn't have the face or the body to stand in front of a green screen in a bandage dress. It turned out the body was much more important than the degree. She was told it would be a "wise investment" to invest in a boob job and a personal trainer. But she didn't tell Murrow any of that.

"A lot more factors go into predicting the behavior of a wildfire than weather forecasting," Alison said. "Like the topography, the plants, the moisture in the soil, what kind of grasses and timber there is, and even with supercomputers crunching all the variables and great minds like mine analyzing the results, we're still wrong nearly half the time. You'd do just as well flipping a coin."

Dot came over, set a slice of coconut cream pie down in front of Alison, and patted her on the shoulder. "On the house, sweetie."

The waitress must have seen Alison crying and knew coconut cream pie was her favorite all-purpose self-medication, at least when she was in Dorothy's Chuck Wagon.

"Thank you, Dot," Alison said, and although she wasn't the least bit hungry, took a bite to show her appreciation.

Murrow asked, "Did being a meteorologist for CAL FIRE at least pay well?"

That was a laugh, not that she could muster even a fake one. "I only made decent money when the mountains were burning, so I supplemented my income with Uber work, which is how I met John. I gave him a ride home from a bar one night . . . and he vomited in the back seat of my car. Six months later, we were married. It was love at first puke."

Murrow made a note on his pad. "You aren't working for CAL FIRE anymore?"

She took another bite of pie, because the thing about pie was, if you took one bite, you were compelled to eat the whole slice. "I took a leave after the accident to take care of John. And then the idea of going back to work for those heartless bastards, after what they did to us, disgusted me."

Murrow nodded. "What did they tell you happened? I haven't been able to get a straight answer out of them. They say it's still under investigation."

Alison had some more pie. It actually made going back over this horrible experience a little less painful to remember. Maybe pie really did have some medicinal qualities.

"John told me it was a freak accident. He was clearing a containment line, the wind shifted, and a burning tree fell on him. Crushed just about every bone in his body. They flew him to a trauma specialist in Los Angeles . . . who tried to put him back together again. But it was like they left a few pieces on the table. He couldn't walk or think straight. He was in the hospital and physical therapy for months . . . but it's what came after that was worse."

"The bills," Murrow said.

"A blizzard of them," she said, organizing some crumbs on the edge of her plate with her fork. "It was $30,000 for the air ambulance, and then $250,000 in hospital charges, from the surgery down to the Jell-Os they served him. That's not counting the five grand for my hotel room in LA, or my meals, or our lost salaries."

"The US Forest Service didn't pay for anything?"

"It was all on us because our claim was frozen pending the results of the investigation, which is still ongoing and probably will be until Jesus comes back," Alison said, pushing the empty pie plate away. "On top of that, we discovered that the government classified John's job as a 'forestry technician,' not as a first responder, so if and when his policy kicked in, it wouldn't fully cover the kind of injuries he sustained."

"That's insane," Murrow said.

"No, it's criminal. And since John couldn't work, there was only a fraction of his base salary coming in. Creditors were all over us. To make some money, John did phone sales, those junk calls everybody hangs up on."

"Were you able to find work as a meteorologist somewhere else?"

"Where? There's not a big demand for them here and anywhere else, either." She wished she'd known that before getting the damn degree. But she'd always been fascinated by the weather and figured if she did what she loved, the money would come. It was stupid. "I did any work I could find, mostly cleaning hotel rooms and waitressing, leaving me maybe three or four hours of sleep a night. But we still couldn't keep up with even our basic expenses. The bank repo'd my car . . . so that sabotaged me as far as getting work . . . and the bank began foreclosing on our house. John was a proud man and he felt he was failing us. He couldn't live with that. So he killed himself. Even that hasn't stopped the bills from coming."

The reporter turned his phone off and closed his notebook. The expression on his face, and even his body language, changed so dramatically it was almost as if he were an actor stepping out of character for a moment between scenes.

"What happened to John wasn't a freak accident, Alison. The Thunderbirds were in a ravine, cutting a firebreak . . . and they came upon a tangle of dead trees that were killed by beetles or something, that had to come down. John was cutting one of them when the tree's crown ignited in flames," Murrow said, and then looked away, as if the moment were playing out on a TV screen beside him and he was watching it. "But he kept working that chain saw, standing in a swirl of embers, as if they were harmless snowflakes. He seemed utterly determined and totally invincible." Now Alison could see it, too, and she felt a surge of love and admiration for her husband. The reporter certainly knew how to evoke a moment. But was it real, or something the reporter was imagining?

Murrow shifted his gaze back to Alison and went on talking. "There was another crew cutting a tree nearby, and when it fell the wrong way, it clipped another tree that toppled into the one John was cutting and it snapped, right on top of him. The crack when that tree broke sounded like the sky tearing open. I'm sure he didn't see it coming . . . but I've often wondered if he heard it."

When he was done, Alison realized that she was crying again. But she didn't try to hide it or to wipe away her tears. "Who told you all of that?"

"Nobody. I was there," he said. "I saw it."

She felt a hot stab of anger in her gut, the heat of it rising up to her face. If there were any tears left, the hot flush on her skin would soon evaporate them. "Why didn't you write about it then, when it could have made a real difference?"

"Because I wasn't there as a reporter." He looked her straight in the eye. "I was one of the men cutting the break."

That was even worse, a deeper, more personal betrayal. Now she understood why his hands felt familiar, because they were just like John's. She was tempted to stab his fucking hand with her fork.

"You were a firefighter and you kept your mouth shut?"

"I was a convict firefighter," Murrow said, "which is why nobody asked me what I saw and why nobody would've listened to me if I spoke up."

Because he was a criminal. A liar. A cheat. And now here he was, proving it once more, pretending to be a reporter, making her relive her personal hell, and for what? But he was still talking.

"No professional firefighters were going to talk about what happened, either, because someone could argue that it was the result of negligence rather than a freak accident. And nobody, not the firefighters or the government, wants to pay *that* price. So, it's in everyone's best interest to keep their mouths shut. The investigation, if it ever ends, will conclude it was an accident."

"Who the fuck are you and what do you really want?"

"I am someone who wants the same thing you do, for many of the same reasons, and who wants to make you financially secure for the rest of your life," Murrow said. "But I need your help to do it."

There could be only one reason a criminal would want her help for anything. "What you have in mind is a crime, isn't it?"

"What was done to you and your family was the crime. You said it yourself."

"Nobody in the Forest Service or the Department of Workers' Compensation will ever go to prison for what they did because it isn't illegal," she said. "But I will if we get caught doing whatever the hell you have in mind, because it certainly is."

"That's true. But you're imprisoned already by your suffering, anger, and debt. I'm offering you a way out. Maybe the only way. You said it yourself: you have nothing left to lose."

He had a point, she thought, and was deft at using her own words to convince her. She couldn't see a way out. But she also didn't know what he had in mind, or if it would work. She was curious, though, and she noticed now that her anger had dimmed considerably. "You're very persuasive. Or I guess I am, since it's my words you're using to convince me. What kind of criminal are you, exactly?"

"A con man," he said.

And that made her smile, a genuine, natural smile. It had been a long time since that had happened. "Of course. At least you're honest. For a criminal, that is."

"I'm also a thief," he said. "While you were absorbed in telling me your story, I stole your wallet."

Alison reached for her purse on the seat beside her, pulled it into her lap, and opened it. Her wallet was still there. She looked up to see the man smiling now, too, a sparkle in his eye that hadn't been there before when he was pretending to be a reporter.

"I'm not that good. How could I have climbed over the table, or crept underneath it, to get to your purse without you noticing? But for an instant, you believed it was possible."

Yes, she did. "It's something in your eyes. Or maybe your smile. It's your talent."

Murrow shook his head. "It's because everyone wants to believe in magic. But magic is just a trick. It's really all about misdirection."

"I'm not a con man, a thief, or a magician," she said. "What do you want me to do?"

"The same thing you did for the Forest Service."

"Wildfire modeling?"

"That's right," he said.

"That's not illegal."

"It will be in this context."

She could only think of one context, given everything they'd discussed, that would make it illegal and it made her heart race. "You're going to start a fire."

"Several, over the course of a few days, right in the middle of a major wind event. But it's essential that we know where and when to start the fires so they behave the way we want them to."

"That's insane," Alison said, too loudly, then lowered her voice to a near whisper. "A fire is a force of nature, it's not something you can control. People could get killed."

The man was prepared for her objection and had his response ready.

"The residents will be evacuated long before the flames get close and those who stay anyway have no one to blame for their fate but themselves. The only people who will certainly be at risk are the professional firefighters . . . and they live for it. Like you said, they don't get paid, or get the excitement they crave, if they aren't facing a huge blaze."

"That's how John died," Alison said.

"That's how my friend died, too, right in front of me. And his family was treated even worse than yours," Murrow said. "Of course there's a risk, a deadly one, but this is how we get justice for the people we lost and for you."

She believed he meant it. But wasn't that how all suckers got swindled by con men? "What's to stop me from going to the police and turning you in?"

"Nothing. But you don't know who I am, or exactly what I'm planning or where. Plus, I'll have a big head start on you when I walk out the door."

"How do you figure that?"

"You'll be preoccupied trying to find your missing phone and your stolen car."

Alison realized now that when she'd reached for her purse to look for her wallet, he'd swiped the car keys and phone that she'd set on the table when she'd sat down. He handed them back to her now because he already knew, even before she did, that he'd convinced her to help him. He was a hell of a good con man, she thought.

"John heard it," she said softly. "The tree snapping. He thought it was the sound of his body breaking."

"Let's take a walk, and this time, I'll tell you a story."

"About your criminal past?"

"About our criminal future," he said. "It begins with Icarus."

She knew what he meant, and that he wasn't referring to the Greek myth about the boy with wings made of feathers and wax who ignored warnings not to fly too close to the sun . . . and paid for his hubris when his wings melted and he plunged to his death.

But even so, the moral of the story merited serious consideration as Murrow, or whoever he really was, laid out his daring plan.

CHAPTER SIXTEEN

Present Day
Friday Night

Walker's second call to an Icarus owner was the California Department of Forestry and Fire Protection's station in Garner's Crossing. He'd identified himself and said, "I'm calling about your Icarus drone. Do you still have it?"

There was a sigh of relief from the CAL FIRE official, whose name was Hunton Credler. "Are you telling me that you found it?"

"Hold on a second." Walker put Credler on hold and called out to Sharpe, who was in his office finishing a call of his own. "I think I've got it. A fire station up in the San Bernardino Mountains is missing an Icarus."

Sharpe came right out, clipping a pile of books and binders on his way, sending them toppling to the floor in his wake as he rushed to Walker's desk. "Put him on the speaker."

Walker did. "Thanks for waiting, Chief Credler. I've brought in my partner, Detective Walter Sharpe. When was your drone stolen?"

"About three weeks ago."

Sharpe said, "Why didn't you report the theft?"

"We did, but not to local law enforcement."

"You went to the FBI."

"Yeah. We didn't want the local press or anybody in Sacramento to find out about it just yet."

"Why is that?"

"The Icarus cost us $100,000 and it generated a lot of media fanfare when it arrived here," Credler said. "We'd like to get it back, or quietly buy a new one, before the public discovers it's missing."

Walker thought that was a dumb move, that the public would be even more upset about the cover-up than the theft itself once the truth came out, and it would, but he kept that opinion to himself. "How did it happen?"

"We got called out on a fire. Somebody torched an abandoned barn. And when we came back, the drone was gone. The fire was obviously a ploy to get us out of the building."

"Nobody was there? Not even a dalmatian?"

"Nope."

"Don't you have a security system?"

"It's a twenty-year-old home security system. The thieves cut the power and phone lines to the station after we left, deactivating the alarm and our cameras."

"You don't have a backup battery to run the cameras and DVR?"

"There's no battery and we have a VCR that records over the tape every couple of hours. Rumor has it the tape was originally a rental copy of *Backdraft* that was never returned."

Walker wanted to reach through the phone line and slap the guy. They spent $100,000 on a drone but couldn't be bothered to spend a couple thousand dollars on a half-decent security system. Even an off-the-shelf system at Costco would be better than what they had. They were practically begging for the Icarus to be stolen.

Sharpe shared a look with Walker. They were both obviously thinking the same thing. But neither one of them expressed their dismay. It wouldn't get them anywhere.

Sharpe spoke up. "When was the last time you used the Icarus to combat a wildfire?"

"Two years ago. The Arrowbear Fire. That was a monster, sparked by lightning. Destroyed sixty thousand acres, two hundred structures, and seriously injured one of our hotshots."

A thought occurred to Walker. "Do you use convict firefighting crews up there?"

Sharpe gave him a quizzical look. Walker ignored it. He was playing a hunch.

"Sure do. We wouldn't have enough manpower otherwise. On Arrowbear, we had to bring them in from all over the state. The Icarus really proved itself on that one. We used the drone to burn up a lot of brush and stopped the fire from advancing. Why are you so interested in our drone?"

Sharpe answered the question. "We think it may have been used down here in an arson."

"Oh shit," Credler said. "Are you talking about one of those big wildfires you're fighting in Los Angeles right now?"

"Both of them."

"From what I hear, they are zero percent contained, tens of thousands of people are being evacuated, and winds are only expected to get worse."

"You heard right."

"If our drone was used to start that catastrophe, you have to keep us out of it. Do you realize how bad this will make us look?"

Once again, Credler was more interested in covering his ass than anything else, which, Walker thought, wasn't exactly proving to be a winning strategy for him.

"We can't control that," Walker said, not bothering to hide his disdain.

"Of course you can, Detective. People only see what you show them. If this gets out, we'll be blamed for everything. That will do real, lasting damage to the US Forest Service and the reputation of every firefighter in the state."

That gave Walker a tickle along the back of his neck. He'd learned not to ignore them. It was either his subconscious needling him or an insect that stings. "The Arrowbear Fire was before my time. What happened to your hotshot?"

"It was a freak accident. He was cutting down a tree to create a fire line and another tree fell on him, broke almost every bone in his body."

"What's his name?"

"John Grayle."

Walker wrote it down. "Where is he now?"

Sharpe gave him a look. He knew what Walker was thinking. *Revenge.*

"He's dead," Credler said.

"He died from his injuries?"

"Not directly. John died later."

"We all die later," Walker said.

Sharpe cringed. Walker shrugged. What he said was true.

"He killed himself," Credler said.

Ouch. Walker walked right into that one. "I'm sorry. I shouldn't have been so crass."

But it was too late. Credler was pissed now, as well as anxious about his job, his reputation, and his pension. It came out as anger. "Do you have any evidence that it was our Icarus that was used in your fire or is it speculation?"

Sharpe said, "It's an educated guess."

"Can you keep your guess to yourself until you know for sure?"

"We never talk to reporters about an investigation."

"CAL FIRE is in Malibu, working your fire, too. They don't need to hear any of your educated guesses."

"You're all in the same agency," Sharpe said. "Surely they know you lost an Icarus."

"Nobody outside of San Bernardino County and some FBI agents are aware of it for now. We'd like it to stay that way."

"We'll do our best," Sharpe said, and Credler hung up.

Walker looked at Sharpe. "Will we?"

"Hell no."

"John Grayle could be our firefighter connection to these two wildfires." Walker circled the name on his notepad twice for emphasis.

"He's dead."

"But maybe it was his crippling injuries from the Arrowbear Fire that made him put a gun in his mouth."

"Nobody said anything about a gun."

"Figure of speech."

"Or that he blamed CAL FIRE for his accident."

"But if his family does, and they believe that's why he offed himself, they might want to humiliate the Forest Service as payback."

"Then why make the fires look like accidents instead of revealing they were started with the stolen drone? And why do it here and not down in San Bernardino County?"

"I don't know," Walker said, "but my gut tells me there could be something in John Grayle's accident and suicide because it's got real emotional stakes."

"Sounds like psychobabble to me. Did you get that from your wife?"

"On-the-job experience. I've seen people take insane risks for money, but usually because there was something personal involved."

"Going broke is personal," Sharpe said.

"It's even more personal if Little Jimmy is going to lose his legs if you can't pay for the operation."

"Who is Little Jimmy?"

"The kid in Scrooge."

"That was Tiny Tim," Sharpe said.

"You get the idea," Walker said. "It's like Al Pacino in *Dog Day Afternoon*. Yeah, he was robbing the bank for the money, but it was mostly so his lover, Leon, could have his dick surgically removed."

Sharpe groaned, pulled over a chair, and sat down. "You think this is all about John Grayle's bereaved family seeking vengeance."

"Or I'm wrong. That's why I'm calling the Department of Corrections as soon as they open up in the morning," Walker said. "I'd like to know the names of the convicts who were up there and saw that Icarus in action."

"That's an even bigger leap."

"The Icarus was stolen by pros."

"Really? Because it sounds to me like a four-year-old could've done it," Sharpe said. "And how does stealing an Icarus drone save someone's legs or get his dick cut off?"

"I don't know yet. But we aren't going to find any of our answers here tonight."

Sharpe scowled with disapproval. "You're going home?"

"I'm going to Garner's Crossing."

"What's there?"

"John Grayle's story," Walker said.

"There's a lot of background we can learn right here off our databases."

"You do that, but I'm still going to Garner's Crossing," Walker said. "But you've convinced me to take a little nap first while you work. Wake me when you're done. I don't want to fall asleep at the wheel."

"We can call the San Bernardino County sheriff's station up in Garner's Crossing to run down any leads we come up with."

Walker got up and took his Stetson with him. "A hunter doesn't catch his prey by asking someone else to follow the tracks."

There was a sleep room, basically a closet with a cot in it, down the hall. Walker went down to it, taking his cell phone from his pocket and calling home on the way.

"Tell me you're not on a stakeout, waiting for some armed killer to come out of a strip club or motel." That was Carly's way of saying hello.

"No, but I'm not going to be home tonight. Nothing dangerous, just dull, plodding detective work, tracking down the backstory on a dead firefighter." Walker quickly filled her in on the investigation. "There's no reason for anybody to take a shot at me. I'm much more likely to die of boredom."

"I like the sound of that."

"Me dying?"

"The boredom part," she said. "I love you, Andy, and I appreciate the sacrifices you're making for us."

"It's no sacrifice. Dying of boredom and dying of a gunshot wound is still dying."

"Yes, but boredom takes a lot longer to kill," she said. "Our son could be out of college by the time you drop dead from it and I'll still be young enough to find a second husband."

"You always see the bright side."

"That's why you love me," she said.

"I do," he said. "Lock the door and keep the Glock within reach."

"Such a sweet bedtime wish," she said.

"It's what my mom used to say to me."

"She was one tough third-grade teacher. But her heart was in the right place."

"So was her Glock." Walker ended the call, went into the sleep room, set his Stetson on a chair, slipped off his shoes, and lay down on the bed.

He was out cold in two minutes. It felt like two minutes later when Sharpe shook him awake, but it had been three hours.

"What have you learned?" Walker asked, getting up stiffly from the bed. He'd have been more comfortable sleeping in his truck.

"John Grayle left a widow behind. Alison. I called her home and cell, but she's not answering. I also ran a credit check on her. At the time of John's death, their car was repo'd, the bank was foreclosing on their house, and he had over $100,000 in medical debt."

"There's Little Jimmy's legs."

"And Al Pacino's dick," Sharpe said.

"It wasn't his dick. It was Chris Sarandon's, but yeah, we've found our emotional stakes."

"And the financial ones."

Walker got up and put on his hat. "They are mixed up together."

"But how do you make money stealing an Icarus drone and igniting wildfires a hundred miles away from home?"

"We'll have to ask her," Walker said, trying to hide his limp as he walked down the hall with Sharpe. "You got the keys to the Tahoe?"

Sharpe tossed them to Walker. "Try not to drive us off a cliff while I'm sleeping."

CHAPTER SEVENTEEN

Two and a Half Weeks Ago

The morning after meeting Alison at the diner in Garner's Crossing, Danny drove her to the Epitome in a panel van with the Icarus drone she'd helped him steal the previous night. The adrenaline high Alison got from that adventure had diminished quickly and she'd crashed, sleeping most of the way back, leaving Danny to his thoughts, going over all the details of the heist again, looking for mistakes and weak points.

Alison didn't awaken until they were driving across the metal-and-glass bridge over the moat and into the Epitome's motor court. She looked back over her shoulder.

"Was that . . . *a moat*?" she asked.

"I was told it's a lazy river," Danny said.

"So, it's safe to assume it's not stocked with piranha or alligators."

"I don't know. I haven't tossed any meat in to find out." Danny drove around the fountain and stopped at the ramp leading to the underground garage.

Alison glanced at the *David* sculpture. "I thought we were keeping a low profile."

"We are. This house is remote." Danny lowered the driver's side window, punched a code into a keypad beside the ramp, and the garage doors rolled up. "Nobody on ground level has a view of us coming or going and the people who live in the three homes on the eastern ridge only see the back of this house . . . and nothing that's going on in front. They don't know we're here. But we have an unobstructed view of them."

"And those are the houses you're hitting."

"That's right."

Danny drove the van into the vast underground garage, which was mostly empty except for a Bentley sedan, a chrome-plated Aston Martin Vanquish, a fire engine, a patrol car, and a flatbed truck carrying a Bobcat mini tractor, along with its bulldozer and jackhammer attachments. A welder was working on the fire engine, the sparks creating lightning-like flashes of light in the vast, sporadically lit space. Four men and one woman were busy doing something, moving among the first-responder vehicles and several boxes of supplies.

He parked, and as soon as they got out of the van, they were met by Adam Horowitz, who was as excited as a child.

"Did you get the Icarus?" Adam asked Danny, ignoring Alison.

"It's in back. But don't start playing with it."

"I just want a peek." Adam opened the back of the van and climbed in.

The black quadcopter looked like a flying gumball machine and was about the same size, but a lot more menacing. It weighed only nine pounds fully loaded and was capable of autonomous flight. It could hold 400 fireballs and drop one every two seconds, or 30 per minute, which would ignite within thirty seconds of release and burn for two minutes. It was more than enough to start an inferno.

Adam picked up the remote, which resembled a PlayStation controller merged with an iPhone, and began examining it.

Danny tipped his head toward Adam and said to Alison, "The Wizard can't resist cool tech."

"The Wizard?" Alison asked.

"That's what he is with computers, hacking, and electronics. So that's what I call him. We're only using nicknames here. It's for your protection as well as ours."

"In case I get caught and blab."

"You can't blab what you don't know . . . and that goes for all of us. But that's not going to be an issue. We're not getting caught." Danny led Alison away from the van toward the other vehicles, but something caught her eye.

She pointed to some devices on tripods that appeared to be elaborate cameras or X-ray machines. "What are those?"

"A laser scanner for mapping the interior of the homes and ground-penetrating radar to see what structures are hiding behind walls and under floors. We acquired the blueprints for the homes we're burglarizing by hacking the computer systems of contractors who built them and Malibu's planning commission, but I doubt they reveal everything that's inside those walls or underground."

They reached the patrol car, which she could now see was from the Los Angeles County Sheriff's Department.

"Stealing a cop car and a fire engine takes guts."

"They aren't real ones, though they are pretty close. They're prop vehicles we stole from a company that rents all kinds of ordinary and specialized vehicles to the studios for TV shows and movies. We're making a few adjustments to them. The Bentley and the Aston Martin are real, though. The Aston Martin comes with the house."

Danny knew that Alison was familiar with fire engines. The vehicle ordinarily had hoses, a water pump, a five-hundred-gallon water tank, ground ladders, and an array of storage units to carry all kinds of firefighting tools and specialized equipment to the scene.

On this fake one, Danny explained to her, half of the water tank and all of the storage compartments were being retrofitted to hold the unique items they would be stealing, everything from paintings and diamonds to antique violins and rare manuscripts.

Logan was applying a giant sticker to the outside driver's side door of the fire engine. It was a logo, meant to evoke an official state seal, for RIGHT GUARD FIRE PROTECTION.

Alison read the company name aloud, then commented, "It sounds like an antiperspirant."

"All the good names for private firefighting services were already taken," Danny said, then introduced Logan to her. "This is Smokey, a car thief with several years of firefighting experience."

"The nickname he gave me does double duty," Logan said.

She said, "I assume for *Smokey and the Bandit* and Smokey Bear."

"You got it, plus I'm a dead ringer for a young Burt Reynolds," Logan said.

"I was just thinking that."

That made Logan smile and he offered her his hand. "Welcome to the crew, Weathergirl."

Alison shook hands with him but glared at Danny. "*That's* my nickname?"

Danny shrugged. "I thought it fit your role in all of this."

"It's sexist and demeaning," she said, letting go of Logan's hand and facing Danny. "What's your nickname?"

"The Saint."

"How does that reflect your contribution to this project?"

Kurt Sabella leaned out from behind the fire engine to reply, lifting his welder's mask so he could be heard. "*The Saint* was an old series of books and TV shows about Simon Templar, the Robin Hood of modern crime. Except this Saint robs from the rich and gives to himself."

"Not this time," Danny said, then turned to Alison. "That's Noah. He builds things."

"Like the ark—I get it."

Kurt continued. "For some reason, the Saint is what everybody called Simon Templar. And whenever they'd introduce Templar, he'd look up and see a halo over his head that nobody else did."

Danny glanced up, just like the Saint would.

"Is that how you see yourself?" she said. "Virtuous and holy?"

"I try to stick to a moral code."

"You're burning up thousands of acres of parkland, endangering hundreds of homes and the lives of who knows how many firefighters, all to commit a heist. Where is the morality in that?"

"I'm also righting the wrongs done to you and to one of our friends."

As he was saying that, Tamiko Harada came over to them and said, "The people we're robbing are titanic assholes who deserve much worse. A good beating at the very least, maybe even a firing squad, but the Saint doesn't like violence as much as I do."

"I don't like it at all, but people tend to get upset when they find out we're conning them," Danny said to Alison, then tipped his head toward Tamiko. "So, that's where she comes in."

"I'm the Muscle," Tamiko said to Alison. "You can just call me Muscle. You don't need the 'the'—that would be pretentious."

"Okay," Alison said.

"She's a black belt and a crack shot," Danny said, "so she handles security while also playing a role in our cons."

"I'm usually the honey trap, because the only thing more fun for me than violence is sex," Tamiko said. "But this time, I'm a sheriff's deputy."

"She likes any excuse to wear a gun," Danny said, "even when it's loaded with blanks."

"I'll just have to find sex somewhere else on this job."

Adam hopped out of the van and waved his hand. "You can stop looking. I'm right here."

"We're talking about guns that fire blanks," Tamiko said to Adam, "not guns that fire way too soon."

Danny led her over to Sam Mertz, who was checking the supplies, which included pneumatic jackhammers, chain saws, drills and various firefighting tools, bags of Ping-Pong balls, containers of antifreeze, bags of pool cleaner, and a small wooden crate of dynamite.

"This is the Locksmith," Danny said. "There's no lock he can't open or safe he can't crack."

Mertz smiled at Alison. "These days, mostly I blow them up to save time. I'm not as patient as I used to be."

"He's got firefighting experience, too," Danny said. "For the first time, the parts we'll be playing in a con aren't really parts at all but jobs we actually did for years. We'll be convincing because we'll be ourselves. It makes it easy."

Alison declared, "I'm Storm."

Danny didn't know what she was talking about. "What?"

"That's my nickname," she said. "Storm."

"I get it," Adam said. "Like the female mutant in *X-Men* who controls the weather."

"That's right," she said, then made an aside to Tamiko. "Just Storm, no 'the' in front. That would be pretentious."

Tamiko grinned and looked at Danny. "I like her."

"Storm it is," Danny said. "Let's go upstairs, Storm. I want to show you the view."

There were two ways to get upstairs: the glass elevator or the floating staircase that wound around it. They took the elevator, a transparent bubble that rose up into the great room beside the foyer. The first thing Alison saw when she emerged was the chrome-plated Lamborghini high above them, revolving atop a crystal pedestal.

"That's ridiculous," she said.

"That's a metaphor."

"Obviously."

"For the house, according to the builder," Danny said. "It's subliminally telling you that this elegant place is securely attached to the bedrock . . . and that you are safe."

"No, it's shouting at you, 'Look at me, I'm filthy rich and I have a big, hard dick.'"

"Would you have a different interpretation if there was a Ford Focus on top?" Danny asked.

"Yes, I would, because it would send an entirely different message, one that's whimsical and self-mocking."

Levi strolled in from an adjoining hallway. "Those are not words that describe the kind of person who can afford this house."

"Meet Levi Brisker, the builder and our host," Danny said to Alison. "He's listing this place for only $75 million."

Levi said, "People with that kind of money to spend would look at a Ford Focus on that pedestal and think I was giving them the finger. Or that I'm cheap and cut corners building the house."

He was as garishly outfitted as the house, Danny thought. Levi wore a yellow long-sleeved Versace Royal Rebellion silk shirt covered with drawings of faux royal crests, seals, and crowns of various colors, a pair of matching shorts, and a pair of yellow-and-black Barocco-print espadrille cotton loafers on his bare feet.

"Have you had any offers?" Alison asked him.

"Not yet."

"So, try a Ford Focus instead," she said. "I could lend you mine."

"Hopefully it won't come to that or my body will be stuffed in the trunk. I'm headed to the bar. Want anything?"

"No, thank you."

He walked past them and went down the staircase. She turned to Danny and said, "It's ten a.m. and he's already drinking?"

"He's facing imminent bankruptcy and he's in debt to a Mexican cartel that has no sense of humor. This gig is going to save him. The fire will spare his house but not those." Danny pointed to the three houses on the opposite ridge.

Alison went to the window to see their targets for the first time. "What about the people in them?"

Danny stepped up beside her and realized this was probably where he'd stood, years ago, when Arnie Soloway was hoisted up into the rescue chopper.

"They will be long gone, forced to evacuate by the sheriff. Then we will go, strip the places of all their treasures, load them into our fire truck, and torch the houses in our wake, hiding any evidence that a crime even occurred."

"And then where do we go?"

"We drive to the coast, head up the Pacific Coast Highway, and on into the sunset. Or, if the fire makes that escape impossible, we come back here and take shelter underground, sipping champagne and snacking on caviar until the fire is contained. Then we leave unnoticed in the smoky aftermath with all other first responders."

"If we don't burn to death in this house," she said.

"Levi says it's fireproof."

"You believe him?"

"I do, though I wouldn't have if there was a Ford Focus on that pedestal," Danny said. "But to be certain, Noah and the Locksmith did their own home inspection and are satisfied enough that they will literally stake their lives on it."

Alison looked back at the homes on the opposite ridge. "Who lives there and why should I hate them?"

Danny said, "The house to the north, the one that looks like a Louisiana plantation, belongs to Orville Kempton, who own dozens of car dealerships in Southern California. He's also a modern-day Jack Benny, a rich cheapskate who fancies himself an amazing violinist but actually sucks at it."

"Who is Jack Benny?"

"That's not important. Kempton made his fortune using predatory lending practices, primarily targeting low-income, non-English-speaking people, that saddle them with lousy cars and enormous debt they can never repay."

"I had a loan like that. It was the only one I could get with my lousy credit. With what I'll end up paying for that Focus, I could have bought a Porsche. What does Kempton have that you want?"

"Even though Kempton has no musical talent, he's able to hobnob with the world's greatest violinists because he owns a collection of rare string instruments by masters like Stradivarius and Montagnana. Those great violinists all want to play with his instruments, which are worth as much as $10 million each. That's what we're taking."

Alison pointed to a house that was all jutting, cantilevered decks and floors, as if the various parts of the building were straining against the I beams to fly apart in seven different directions. "Who is in the house that looks like a freeze-frame of an explosion?"

"I never thought of it that way, but you're right. It belongs to Arseny Pletov, a steel-making oligarch with ties to the Russian mob who also owns a string of marijuana dispensaries in Southern California. He has other homes in Moscow, London, Berlin, Hawaii, and Sardinia and owns a three-hundred-foot yacht that's presently anchored in the Seychelles."

"He sounds rich, but not evil."

"His Russian miners all live in remote company-owned towns so every ruble he pays them goes right back into his pocket for their over-priced food, cheap housing, and substandard medical care. They aren't able to save any money, essentially making them slaves who can never leave."

"What a lovely person," she said. "What's his treasure?"

"He's in love with American popular culture and owns millions of dollars' worth of sports and music memorabilia."

"Like what?"

"Handwritten, original song drafts by John Lennon, Paul McCartney, and Bob Dylan. Kirk Gibson's home run baseball. Muhammad Ali's Olympic gold medal. Guitars that belonged to Kurt

Cobain, Elvis Presley, and Prince. Honus Wagner's baseball card. That kind of thing. I have a shopping list."

"You can resell that stuff?"

"Easily. There's a thriving black market for it, especially among Russian oligarchs, who would probably pay a premium just to own a rarity that once belonged to one of their rivals."

"Who lives in the house that's surrounded by palm trees?"

"Roland Slezak, a hedge fund maverick who devised a clever strategy for making his fortune," Danny said. "He targets biotech companies that make obscure specialty drugs, shorts their stocks, and then acquires the companies on the cheap."

"What are specialty drugs?"

"They are highly effective medicines made by only one supplier to treat maladies with only a small number of sufferers. So, there's no real financial incentive for other pharmaceutical companies to develop alternative treatments. He's acquired dozens of biotech firms with a specialty drug or two in their portfolio."

"Why does that make him a rat bastard?"

"Because once he owns the companies, he immediately jacks up the prices on those essential drugs," he said. "For example, Nevrasol, a drug that is the only treatment for a rare immunity disorder, used to cost $13 a pill. But then Slezak acquired the only company that makes it and immediately raised the price to $750. He did the same with Reevec, the one drug that cures a brutal strain of tuberculosis, inflating the price of a month's supply of pills from $500 to $10,800. Those are just two of dozens of examples. And if you're somebody with any of those atypical, brutal maladies, you either pay up . . . or die."

"That's extortion," Alison said. "How can he get away with that?"

"Because it's entirely legal and he makes huge political contributions to local, state, and national members of both parties to make sure it stays that way."

"I can live with burning down their houses, as long as no innocent people get hurt," she said. "Which one of those three men do you blame for your friend's death?"

"Slezak. During the Crags Fire, his mansion was the only one out here and it meant more to him than anybody's life," he said. "And kowtowing to him was a higher priority to the fire department than the safety of a crew of convict firefighters. So Slezak's house was saved, but a man was killed and his family got nothing in compensation. Not even an apology."

He was sure that Alison knew how that felt, and how the rage and heartbreak never went away. Maybe, Danny thought, if they pulled off this heist, and got some measure of revenge and compensation, it would dim just a little for him. Maybe for her, too.

"What does Slezak have that you want?" she asked.

"His house. I want to see it in ashes. But the rest of you can divvy up his collection of million-dollar watches."

"I don't own a watch and I already know his time is running out," she said. "The Santa Anas will be blowing through here in a few days."

Danny looked away from the view and faced her. "Can you tell us exactly when . . . and how long the winds will last?"

"Yes, but I will need real-time access to meteorological data."

"The Wizard has hacked into the National Weather Service, so you have access to all of their resources, including Doppler radar, satellite imagery, and computer modeling."

"I'll also need topographical maps of the Santa Monica Mountains, data on soil moisture levels, the various types of ground cover, the historical paths of previous fires that came through here, and a ton of other stuff."

"The Wizard has it all for you," Danny said. "And whatever he doesn't have now, we can get. You'll have all the data you need, in real time, for us to set fires with Icarus where and when we need them . . . and that we can be reasonably certain will go where we want them to."

There was already a fire raging in Stevenson Ranch that someone else had started and that the Santa Anas were blowing their way, which was very helpful and which Danny saw as a good omen. For his plan to work, they needed to start a fire in Ventura that was ferocious enough to keep the fire crews up there busy, and one more within the City of Los Angeles that would overburden LAFD's resources, before setting the one that counted, the one that would create jurisdictional chaos, merge with the oncoming Stevenson Ranch blaze, and then rampage through the largely unpopulated areas of the Santa Monica Mountains . . . to right where they were standing.

Alison said, "There's nothing reasonable about this. They are called *wild*fires for a reason. There are too many variables I can't predict or control."

"That's what makes it exciting," Danny said.

"I don't need any excitement."

"We all do," he said. "It's how we know we're alive. Tell me your heart isn't racing already."

Danny was sure it was, but he hoped that it was from excitement and not terror.

CHAPTER EIGHTEEN

Present Day
Saturday Morning

On the outskirts of Garner's Crossing, deep in the woods of the San Bernardino Mountains, Walker pulled up in front of a row of duplexes with fake half-timbered facades meant to evoke a ski lodge. It was early morning. There was a light dusting of frost on the ground and Walker realized he hadn't brought a coat.

Sharpe was snoring away and had been almost since they'd left LASD headquarters, despite the country music Walker had blaring from the radio to keep himself entertained on the four-hour drive.

He turned off the radio and nudged Sharpe awake. "We're here."

Sharpe yawned. "Where's here?"

"This is Alison Grayle's place."

Sharpe peered out the window at the duplex. "We're supposed to check in first with the sheriff's office or police station to let them know we're operating in their jurisdiction."

"That's only necessary if you're making an arrest and might need backup."

Sharpe gave him a hound-dog look that reminded Walker how his partner earned his nickname. "No, it's not."

"Trust me, they don't care if we're just driving around, looking things over, and asking a few questions. In fact, they'd rather not hear from us, because then they'd have to take a uniform off the street to play tour guide," Walker said. "They only care we're here if there's gonna be a shoot-out. Or a car chase. Or if you commandeer a school bus and drive it through a house, and the house collapses, and the bus ends up in a swimming pool."

Those were the good old days, Walker thought, before marriage and imminent fatherhood and bad knees smothered all the excitement in his life.

Sharpe stared at him for a long moment. "Was the school bus empty?"

"For the most part."

"There were still some kids on it?"

"No, of course not. Just the driver," Walker said. "And he only had a mild heart attack, which probably saved his life."

"How do you figure that?"

"He had no idea he had any coronary issues until then. Turns out his arteries were blocked tighter than the drain in a gas station toilet. Thanks to me, he made that discovery with a mild heart attack instead of the widow-maker he was in line for." Walker put on his Stetson and got out of the Tahoe but kept the engine running so the interior would stay warm and toasty.

The mailbox on the curb in front of Grayle's duplex was overflowing with envelopes, magazines, and fliers. He took it all out and sorted through it, Sharpe stepping up beside him to see what she'd received. There were lots of bills marked PAYMENT DUE and FINAL NOTICE on the envelopes. The postmarks went back over three weeks. "She's been away for a while."

"Probably running from bill collectors," Sharpe said.

"Or she offed herself, too." Walker shoved the bills back in the mailbox and went up to the front door, sniffing.

Sharpe followed behind him, shivering in the cold. "What are you doing?"

"If her body is decomposing in there, we might catch a whiff of it, unless the cold has kept her fresh. You should sniff around, too. You're probably better at it than me."

"Is that a Shar-Pei reference?"

Yes, it was.

"No, and I'm surprised you went there," Walker said. "I thought we were developing mutual respect and trust."

They continued around her half of the unfenced duplex, but the window shades were down, and the back door was locked. There were no signs of any disturbance. As they returned to the front of the duplex, they were met by a woman, easily in her fifties, wearing a heavy pink bathrobe and fluffy sheepskin slippers, who was letting her little french poodle pee on the mailbox post. She said, "Where's the fire?"

Her comment reminded Walker they were still wearing their arson investigator uniforms and windbreakers from the day before.

Sharpe smiled and said, "No fire, ma'am. We're looking for Alison Grayle."

He introduced themselves and asked her for her name. It was Esther Radcliffe.

The door to the adjoining duplex was ajar, so he assumed Esther was the next-door neighbor.

Esther said, "Alison won a trip to Hawaii and asked me to look after the place until she gets back. I'm a little behind."

"When is she coming back?" Sharpe asked.

"If I were her, I never would. Not a lot of happy memories for her here. It's horrible what happened to John."

"Yes, it is. CAL FIRE has a lot to answer for."

"All of this, for starters." Esther took the bills out of the mailbox and waved them in front of the detectives. "It's despicable."

Walker asked, "When did she leave?"

"About three weeks ago, but she'll be back next week," Esther said. "Are you here to hire her again?"

"Again?" Sharpe said.

"As your CAL FIRE weather expert. You should, because she's wasting her expertise in the kitchen at Pizza Pete's. There aren't a lot of opportunities for her there to use her meteorology degree, unless the weather has something to do with how quickly dough rises."

"Does pizza dough have to rise?"

"I wouldn't know," Esther said, watching her dog take a dump on the grass. "I've never made a pizza that wasn't frozen first."

"Me neither."

Sharpe said, "Thank you, Mrs. Radcliffe. You've been very helpful."

"Do you want to leave your card for her?"

"We'll catch her instead," Walker said.

"Catch her?"

"He meant catch up with her," Sharpe said. "When she gets back."

The two detectives got back into the warm Tahoe, but Walker didn't immediately drive away. Esther Radcliffe, who was picking up her dog's droppings with a poop bag, had given them a lot to consider.

"Alison Grayle was a CAL FIRE meteorologist," Walker said. "And she was married to a hotshot. She certainly knows about wind and fire."

"And fire modeling."

"What's that?"

"Predicting how a fire moves, based on weather and geography," Sharpe said. "I'm now convinced that someone strategically selected the Chatsworth and Skirball locations, and chose to set them aflame precisely when there were the optimal weather conditions for a fast-moving wildfire, to achieve a purpose."

Walker waited expectantly for the big reveal, but Sharpe was taking his sweet time. "Go on already," he prodded. "What's her purpose?"

"I have no idea," Sharpe said.

That was a disappointment. He was counting on another detergent or Ping-Pong ball moment. "Why not?"

"Because we need more evidence to figure it out."

"No, we don't. We have plenty," Walker said. "But I think better on a full stomach and I'm sure you do, too. Let's get a pizza."

"It's not even nine a.m. They won't be open yet."

"They will be for us. You find out where Pizza Pete's is and plug the address into your GPS while I call the Department of Corrections."

Walker took out his phone and called the Department of Corrections while following the GPS directions on Sharpe's screen at the same time. He got switched around to several departments before finally reaching someone who could email him a list of all the convict crews that worked the Arrowbear Fire. The call ended just as they arrived at Pizza Pete's, which was an odd building, half–log cabin and half–Quonset hut. Walker couldn't tell which structure came first. There were two cars parked behind the building, so that's where Walker parked, too.

The detectives got out and Walker banged on the back door. A bearded man wearing a puffy Patagonia jacket over a sweatshirt and jeans opened the door. His nose had been used as a punching bag so many times over the years that his nostrils were crooked.

"We're closed," he said, but he didn't slam the door in their faces.

Walker said, "We're sheriff's department arson investigators."

"That would explain the words ARSON INVESTIGATORS on your windbreakers."

"You're very observant. Are you Pizza Pete?"

"Yeah," he said.

"Do you prefer to be called Pizza or Mr. Pete?"

Sharpe spoke up before the man could reply or Walker could intentionally irritate him any further. "We only need a moment of your time, sir. Does Alison Grayle work here?"

"She did."

"What's that mean?"

"I fired her."

"When, exactly, did you do that?"

"About two weeks ago," Pizza Pete said. "She called up, said her luck had changed, she'd won a trip to Hawaii, and didn't know when she'd be back."

Walker said, "And you fired her for that?"

"She's not squeezing out a kid or having a brain tumor removed. She's taking a trip. I don't have to keep her job for her. Do you think anybody here gets a monthlong vacation? I own the place and I don't get one, certainly not now when I have to do her job *and* mine. So, fuck her. She can go back to being a maid at Motel 6."

"Or being a meteorologist with the fire department."

"Is that why you're here? To ask her back? Good luck with that. Everybody in the kitchen knows how she feels about you people."

Sharpe said, "What did we do?"

"You killed her husband."

Walker didn't see the point in arguing that the Los Angeles County Sheriff's Department had absolutely nothing to do with Grayle's accident. There were more pressing matters to deal with. "One more question. Is it too early to order a pizza?"

Pete closed the door on them. Walker turned to Sharpe. "I guess that's a no and I forgot to ask him if pizza dough has to rise."

They got back in the Tahoe, and Sharpe held his hands in front of the hot air jets as if he were warming them over a campfire.

"Alison fits both the wildland and urban arsonist profile," Sharpe said, "but there's no evidence that she stole the drone and used it to start the Chatsworth and Skirball fires in LA."

"She left here the same time the Icarus drone did," Walker said, driving out of the parking lot and making a left onto Main Street, figuring it would lead to an open restaurant. "She's our perp. I don't believe in coincidences."

"A coincidence isn't proof."

"It is for me."

"We need to find out if she's in Los Angeles."

"That's easy enough," Walker said. "We can track her cell phone, credit card transactions, or ATM withdrawals."

"Not without warrants," Sharpe said. "And I don't think we have enough probable cause to convince a judge to give us one."

Main Street had a village feel and all the buildings were designed, it seemed to Walker, to look best with snow-covered rooftops but were bleak otherwise, which was also how he thought about Las Vegas, which was made to be seen only at night. All the shops were closed except for a hardware store and a sporting goods store that offered live bait.

"We don't need warrants," Walker said. "All I need are her cell phone and credit card numbers. I have a hacker friend in the skip-tracing business who owes me a lifetime of favors who can do the rest."

"Illegally."

"I don't know what his methods are, but it's probably whatever that hot British woman does on her iPad while the Latino Magnum PI, not Tom Selleck, drives them around Oahu in his Ferrari."

Sharpe gave him that hound-dog look again. "You're talking about a TV show."

"That's why I wouldn't mention this investigative tactic in a police report or courtroom."

"Then how are you going to explain to the DA how you found her?"

"Cunning, instinct, and deduction," Walker said.

"Nobody will believe it."

"It's always worked for me before," Walker said. "I think it's the hat."

Walker's phone dinged. He checked the screen. An email had arrived. He opened his mail app while he was driving to see what it was, earning a disapproving frown from Sharpe. "I just got the list from the Department of Corrections of convict firefighters who were here for the Arrowbear Fire."

"What do you hope to glean from that?"

"I don't know," Walker said. "But it will give me something to read over breakfast or in the bathroom afterwards."

There was a diner at the end of the block, Dorothy's Chuck Wagon. Walker loved diners, especially old ones. He pulled into a parking spot close to the door and they went inside. The place was warm and had the comforting, inviting aroma of bacon, eggs, and hash browns. Best of all, the interior hadn't been redecorated since the Kennedy administration.

Walker and Sharpe found a booth and sat down opposite each other. A waitress named Dot, which also seemed just perfect to Walker, handed them menus and poured them cups of coffee without being asked. The detectives both ordered the American Breakfast, then Walker got Alison's cell phone and credit card numbers from Sharpe, called his hacker friend, and asked him to follow her digital tracks.

When Walker ended the call, Sharpe said, "I don't feel good about this."

"You will when we catch her." Walker had a sip of coffee, which tasted like Folgers Classic Roast to his educated palate, and then pulled up on his phone the list of convict firefighting crews, and the convicts who were on them, that fought the Arrowbear Fire. "The convict crews came here from all over the state for the Arrowbear Fire. I can't believe these felons not only get out of jail but get to travel, too."

"It's not a vacation." Sharpe took a sip of coffee, then scowled at his coffee cup, as if it had just insulted him. "They don't leave the fire or the staging area. It's exhausting work in hellish conditions. Literally. They could spend days covered with soot sleeping on the ground with their backpacks for pillows."

"Boo-hoo. I need more napkins to wipe away my tears. These are hardened criminals." Walker could see that two of the convict crews came from the LA area. One crew was from a conservation camp in the Angeles National Forest, the other from the Santa Monica Mountains. He started scrolling through the Angeles Forest crew's list of convicts, not that he really expected to recognize anybody.

Sharpe was also reading something on his phone. "Last night, while we were driving up here, the Chatsworth Fire and Stevenson Ranch Fire merged. It's zero percent contained. It's jumped the 101 freeway at Las Virgenes and is heading for the Pacific. Calabasas, Agoura, and Malibou Lake are being evacuated. That's tens of thousands of people who are being displaced, more if you throw in everybody who had to flee Bel Air and Brentwood."

"Do you think the fire had help from Icarus crossing the freeway?" Walker opened up the list of Malibu-based convicts who were working the Arrowbear Fire and began idly scrolling through the names.

Sharpe set his phone aside. "I'm thinking about how two big fires, seemingly started by faulty power lines, erupted within two days of each other in urban wilderness areas within Los Angeles County during a high-risk Santa Ana wind event. I'm thinking about how unlucky it was that one fire started in the middle of two of the wealthiest neighborhoods in the city and forced the shutdown of one of the busiest highways in the nation. And how the next fire started in a spot that not only crosses multiple firefighting jurisdictions but where the wind and terrain create a natural wildfire speedway to the sea. You couldn't pick better locations to create chaos and strain the firefighting resources in the region to the breaking point."

"You're wondering if that was the goal."

"Or, worse, if it's all part of a bigger plot."

Walker scrolled past a name on his screen and, for an instant, thought he'd imagined it.

But no, there it was, in black and white, a name from his distant past, when his knees didn't ache, when there wasn't buckshot in his flesh, and when fatherhood wasn't roaring toward him like a runaway train.

"It's definitely a bigger plot." Walker stared at the name and all that it implied and all the questions that it answered. "A daring heist or an outrageous swindle . . . or maybe both."

"How do you know?"

"Because Danny Cole is involved," Walker said. "He was a convict firefighter in Malibu and he was here for the Arrowbear Fire. He probably saw the Icarus in action and realized its criminal potential."

"Who is Danny Cole?"

Walker opened up his photo app, accessed his picture library in the cloud, and quickly searched for shots from eight years earlier. It took him a moment, but he found the booking photo he was looking for.

He held up his phone so Sharpe could see Cole's face. "Him."

That's when Dot the waitress arrived with their breakfasts, setting the plates of eggs, bacon, and pancakes down in front of them. She glanced at the photo on Walker's phone as she did so. "There's a familiar face. Is he a friend of yours?"

Sharpe and Walker shared a look, then Walker said, "You know him?"

"No, but he was sitting right where you are a few weeks ago."

"And you remember him?"

Dot smiled at the memory. "Of course I do, honey. He was good-looking, a big flirt, and left me a very nice tip."

Sharpe said, "Was he alone?"

"He was with my friend Ally, which is also why I remember him. They left together and I haven't seen either one of them since. They probably ran off on a whirlwind romance. At least, that's what I like to imagine, except when I do, it's with me instead of her." She winked at Sharpe. "A girl is allowed to dream. Do you need anything else, boys?"

"No, thank you, we're good," Sharpe said, and as soon as she left, he looked at Walker, who'd set down his phone and started devouring his bacon and eggs, dragging the strips of meat through the yolk like it was dipping sauce. "Do you believe in coincidences now?"

"Do you still think coincidences aren't proof?" Walker gobbled his yolk-slathered bacon.

"Okay, it's a draw," Sharpe said, cutting into his pancakes. "How do you know Danny Cole?"

Walker kept eating as he talked. "He's a slick con man and a master thief. I arrested him after he ran a big banking scam on a drug lord up in Ventura."

"Where there's another wildfire raging right now."

"It's no coincidence, either. The fires are all connected, they are a key part of his scheme, and he needed Alison's expertise, and the Icarus, to pull it off."

"Now we have enough to call a judge and get a warrant for Alison's phone, credit card, and banking activity," Sharpe said. "We don't need your friend."

"He's already on it," Walker said, mopping the remaining yolk off his plate with a piece of pancake speared on his fork. "But it's going to be a dead end with or without the warrant."

"How do you know?"

He ate the yolk-smeared bite of pancake. "Because Danny Cole is smart. I guarantee you that he told Alison Grayle to toss her phone and credit cards and that she's been using a burner and cash from the moment she left this diner. There won't be any digital trail."

"We have to get back to LA." Sharpe pushed aside his plate, his pancakes hardly touched. "Now."

Walker hated to leave any of the food behind, but Sharpe was right. There was no time to waste on a leisurely breakfast. That's why he was devouring his meal so fast. He finished his coffee and tossed Sharpe the car keys.

"You drive this time. I need to work the phone, find out about the other convicts on that crew and where they are now. They could be in it with him, whatever the hell it is."

It wasn't the fires—they were already blazing and probably wouldn't stop until they hit the beach and there was nothing left to burn.

"By the time we figure out what he's doing," Sharpe said, "it could be too late to stop him."

"But not to catch him," Walker said.

PART TWO

PRESENT TENSE

CHAPTER NINETEEN

Present Day
Saturday Morning

The Chatsworth and Stevenson Ranch fires merged on Friday, creating a massive wildfire, but the winds had ebbed a bit during the night, and Danny was worried the blaze might stall in upper Las Virgenes Canyon, between the evacuated gated communities of Mountain View and Hidden Hills, and not cross the 101 freeway.

And if that happened, there would be no heist.

So last night, under the cover of darkness, he'd launched the Icarus from the roof of the Epitome and dropped fireballs along the rolling hills in Anza Calabasas Canyon, the open space south of the 101, where the winds would naturally be expected to carry embers. And maybe they would have, eventually, but Danny needed to eliminate any doubt.

And he did, in a big way.

The Icarus performed like one of Daenerys Targaryen's fire-breathing dragons. The dry hillsides east of Las Virgenes Canyon Road erupted in flames with astonishing ferocity that seemed to drag the existing wildfire across the freeway, over a defensive line of fire engines, with some kind of magnetic, fiery force.

By sunrise on Saturday, the fire didn't need any of Danny's help. It was being pushed by blistering fifty-mile-per-hour winds and single-digit humidity and was devouring acres of parched brush by the minute in its charge toward Wishbone Canyon.

A mandatory evacuation order had been issued to residents by phone, email, and media reports as a precaution on Friday, and now sheriff's deputies, forest rangers, and California Highway Patrol officers were going door-to-door, even in the most remote areas of the Santa Monica Mountains, to make sure people fled while they still had the chance.

One of the Epitome's two safe rooms was in the underground garage, and the other was off the master bedroom. The safe room upstairs was primarily designed as a haven from armed invaders. The one downstairs was more of a long-term refuge from any catastrophic natural and man-made disasters, such as wildfires, nuclear war, or a zombie apocalypse, so that's where Adam set up the war room for the fire heist.

Adam and Alison, wearing headsets that allowed them to listen to dispatches from the Los Angeles County Fire Department's Incident Command center, sat at a table facing a bank of a dozen flat-screen monitors mounted on adjustable stands. Danny and the others stood behind the two of them, watching the relentless advance of the firestorm play out on the screens on multiple fronts.

The monitors, divided into windows, showed them satellite images, Doppler radar, numerous live television newscasts, a live view of the opposite ridge of Wishbone Canyon, and thanks to Adam hacking the Incident Command System's computer network, the real-time deployment of fire and law enforcement resources superimposed on a map of the Santa Monica Mountains fire zone. Another separate screen tapped into the live video feeds from the exterior surveillance systems at each of the three Wishbone Canyon homes they were targeting. And one more screen was devoted to the surveillance of the Epitome itself, and on that one they could see an LASD patrol car crossing the moat and driving into the motor court.

"It's showtime," Danny said and they watched, from various camera angles, as the scene unfolded.

◆　◆　◆

A sheriff's deputy got out of the car, his face covered with a bandanna against the smoke and ash already swirling in the air, went to the front door, and rang the bell. It was odd to Danny to see a cop masked like he was about to hold up a liquor store.

But Levi didn't seem to notice or care about that when he answered the door. He was casually dressed in a white Armani polo, red Peter Millar polyester golf pants, and a pair of Duca del Cosma Nappa leather golf shoes for a nice Saturday afternoon at the country club.

"Good morning, Deputy. What can I do for you?"

"Didn't you get the mandatory evacuation order?"

"No, I didn't."

"It was sent out by phone and email and is all over the news."

"I don't answer robocalls, I wasn't on my computer, and I don't watch TV."

The deputy pointed to the monster cloud of smoke hanging over the mountains and blotting out the sun. "You didn't notice all of the smoke and ash . . . and the smell of thousands of acres burning?"

"I was in the VR studio, golfing at Augusta with Tiger Woods."

That was true. It was how Levi had spent most of his days lately, when he wasn't drinking in the pub. Danny couldn't blame him for being anxious. Levi's time was running out and his life depended on whatever Danny was up to.

The deputy asked, "Are you alone or are there other people in the house?"

"Just me and Tiger."

That was a lie, but Danny thought Levi was totally convincing.

"It's not safe here. You have thirty minutes to pack whatever you need and get out," the deputy said in a tone that didn't invite disagreement.

Apparently, Levi didn't pick up on that. He smiled and said, "I'll stay and take my chances."

"It's not a request. That's why it's called a *mandatory* evacuation. Being here will put first responders at risk. You can go on your own in thirty minutes or we can arrest you. That's the law. Either way, you're leaving. We'll be waiting at the checkpoint on Latigo Canyon Road and PCH, the only way out of here. If we don't see you, we're coming back with handcuffs and dragging you out."

The deputy left.

◆ ◆ ◆

Danny put his hand on Adam's shoulder.

"Shut down all communications in Wishbone Canyon, but don't cut off their electric power yet. We want them to be able to open their garage doors and drive away."

Adam tapped a few keys on his keyboard. "Done. The only way they can communicate with the outside world now is with smoke signals."

Alison turned to Adam. "How did you do that?"

"Easy. A few days ago, we dug up the road and hijacked their shared cable, telephone, electric, and fiber optic lines. We also have powerful antennas on the roof that are jamming all radio, cellular, and even satellite communication capabilities."

"Except our own," Danny said, holding up a flesh-colored earbud between his right thumb and forefinger. "We'll be in contact with you, Adam, and each other with these earbuds, starting now." He put a set in his ears and turned to everyone else. "Time to suit up. We roll out in five minutes."

Everyone but Adam and Alison left the war room. Logan, Mertz, and Kurt went to the fire engine to get into their gear, and Tamiko, who was already dressed in her sheriff's deputy uniform, went to her patrol car to await her deployment.

Danny strode over to the glass elevator as Levi emerged, looking rattled.

"You can relax now," Danny said to him. "Your troubles are over. Tomorrow your debts will be erased, your life won't be in danger, and you'll be a very wealthy man. It will be a fresh start for you."

"If your scheme works," Levi said. "Whatever it is."

"It already has as far as you're concerned. The fire is coming, when and where I said it would. Those houses will burn. This one won't. You'll be saved."

Levi offered Danny his hand. "Good luck, Mr. Templar."

"You too."

Levi walked over to his Bentley, got inside, and drove out of the garage. Danny watched him go, then heard Adam's voice in his ear.

"We have action across the ravine."

"On my way." Danny went back to the war room. On one of the screens, he saw the deputy who'd just visited them arriving at the gates of the three-home neighborhood on the opposite ridge.

"The deputy just arrived to tell them to go," Alison said.

"But Kempton clearly got the message already," Adam said. "I've been watching him and his family on his surveillance cameras packing up their two Range Rovers."

Alison pointed at the screen, where they could see a man confronting one of the deputies. "Looks like Roland Slezak is already arguing with the deputy."

"Maybe the deputy will shoot him and make things easier for us," Danny said. "How much time do we have before the fire gets here?"

"Five, maybe six hours," she said. "But that could change in an instant."

"It would be nice if you could give us a little more warning than that."

"I'll do my best," she said.

◆　◆　◆

For most of the drive back to Los Angeles, Walker and Sharpe were both talking on their phones at the same time.

Walker's first call was to the Department of Corrections. He learned that two of Cole's fellow convicts on the firefighting crew—a safecracker named Sam Mertz and a car thief named Bobby Logan—were also back on the streets and hadn't reported to their parole officers in two weeks. And his second call to Walker's hacker friend confirmed what he'd already guessed—that Alison Grayle went off the grid two and a half weeks ago in Garner's Crossing. His third call was to Carly, letting her know he was on his way back to headquarters for another dull day of desk work.

He got off the phone as they were on the 10, passing through West Covina, and he picked up the thread of Sharpe's ongoing call.

"Just because they didn't find more Ping-Pong balls doesn't mean we're wrong, Lieutenant," Sharpe said, holding the phone to his ear with one hand and driving with the other. "We think a firefighter's widow stole the Icarus." There was a pause while Sharpe listened to a question. "Revenge, sir, because her husband was seriously injured in a fire and then killed himself . . ."

Walker could guess the gist of what their commanding officer said next and whispered it: "That's a motive, not proof. What proof do you have?"

That earned him a glare from Sharpe, who kept talking. "We know she had lunch three weeks ago with Danny Cole, a thief who was on a convict firefighting crew that saw the drone in action, and then she disappeared right after it was stolen. The timing all lines up."

Walker whispered, "How does any of this connect them to any fires in Los Angeles?"

Sharpe mouthed "shut up" to Walker, then said into the phone, "Cole was originally arrested in Ventura and spent years on the Malibu convict fire crew, so Los Angeles is the area he knows. That's why they've set the fires here."

"To what end?" Walker whispered.

Sharpe said, "A heist."

Walker whispered, "How do you know?"

Sharpe said, "Because that's Cole's profession."

But what were the emotional stakes for Cole? That's what Walker wondered. You don't set fire to half of Southern California just to make a score. It was too risky. But that wasn't what he thought the lieutenant would ask. Rather, it would be:

"What are they stealing?" Walker whispered.

Sharpe said, "We don't know."

"In other words, it's all guesswork," Walker said, forgetting to whisper. "You don't know anything. It's a big fat nothing burger."

Sharpe silently mouthed "shut up" at him again and then said, "Nobody is calling you big and fat, sir. Walker is on the phone with his wife."

Walker whispered, "He's calling his wife fat?"

Sharpe said, "She's eight months pregnant."

Sharpe listened, nodded, then said, "The LAFD is saying that because power-line failure is the easy, obvious explanation. They didn't see what I saw."

He looked frustrated as he listened to what the lieutenant said next, which Walker couldn't guess, so he kept quiet.

"Understood. Thank you, sir. We will." Sharpe ended the call and tossed his phone on the seat. "He doesn't buy our theory. The other investigators didn't find any bits of Ping-Pong balls in Skirball or Chatsworth."

"Just our luck."

"The LAFD says the fires were caused by damaged power lines and the lieutenant thinks the evidence backs that conclusion."

"He's an idiot," Walker said.

"Because he believes a conclusion that's based on evidence over one that isn't? Do you hear yourself?"

"Evidence isn't everything. Besides, you know I'm right."

Sharpe didn't respond to that. Instead, he said, "He thinks we both need sleep and is giving us the day off."

"We need to see exactly where the fire is, where it's been, and where it's headed. That will point us to Cole's target."

"All of that information, which is fed to Incident Command, will be at the Emergency Operations Center downtown," Sharpe said.

"Then that's where we have to go."

CHAPTER TWENTY

The fire engine, with Danny, Logan, and Mertz inside, rolled into the gated Wishbone Ridge neighborhood first, followed by Kurt driving the flatbed truck that carried the Bobcat with the scoop attached.

The private gated community was a single, long cul-de-sac, with Slezak's house first, Arseny Pletov's in the middle, and Orville Kempton's at the end, each house sitting on a five-acre property carved out of the rolling hills that formed the western slope of the eastern ridge.

Danny's crew passed Slezak and the deputy, who were arguing in the street beside the patrol car. It was the same deputy who'd come to Levi's door.

Danny parked the fire engine below the water tank on the ridge above the homes and turned to Logan and Mertz. "I'll go make the introductions. You two hook the engine up to the water tank and prepare the hoses like we're getting ready to actually fight the fire."

"I wish we were," Logan said.

"Try not to knee Slezak in the balls," Mertz said.

Danny got out. The wind was blowing hard from the north. Ashes were raining all over, like dirty snowflakes, and gathering on the ground. There was a strange beauty to it.

The deputy was pointing at the open gates and, beyond them, to the dark, churning cloud of smoke billowing out over the mountains to the north. "That fire is heading right this way. That's why it's a *mandatory* evacuation and not a voluntary one."

"This is my property," Slezak said, gripping a cell phone in his hand like a rock he intended to throw. "You can't make me leave, and if I were you, I wouldn't try, unless you are looking for an immediate career change."

The deputy looked past Slezak to Danny, and then to the two firefighters running a hose from the engine up to the water tank, and to Kurt, who was out of his truck and unlatching the Bobcat from the flatbed.

"Who are you people?"

Danny held out his hand to the deputy. "Captain Spike Reardon, Right Guard Fire Protection. We're private firefighters. The insurance companies that have the policies on these $50 million homes sent us to protect them."

Slezak snorted. "My home is worth nearly twice that."

Danny looked at him. "I'm sure it is, sir. And the insurance company doesn't want to pay out that kind of money if they can avoid it. So here we are."

"It's about time," Slezak said. "You should have been here hours ago, clearing brush and creating firebreaks with that Bobcat. But that's not enough. We need real firefighters out here . . . and retardant drops from helicopters. I'm making the call." He lifted his phone to his ear.

"You do that." The deputy waved Danny over toward his patrol car. "Can I have a word with you?"

"Of course." Danny and the deputy stepped out of Slezak's earshot.

"Before this private gig, did you work for a city, county, or state fire department?"

"We all did," Danny said, and that was true.

"Then you have an appreciation of the risks and the politics involved here. Do you know how seriously overextended CAL FIRE, LAFD, and LA County resources are right now fighting all of these fires?"

"That's why we're here, Deputy."

"Once Incident Command knows that a private firefighting crew is here, they'll allocate their limited resources elsewhere."

"Makes sense," Danny said. "They can't be everywhere at once."

The deputy took a step closer and lowered his voice to a near whisper. "The thing is, they may not be here at all, even if you're in desperate trouble. They are spread too thin and getting here to save you could be impossible or suicidal. And that's assuming you can even manage to send out a call for help. This area has become a dead zone. We can't get a radio signal here."

"Thank you for the warning, Deputy. We understand the risks and if it comes down to us or those houses, we'll choose us."

The deputy smiled and took a step back. "I'm relieved to hear it."

"The thing is, we are strictly in the structure protection business. If any residents stay, they will be a dangerous distraction that could get us killed. We need them gone."

"I understand. The second house appears to be empty and the family at the end of the street is about to go. This guy Slezak is the only straggler. But don't worry. I'll show my fangs and scare him off."

The deputy and Danny returned to Slezak, who was shaking his phone as if it might change its performance.

"I can't get a signal." Slezak pointed to the patrol car. "I need your radio. Now."

The deputy ignored the request. "The firefighters are here. Your home is protected. What you need to do now is leave."

"I'm staying to make sure they do their jobs." Slezak looked Danny right in the eye, daring him to argue. But Danny remained silent, content to let the deputy fight for him.

"You aren't a firefighter, sir," the deputy said.

"No, but I'm a lot smarter than they are"—he jerked a thumb at Danny—"and I've been through this before. They need my experienced leadership."

The deputy checked his watch. "You have fifteen minutes left to evacuate. If I don't see you at the Latigo Canyon checkpoint, I will come back and arrest you."

"The hell you will. Sheriff Lansing is a close, personal friend. I'd call him now if I could get a damn signal. But he gave me this." Slezak reached into his pants pocket, pulled out a gold Los Angeles County sheriff's badge, and thrust it in the deputy's face. "I am an honorary deputy chief. I'm exempt from any evacuation. So fuck off."

The deputy nodded and appeared to give the suggestion some thought. "Have you ever been tased, Mr. Slezak?"

"No."

"The sphincters often let go." The deputy took a step forward and pulled his bandanna down so Slezak could get a good look at his face and the cold determination in his eyes. "So, if you intend to resist arrest, you might want to wear a diaper or have a clean pair of pants handy."

Without waiting for a reply, the deputy tugged up his bandanna again, went back to his patrol car, and drove off.

"He doesn't scare me," Slezak said. "He's all talk. There's no way they are coming back for me. It's too dangerous."

"You're right, it is," Danny said. "That's why your insurance policy says that if you ignore a mandatory evacuation order or the instructions of firefighting personnel, your coverage will be instantly revoked and you won't be compensated if your home is damaged or destroyed by fire."

"That's bullshit. Did you see this badge?" Slezak held it up in Danny's face. "I'm a first responder."

Danny wanted to respond first with a knee to Slezak's groin. Instead, he said, "If you're not gone in ten minutes, I will void your homeowner's insurance policy. I have the authority."

"If you do that, you're finished as a firefighter. I'll destroy you. You'll be lucky to get a job checking receipts at Walmart."

"Maybe, but I doubt that will ever ease your misery over losing $100 million because your uninsured house went up in flames. It's your call."

Danny didn't wait for an answer. He walked back to the fire engine, where Mertz and Logan were going through the motions of hooking up the line from the water tank and checking the pressure. They might actually need the water if the fire got too close too soon. Slezak watched them for a moment, then stomped back to his house in a huff.

Mertz watched Slezak go. "Think he'll evacuate?"

"Oh yeah," Danny said. "He won't risk $100 million."

Logan looked off in the direction of the fire, miles to the north. "I'd give up my share of this heist to be up there, fighting the fire."

"You may still get your chance," Mertz said. "If everything goes wrong."

Two Range Rovers came their way from the end of the cul-de-sac. The lead car stopped beside the fire engine and Orville Kempton rolled down his window to speak to Danny. Two Dobermans sat on the back seat.

"I'm so glad to see you guys," Kempton said. His hairline was receding and he was compensating for the loss by growing a ponytail with what he had left. It made him look like an aging hippie who'd come into a lot of money. "It's a huge relief."

"That's why we're here," Danny said.

"After you save my house, bring this to any of my dealerships." He handed Danny a business card with his signature on the back. "I'll show my appreciation by giving each of you guys an incredible deal on a new car."

"We don't make a lot of money," Danny said.

"Don't worry. We offer unbelievable financing. You'll pay so little each month, it will feel like the car is free." Kempton smiled and drove off, followed by his wife and kids in the second Range Rover.

Danny turned to Mertz and Logan. "We can start with Kempton's place."

Mertz said, "How many violins do you think he managed to stuff into his car with his family and his dogs?"

"A few, but not all. Even if he only left one or two behind, we could leave here with them and nothing else and still be set for life."

"But we won't," Logan said. "Because we're greedy bastards."

"And it would be a tragedy if those instruments burned," Danny said. "They are important historical and cultural artifacts."

Mertz stepped up beside him. "So, you're not simply stealing them, you're saving them."

"That's right."

"From a fire you started," Mertz said.

"Let's not get bogged down in the details." Danny tore Kempton's card up and dropped the pieces on the ground.

There was a screech of burning rubber, and the men turned to see Slezak speeding out of his property in a vintage 1965 Corvette Stingray convertible. He skidded to a stop inches away from Danny and said, "If my house isn't standing tomorrow, the next uniform you'll be wearing is a blue vest. Remember that."

"You certainly know how to motivate people to do their best work," Danny said. "And I can promise you that's exactly what we'll do."

Slezak gave him the finger and sped off. As soon as he was gone, Mertz and Logan unhooked the hose from the fire engine. Kurt went to work removing the scoop attachment from the Bobcat and replacing it with the jackhammer.

Danny turned to look at the Russian's cantilevered house. The deputy said it was empty, but he needed to be sure.

"Mr. Wizard, are all the houses empty?"

Adam had installed a thermal-imaging camera on top of the Epitome for exactly this situation. He promptly replied through the earbud from the war room: "Nope. I'm reading three heat signatures in the Kremlin and they'll see you coming. They have a closed-circuit surveillance system with a battery backup at the house that I can't jam or shut down, but at least they are the only ones seeing the feed."

"Give me ten minutes, then send over the Muscle."

Tamiko replied on the earbuds, "Roger that."

Danny knew that meant she'd be there in five minutes. She didn't like to wait.

He went to the fire engine, opened a storage compartment, and removed the handheld battering ram. As he walked to Arseny Pletov's house, Mertz and Logan got into the fire engine and drove it up to Kempton's house to begin their pillaging. Kurt followed them a few moments later in the Bobcat in case any walls, floors, or vault doors needed to be demolished.

Danny strode across Pletov's motor court, with its obligatory fountain, to the front door. He looked up at the security camera mounted on one of the porch pillars as he rang the doorbell and said, "Anybody home?"

He waited a second for a response, then used the battering ram to bash the door open. It took only three swings to splinter the door apart at the jamb. He pushed the door out of his way and strode into the entry hall. Almost immediately, three muscular men in tailored suits and holding guns surrounded him.

"I rang the bell," Danny said, still holding on to the battering ram. "Nobody answered."

"Out," one man said with a heavy Russian accent that matched his heavy head, heavy body, and heavy gun.

"Why are you pointing a gun at me?"

"You broke in."

"Clearing the houses is part of my job. I'm saving this place and you from the fire."

"I don't see a fire," the Russian said.

"By the time you do, it will be too late."

The Russian poked Danny's forehead with the barrel of his gun. "Out. Now."

Danny walked out, the three Russians right behind him. The moment the lead Russian stepped outside, Tamiko emerged from hiding behind a pillar and put her gun to the man's head. She wore a pair of dark sunglasses, even though there wasn't any sunlight to get in her eyes. It was purely for intimidation.

"Police. Give the firefighter your gun, Putin." He did. She kept her gun pressed to his head and looked at the others, who hadn't lowered their weapons. "Tell Lenin and Yeltsin over there to drop their guns and kick them aside."

Putin said something in Russian and the other two men dropped their guns.

Tamiko holstered her gun. "Now get the hell out of here, and let these firemen do their jobs. Or, and I'm begging you to do this, resist so I can shoot you in self-defense and leave your corpses to burn."

Putin said, "We will go."

"Pussy." Tamiko looked at Lenin and Yeltsin. "Go get your car. Putin will wait for you here in case you're thinking about rearming and making a stand. You can pick him up on your way out."

She led Putin toward her patrol car, which was parked in the motor court.

Danny dropped the battering ram, scooped up the other guns, and tossed them all in the fountain while he whispered just loud enough for his earbuds to pick up what he was saying. "Those three gorillas didn't stick around just to protect Muhammad Ali's Olympic gold medal and Kurt Cobain's guitar. There must be something more valuable here we don't know about. Locksmith, bring over the ground-penetrating radar and let's see what they're hiding."

Mertz replied in his ear, "On my way."

A black Escalade emerged from Pletov's underground garage and stopped beside the patrol car.

Tamiko pushed Putin toward the SUV and then kicked him in the ass for good measure. "Don't come back or the firemen will let your house burn. Imagine how happy your boss would be with you after that."

Putin got into the back seat and the Escalade drove off.

"They were no fun," Tamiko said.

"Did you have to kick him?" Danny asked.

"I had to get something out of it," she said.

CHAPTER
TWENTY-ONE

The Emergency Operations Center, located in a seismically safe build-ing on Temple Street in downtown Los Angeles, looked just like every depiction of NASA's mission control that Walker had ever seen in the movies. There were occupied workstations with computer screens every-where, all of them facing a massive wall of even more screens, showing all kinds of video, data, and maps, while people wearing uniforms repre-senting every first-responder agency he could think of scurried around, looking grim, determined, and busy.

Sharpe elbowed him in the ribs. "Take off your hat."

"Why? It's not a church."

"We're allowed to be here, but since we're supposed to be off duty, we shouldn't draw attention to ourselves."

"I think better with my hat on," Walker said. "And if a really great cowboy hat is all it takes to distract these disaster response professionals from battling a cataclysmic inferno devastating Los Angeles, then we have bigger problems."

Sharpe gave up and gestured to a matronly-looking Black woman in a Los Angeles County Fire Department uniform sitting at a computer console and wearing a headset/microphone combo.

"That's Yvonne, one of the county fire's crisis technicians. She deals primarily with logistics, getting deputies and resources from point A to B, depending on ground conditions. Let me do the talking, okay?"

"You're the boss."

They approached Yvonne, who broke out in a big smile when she saw Sharpe.

"Shar-Pei, what are you doing here?"

"My new partner and I are working the arson angle on all of this."

"There's an arson angle?" Yvonne gave Walker the once-over, starting with his hat and not getting much farther. She didn't seem to approve of what she saw.

"That's what we're trying to nail down," Sharpe said, "but we need your help."

"Of course. What can I do?"

"Can you please show us the geographical scope of the Skirball and Chatsworth fires as they grew over time?"

"Sure can. First up, Skirball." She hit some keys, and a Google Earth satellite view of the Sepulveda Pass appeared on her screen with a red overlay that spread like an oil slick across the geography as the timeline counter in the upper corner of the screen ticked away. "The red represents the geographical scope of the fire from when it started to this moment. It only licked the Getty before moving into Brentwood, where it is now."

Walker asked, "Are any alarms going off at the Getty?"

Sharpe gave him a cutting look for speaking up.

"It's all quiet," Yvonne said. "In fact, the security personnel and some of the staff refused to leave to make sure the collection is safe."

Scratch the Getty as a target, Walker thought. "Aren't the staffers worried about their own survival?"

"That may be the most fireproof building in Los Angeles," she said.

Walker pointed to the residential areas west of the Getty. "How about household alarms in those evacuated homes? Any of them going off?"

"Dozens, mostly in the homes that are burning or getting pelted by water or retardant drops," Yvonne said. "But LASD's not rolling on them, if that's what you're asking."

"You're not worried about looters?"

"We're more worried about loss of life," she said. "We're not going to send a deputy into an inferno to respond to what 99.9 percent of the time are false alarms."

"How do you know that?"

Sharpe and Yvonne both looked like they wanted to smack him for asking such a stupid question.

Sharpe said, "Think about it, Walker. How is a burglar going to get in and out of a neighborhood that's surrounded by firefighters, cops, and flames?"

It was a good question but it was also giving Walker a mental tickle. It was just the kind of challenge that would excite Danny Cole . . . and there were a lot of riches out there for the taking. He could be robbing those homes in Brentwood or Bel Air right now. But which one?

Sharpe turned back to Yvonne. "Can you please show us the progression of the Chatsworth Fire?"

She did, putting it on her screen. The boundaries of the fire spread like an ever-growing amoeba from Chatsworth south toward Malibu. "The fire joined up with the Stevenson Ranch blaze and is moving straight toward the ocean, which is no surprise."

Walker asked, "Why not?"

She rolled her eyes and looked at Sharpe. "He really is new, isn't he?"

He sighed and took on a professorial tone. "The geography of the Santa Monica Mountains, combined with the atmospheric conditions that create the Santa Ana winds, makes the area a natural fire highway to the Pacific, and the geologic evidence proves it has been ever since

California rose up from the sea. In fact, blazes through there are such a regular part of nature that some native plants evolved to require fire to thrive and promulgate, as strange as that may seem."

Walker had never heard anybody use the word "promulgate" in conversation, but he got the idea. "That means a wildfire's path in this area is predictable."

"In general, yes, but not entirely. There isn't just one narrow path through the mountains and there can be freak shifts in wind direction that can change everything in a split second," Sharpe said. "Or the fire can become so intense that it creates its own weather system, and then anything can happen . . . including fire tornadoes."

"Fire tornadoes?" Walker said. "Really?"

Yvonne spoke up. "That's why we evacuated all of Calabasas, Agoura, and Malibu on Friday and assigned key firefighting assets to cover the developed pockets in the mountains and canyons where there are multiple structures. But otherwise, we're letting the fire burn."

"Why?" Walker asked.

"Because it's too dangerous to get in there and try to fight a force of nature where very few structures and no lives are in danger. We have to pick our battles, Cowboy." Yvonne pulled up a map on her screen and, using her finger on her touchpad, was able to draw a white circle around an area north of the Pacific Coast Highway and along the beaches of Malibu. "This is where we're drawing the line."

Of course it was, Walker thought. Because the homes, which were either overlooking the beach or right on it, were some of the most expensive and exclusive properties in the United States, an area collectively known as Billionaire's Row.

But Walker could still see homes, big ones, dotting the ridges and valleys in the vast area between Topanga Canyon to the east and Latigo Canyon to the west.

"There are lots of homes in the mountains between the 101 freeway and PCH, all scattered among the ridges and in the canyons, that could burn before the fire gets to that billion-dollar line in the sand."

"That's the problem," Yvonne said. "The homes are spread out and hard to reach. Getting firefighters in and out of there is highly dangerous."

"Isn't that their job?" Walker asked.

Sharpe winced.

Yvonne replied, a defensive stiffness behind her words. "Yes, it is, Detective. And we'd like to protect every single structure. But we've got three big fires going in the county, and another one up in Ventura, taxing the entire region's firefighting resources. We only have 50 percent of the manpower and equipment we need to battle this wildfire. Luckily, most of the area is still open space or parkland . . . and most of the idiots who built isolated, impossible-to-protect homes out there are zillionaires who can afford to lose them."

"But that's not what happens, is it?" Walker said. "The zillionaires get on the phone and scream at the politicians who are beholden to them for campaign donations and pretty soon you get a call from your boss telling you to rethink your priorities when it comes to allocating resources."

Yvonne nodded. "Yes, there are times when some firefighting resources are moved from protecting a neighborhood to protecting an individual home . . . and then you pray the neighborhood doesn't burn as a result."

Walker asked, "How often are your prayers answered?"

"Not enough."

Walker looked again at the satellite image of the Santa Monica Mountains. "Can you show us where the firefighters are positioned now?"

Yvonne typed a few keys and clusters of multicolored dots, widely dispersed, appeared on the satellite image. "The white squares and orange dots are various firefighting battalions and crews. The yellow dots indicate Los Angeles County sheriff's deputies on patrol or manning road closures or checkpoints. The blue dots indicate convict firefighting crews."

Walker saw smatterings of white and blue dots, clustered together, near some structures in the mountains, but most were in neighborhoods of a dozen or more homes. He also saw a few gray dots among the outlying homes, mostly on ridges or deep in canyons, far from where firefighters or deputies were positioned. "What are the gray dots?"

"The locations of independent firefighting forces," she said. "Either they notified us directly where they are stationed or their locations were passed along to us by law enforcement or our firefighters."

"What are independent firefighting forces?"

Sharpe answered the question. "Freelance firefighters working for insurance companies to protect their assets, which are usually homes in the ten- to one-hundred-million-dollar range."

"What happens if those private firefighters see another home burning down the road that's not covered by their insurance company? Will they do something about it?"

Sharpe shook his head. "Not unless they think it presents an immediate threat to the homes they are paid to protect."

"That's bullshit."

"That's the way firefighting used to be done in eighteenth- and nineteenth-century England. The rich hired professionals and the poor were on their own with a bucket brigade," Sharpe said. "But as cities grew, the rich soon learned that fires, like viruses and tsunamis, don't respect property lines, so firefighting became a public service, funded by taxpayers."

"Except the rich can still pay for concierge firefighting services," Walker said.

Yvonne shrugged. "I'm fine with that if it means more of our limited public resources can go where they are most needed. The problem is, when the private guys get into trouble, they call us to save their asses, taking our resources and manpower away from protecting other homes and jeopardizing the lives of our first responders."

"And the little guy gets screwed again," Walker said.

Yvonne's expression hardened with determination. "Not today, Cowboy. Not this fire. We don't have the resources to spare. We've warned the private firefighters that they are on their own. Nobody is coming to their rescue."

"Thank you, Yvonne," Sharpe said. "You've been a big help."

"Anytime, Shar-Pei."

Sharpe took Walker by the arm and led him off to one side, out of Yvonne's earshot and out of everybody's way. "What happened to letting me do the talking?"

"You weren't asking the right questions."

"You mean I wasn't asking the dumb ones."

"The fires are a distraction for a heist."

"Where? Besides the Getty, which is occupied and thoroughly secured, I don't see any museums or banks that Cole can rob while everybody is busy fighting the fires."

"Malibu is wide open. There are dozens of mansions in the mountains that are stuffed with cash, jewels, and artwork that are empty and unprotected, each one the equivalent of a museum or a bank," Walker said. "I think Cole started these fires to evacuate a neighborhood and spread firefighters and law enforcement resources so thin that he'd be free to pillage the homes with impunity."

Sharpe mulled that for a moment. "Even if you're right, which homes are they hitting? And how are they going to get out with their loot without being caught or burned alive?"

"I don't know, but I guarantee you that Cole has found a way to do it."

"It's an enormous risk. There's got to be other things he can steal that don't require him to create and survive an epic wildfire."

"That means there is something else driving him besides just greed and the thrill of the score."

"You're talking about emotional stakes again."

"That's right. But not just for him," Walker said. "For all of them."

"All?"

"It's not just Danny Cole and Alison Grayle doing this. He's got a crew that probably includes two of the convicts who fought fires with him in Malibu." Something occurred to Walker and he rushed back to Yvonne's desk. "I'm sorry to bother you again. I promise this will be the last time, but it's very important. Can you please pull up that map of Malibu again with all the overlays on it?"

"I have a job to do here, you know," she complained, but she did as Walker asked.

"Thank you." He looked back at Sharpe. "Were there ever any fires in this area that Cole and those convicts would have fought?"

Sharpe studied the map and Walker saw the man's expression suddenly change. Something had clicked in that Sherlockian brain of his. "That's it."

"What's it?"

"The Crags Fire swept through here five years ago," Sharpe said. "A convict firefighter was killed."

"I remember that," Yvonne said. "It was a horrible accident."

Cole is getting revenge. That was the emotional hook, Walker thought, one Cole shared with Alison Grayle. That had to be how Cole had roped her in. "Where exactly did the accident happen?"

"Southeastern end of Wishbone Canyon. Right about here." Sharpe pointed to a gray square that indicated the location where a private firefighting unit was protecting some homes right now, all by themselves, without any support or backup from county firefighters or deputies.

Or anybody around to see what they were doing.

And now Walker knew exactly where Cole was . . . and how he planned to get in and out with his bounty . . . and why he was doing it.

And Sharpe knew it, too.

◆ ◆ ◆

Sam Mertz set up the ground-penetrating radar device in the middle of Pletov's living room and fired it up while Kurt did a preliminary scout inside Slezak's house and Danny, Logan, and Tamiko removed the violins from Kempton's house and loaded them into the fire engine.

Kempton's house was vast and unusual. It had a hookah bar, a beauty salon, and an indoor gym with a rock-climbing wall that Tamiko couldn't resist trying.

Danny was outside, gently placing a Stradivarius into a padded storage compartment in the fire engine, when he heard Mertz's voice in his ear.

"There's a hidden room down in Pletov's garage. It's got to be 1,500 square feet and surrounded with reinforced concrete. It could be a vault or a bomb shelter."

Danny said, "I'll be right down."

He left Logan and Tamiko to finish up at Kempton's and drove the Bobcat down to Pletov's house and into the underground garage, where Mertz was waiting. Danny expected to see a collection of exotic cars. What he saw instead were two forklifts and several stacks of empty pallets. It didn't make any sense.

Danny looked at the floor and saw tire tread marks that ended at a wall covered with storage units, a pegboard of garden and woodworking tools, and a pristine built-in workbench. Pletov might as well have painted arrows on the floor and added a sign reading HIDDEN ROOM.

"Not very convincing, is it?" Mertz said.

Pletov should have messed up the workbench so it looked like someone had actually used it, but Danny understood why he'd cut corners. The odds of someone making it down here uninvited were slim. And Danny wouldn't have, either, if not for a hunch and the GPR.

"True, but it helps if you already know there's a secret room."

Danny ran his fingers along the underside of the workbench and along the shelves until he found the hidden button. He pressed it. A section of cabinetry slid away to reveal a bank-vault door that covered a space just large enough for a forklift to pass through.

It raised a lot of questions for Danny. "What could be so valuable that Pletov needs a forklift to move it, an underground vault to store it, and three armed guards to watch over it, even during a wildfire?"

Mertz cracked his knuckles. "Give me an hour with the Bobcat's jackhammer and a few sticks of dynamite and we'll find out."

CHAPTER TWENTY-TWO

Sharpe pulled Walker to a corner of the Emergency Operations Center where they could talk without being overheard. "We need to get to Wishbone Canyon."

"I was hoping you'd say that," Walker said. "I didn't think you would, though."

"I'm not wearing this badge as a fashion accessory, Walker. The problem is, Wishbone Canyon is in an extremely high-risk fire zone. We'll need to be dropped in by a chopper as close as possible to the canyon and then hike the rest of the way."

"Are you up for it?"

"The arson and explosives unit is a division of SWAT. It's what I'm trained to do."

"Yeah, but when was the last time you did anything like this?"

"Don't worry about me," Sharpe said. "I'm not the one with bad knees and a gut full of buckshot."

"Which I got from years of doing this kind of shit."

Sharpe pressed on, ignoring Walker's implication that he didn't have the necessary experience. "Once we're on the ground, we'll be on our own. There's no guarantee there will be another chopper or any ground units available to get us out. It all depends on how the wind and fire behave."

"I am counting on Cole to have a way out," Walker said.

Sharpe looked at him in disbelief. "Do you really think relying on the bad guys to save our lives after we've arrested them is a wise exit strategy?"

"It is if you know Danny Cole. He'll have a brilliant escape plan."

"One that doesn't include the two of us," Sharpe said.

"What do you mean *two*? We need at least four others."

"Nobody is going to authorize you, me, or anybody else in law enforcement to go into those mountains." Sharpe gestured to everyone working around them. "Right now, all these people care about is controlling the wildfire, not catching bad guys."

"Because most of them are firefighters, not lawmen," Walker said. "What about reaching out to the sheriff?"

"Even if we could convince Lansing that a heist is going down, he isn't going to drop deputies into the path of a rampaging wildfire to stop it."

"Even if one of the rich homeowners calls him and exerts some pressure? The sheriff is a politician who'd like to be mayor. Maybe even governor someday. That takes money."

"But if a bunch of deputies die trying to save some millionaire's jewelry, Lansing's political future will die, too," Sharpe said. "No, he won't send us or anybody else in to stop the crime. He'll say it's not worth risking anybody's life."

"It is to me and you. Because arresting bad guys is what we do," Walker said. "The risk comes with the job. If that's a problem, you shouldn't be a cop."

"That's not going to be an issue for us, though, since nobody is going to fly us into a wildfire."

"Leave that to me," Walker said.

Alison was getting increasingly worried as she and the Wizard watched the data stream from Incident Command on her screens and listened to the frenzy of fire and police radio traffic.

The Wizard had muted the microphones in the war room so the Saint and his crew wouldn't be distracted by all the noise the two of them were listening to. If she or the Wizard wanted to talk to the crew, they had to hit a button to activate their mikes.

So only the two of them knew that over two thousand firefighters supported by a pair of Super Scooper air tankers holding 1,600 gallons of water each, a helitanker capable of releasing 2,650 gallons of water, and three other water-dropping helicopters hadn't been able to slow the wildfire's relentless march. The aircraft had been grounded Friday night, when the fire made its biggest gains in acreage, and today there weren't nearly enough personnel and equipment to cover the vast terrain being incinerated. Even now, with the aircraft back in the battle, the topography, the winds, and the smoke were making it too dangerous to fly into the most critical areas.

More than twenty thousand acres, mostly of open space and parkland, had already burned, along with more than a hundred homes and other structures. Luckily, there had been no fatalities or serious injuries to weigh on Alison's conscience.

Yet.

The winds had picked up, and the Los Angeles County Fire Department's experts had issued a new forecast, for internal use only, showing the fire's projected path through Malibu. A tsunami of flames would wash through Wishbone Canyon in the next four hours and hit the beach by sunset.

Their forecast was more conservative than her own. She thought it could hit them in three hours or less if the inferno got a nice wind-driven run through the canyons. But that was still plenty of time for the Saint's crew to clean out all the houses and go.

But why wait?

The thieves had already scooped up all of Kempton's violins and bunch of Pletov's memorabilia. The Saint had said it himself an hour ago—they could leave now and escape with tens of millions of dollars' worth of stolen goods.

What was the point of staying until the inferno arrived?

But she could hear Ed Murrow—or Simon Templar, or whatever his name really was—and the others talking and sense the excitement in their voices. She knew they wouldn't leave yet. Not until they had everything there was to get . . . or unless doom was right on top of them.

Kurt found a safe in Roland Slezak's master bedroom and now he drilled into it with a pneumatic drill secured over the safe by a tripod attached to the wall. The device looked to Danny like some kind of mechanical spider.

Danny and Logan watched Kurt work, dividing their attention between the drill and the two blacktip sharks swimming in the eight-foot-long, six-hundred-gallon saltwater aquarium in the ceiling above Slezak's bed. The sharks were clearly agitated by all the noise and shaking.

"How would you like to sleep under that?" Logan said, sitting beside Danny on the edge of the bed. "I'd be afraid there'd be an earthquake and they'd land in bed with me."

"Yes, but you aren't a shark," Danny said. "Maybe Slezak is counting on them not to eat one of their own."

From Danny's standpoint, the heist couldn't be going more smoothly. They'd already cleaned out Kempton's place, and Tamiko was packing up the last of the memorabilia at Pletov's house while Mertz worked on opening the vault in the oligarch's underground garage.

Kurt shut off the drill, removed the tripod apparatus, and opened the safe. Inside were a mahogany watch box, various papers, and four gold bars. He whistled. "If this is what was left behind, imagine what he took with him."

Danny stepped up beside Kurt, removed the box, and opened it. About a dozen watches were inside, safely and snugly stored in foam cutouts, but several slots were empty where other watches had once been.

"Slezak took three of his Patek Philippes, the $11 million Supercomplication, the $5.5 million Calibre 89, and the $4 million World Time, and also the $4.5 million Louis Moinet Meteoris that has an actual piece of moon rock in it."

"What's left?" Logan asked.

"Just the dregs, like this lousy Vacheron Constantin." Danny tossed it to Logan, who caught it. "And this Lange & Söhne Grand Complication." He tossed that watch to Kurt. "And this Franck Muller Aeternitas Mega." Danny took it out for himself.

Logan slipped the Vacheron Constantin onto his wrist. "It's not bad looking. What's it worth?"

"The Vacheron? Only a million."

Logan blinked hard, then nodded toward Kurt. "What about his?"

"Two million," Danny said.

Logan gestured to the Aeternitas Mega on Danny's wrist. "And yours?"

"About the same."

Logan looked at his watch. "Why am I getting cheated?"

"We're splitting everything evenly among all of us, but if you want another one to wear out of here, try this." Danny tossed him another watch. "A Rolex Daytona Oyster Albino."

"What's this one go for?"

"Four million."

Kurt admired the watch on his wrist. "Why didn't Slezak take the whole watch box with him?"

"Probably figured the watches were safer in the vault, even if the house burns down," Danny said. "Besides, they're all insured."

That's when they heard an explosion, which was much louder in their ears than it would have been if they'd heard it outside, where the sound was muffled by the concrete and bedrock that surrounded Pletov's underground garage.

The sound was so painfully loud, for the three of them as well as Adam and Alison back at the Epitome, that they plucked the earbuds out of their ears and missed hearing Mertz the first time he spoke.

Danny's ears were still ringing when he put the buds back in and asked Mertz, "Are you all right?"

Mertz responded a moment later. "I'm great. I've got something here you've all got to scc."

◆　◆　◆

Every bolt and rivet rattled in the decades-old Bell 206 helicopter carrying Sharpe and Walker as it wove wildly through the canyons, under a blanket of smoke, toward the ferocious inferno only a dozen miles ahead of them.

Sharpe and Walker were suited up in tactical Kevlar and armed like soldiers going into battle.

Their pilot was Buck Tatum, who'd bought the retired news chopper from a local TV station. Even on a good day, it would be a bumpy ride in the old workhorse. But now they were being batted around by the rough atmosphere, a ride made even worse by the pilot's sudden moves to control the aircraft and avoid obstacles in the poor visibility created by the smoke.

For Walker, the flight was pure fun, as safe as a Disneyland ride, because the excitement of being back in action was smoothing out any justifiable concerns he might otherwise have had about crashing.

It wasn't the same for Sharpe, as Walker could see. Sharpe's knuckles were white as he gripped the armrest on his seat and gritted his teeth through every bump and turn of the aircraft.

That's because, Walker thought, police work for Sharpe was an intellectual pursuit, a mind game, analyzing the clues to get to the bad guy. It wasn't about the chase. It was about being smarter than his quarry and everybody else.

For Walker, police work was all about the hunt, and the risk that came with it. As long as he was wearing a badge and carrying a gun, there was no way to truly mitigate the risk that came with a job in law enforcement, which was something Carly either didn't understand or didn't want to.

But this time, the risk was one he could have chosen not to take. He did it anyway, because *not* doing it would have meant giving up the hunt, too, and then who was he and what the hell was he doing on the job?

He knew why he was here, but he wondered why Sharpe was in the chopper, flying into a wildfire. This wasn't a mind game anymore. This was action.

Maybe Sharpe just wanted to see what his new partner was made of, Walker thought. Or maybe he didn't want to appear cowardly. Whatever Sharpe's reasons were, Walker realized he was glad to have him along. He knew that Carly would have considered that an epiphany, a loner finally accepting a partner, but he doubted he'd ever tell her about it.

Sharpe looked at Walker and gestured to Tatum, a former TV news photographer who'd been downsized out of a regular paycheck and who now made his living by selling breaking news footage to TV stations and stock footage to movie studios. Tatum was talking animatedly to someone on his headset, but Sharpe and Walker were wearing headsets themselves and couldn't hear any conversation but their own.

Sharpe asked, "Isn't your friend worried about his license being revoked by the FAA and facing criminal charges for flying into restricted airspace?"

"I'm sure he's talking to them now, telling them I shoved a badge in his face, told him I had an emergency and that I was confiscating him and his chopper to fly us into the fire zone," Walker said. "Which is basically the truth, but he's getting footage nobody else in town has, so everybody wins."

"He might keep his license, but we could lose our badges."

"I haven't had this one long enough to get attached to it and you're old enough to retire anyway. But it's not going to be an issue for either of us."

"Why's that?"

"Because we're flying into a monstrous wildfire and will probably get killed."

"That's reassuring."

The chopper came to a stop, hovering in place, and Tatum's irritated, gravelly voice came through their headsets.

"I'm setting you down here. The smoke is too dense. We're about three miles south of Wishbone Canyon, below the tip of the eastern ridge. This is as close as I can get without losing visibility. I don't want to collide with a mountain or another chopper."

"Coward," Walker said. The pilot gave him the finger. Walker smiled at Sharpe. "He loves me."

"That's obvious."

The chopper landed on a flat, weedy piece of land and Sharpe and Walker spilled out. The chopper rose and arced away, leaving the men behind in near darkness amid a swirling flurry of falling ash.

Sharpe looked around for landmarks and checked his paper map. They were in the middle of the wishbone created by the two ridges, which weren't edged by sheer drops. Instead, the ridges were buttressed by rolling hills with some low folds and deep ravines and crisscrossed with hiking and deer trails.

Walker checked his phone. No signal. So much for calling his wife and lying to her about how little danger he was in. At least they had radios they could use to monitor communications and learn what was happening with the fire. And, if they got into a tight corner, to call for help, not that there was any guarantee anyone would answer.

"That way." Sharpe pointed north, where the wishbone ridges stood in sharp contrast against the dense smoke, which resembled a violent approaching storm, the billows constantly churning, revealing flashes of the tall, intense flames incinerating the mountains.

The two detectives hadn't walked far when they both started hearing the radio chatter about a new fire.

"Oh, joy," Walker said.

CHAPTER
TWENTY-THREE

Danny, Logan, and Kurt hurried over to the Russian's house and down to the underground garage, where Mertz and Tamiko were waiting. Mertz was powdered with concrete and plaster dust. Tamiko stood beside him wearing Michael Jackson's sequined white glove. The drilling and the blast had created a big, jagged hole in the wall where the vault door once stood. Beyond it, in the settling mist of dust and charred bits of green paper, was the hidden 1,500-square-foot space, now revealed. The room was filled, from floor to ceiling, with pallets of shrink-wrapped cash.

Two of the pallets, close to the vault door, had been partially obliterated by the blast, and Danny realized the bits of paper fluttering around were money.

Danny stepped inside the vault, picked up a stack of cash from one of the torn pallets, and flicked through the bills. They were used hundred-dollar bills. He looked up again at all of the pallets, at all of that cash, and realized he was looking at millions of dollars. Maybe tens of millions.

The four other members of his crew came inside behind him.

Kurt said, "I may break into tears."

It was a burglar's fantasy come true. Riches beyond their wildest dreams, right there in front of them. Everybody was grinning.

Adam's excited voice came over the earbuds. "What is it? What are you all looking at?"

Tamiko replied, "Pallets of cash."

Alison said, "Did you say . . . *pallets?*"

Kurt picked up a packet of money and sniffed it like a cigar. "More cash than you can possibly imagine."

Mertz said, "It's like we just broke into the US Mint."

"I wish you guys were wearing cameras," Adam said.

"Me too," Alison said.

Logan asked, "What's Pletov doing with so much cash?"

Danny made an educated guess. "Pletov owns a bunch of pot dispensaries as a sideline. It's a mostly cash business. Even though selling pot is legal in California, dispensaries can't find any banks willing to accept their money. That's a big problem for a legitimate business, but it's even worse if you're a Russian mobster. So he's been hoarding it."

Tamiko said, "Forget about stealing Dorothy's ruby slippers and Babe Ruth's bat. Let's stuff as much cash as we can into the fire engine."

Kurt nodded in agreement. "We can bring in the flatbed, too, and load it up with all the pallets it can carry."

"We'll still be leaving a lot of money behind," Logan said.

"The Epitome is close by. We can come back for more," Kurt said. "Maybe we'll be able to empty out all of this before the fire gets here."

"There's another problem." Mertz brushed the dust off his face. "We don't have anything to cover the pallets with. We'll be driving on the road between here and the Epitome with all of that shrink-wrapped cash out in the open."

"So what?" Kurt said. "Who is going to see us? Squirrels? Deer? Nobody is out here."

For Danny, the wonderment of the discovery was wearing off fast and the reality of how to handle all that cash was setting in, along with all the practical implications and consequences. "That's fine here and now. But how do we get out of Malibu with all of this cash?"

Kurt said, "We'll keep it in the Epitome's garage and come back for it later, maybe with a couple of moving trucks."

Danny shook his head. "The beauty of this heist is that we can get away now, or in the immediate aftermath of the fire, without a trace. Like we were never here. But now you want to return to the scene of the crime. That's asking to get caught."

"Not if we're smart about it," Tamiko said.

"The Epitome is going to be the last house standing after the fire and will become the center of media attention," Danny said. "How do we get all of these pallets of cash out of the garage before someone discovers them?"

Kurt patted Danny on the back. "You're brilliant. You'll think of something. You always do. We can't leave this behind."

"Yes, we can," Mertz said. "We should stick to the plan."

Kurt looked at him incredulously. "You want to burn five, ten, maybe twenty million dollars? It's right here for the taking."

Danny said, "We don't need it. You're wearing $2 million on your wrist right now. That's a pallet of cash, only it's a lot easier to carry and to hide."

"You're going to have to fence the watch, for ten cents on the dollar," Kurt said, then picked up a packet of cash. "These are actual dollars. Nothing to fence. No middleman necessary."

Alison spoke up, a voice in their ears from afar, almost like their own conscience. "It's a moot point. You don't have time to take the money anyway."

"What's changed?" Danny asked.

"Another fire," she said. "Someone torched a house in Topanga, and the blaze is spreading fast, heading southwest, pushed by the Santa Anas."

Topanga Canyon was only ten miles east.

Logan said, "Why would anyone burn down their own house during a wildfire?"

Adam answered the question. "According to the cop chatter, it was a crime scene. Soaked in blood."

Alison added, "You need to leave before the new blaze merges with the Chatsworth Fire."

"Where will that happen?" Logan asked.

"Right on top of us," Alison said. "In two hours, probably less."

Danny clapped his hands. "That's it. We're done. We just have time to open the doors and windows of the houses to let the embers in, splash the floors with gasoline, and off we go."

Everyone except Kurt took a packet of money, more as a souvenir of their amazing discovery than anything else, and left the room. He lingered behind for a moment, staring wistfully at all of that money, soon to be ashes.

◆ ◆ ◆

Nature was fleeing.

Deer, rabbits, racoons, even coyotes dashed past Sharpe and Walker, away from the coming apocalypse from the north, blowing with the wind, the promise of death in the air. The animals weren't concerned about the two humans in their midst, not with a far worse terror approaching, though Walker could have sworn he saw a few of them glance at him with incredulity.

Who walks toward death instead of running away from it?

Cops, that's who.

The two detectives hiked in silence along a well-worn trail, the sky getting darker, and the air thicker with ash, with each step.

Sharpe's attention was on the radio chatter from Incident Command. There was a house on fire in Topanga Canyon, intentionally set by somebody to destroy the evidence of a bloody massacre. The fire sparked a new blaze that was moving rapidly southwest.

"That Topanga fire worries me," Sharpe said as they neared the trailhead located off Latigo Canyon Road. "If it merges with the Chatsworth Fire, it will come barreling down this canyon right into us."

"I'm sure Danny Cole knows that, too."

"Is that supposed to reassure me?"

"He'll have a plan."

"You keep saying that," Sharpe said, "but we're the ones who should have a plan."

There was a Bentley sitting on the side of the road, the engine running. Without thinking, Walker drew his gun.

Sharpe stared at Walker with an expression similar to the one a deer had given him a few minutes ago. "Why are you holding a gun?"

"Instinct."

Sharpe stopped and looked around. "All I see is a Bentley idling on the side of the road. Where's the threat to us in that?"

"There's a fire coming," Walker said, "so why is he just sitting there instead of getting the hell out? It feels wrong."

"It doesn't mean you're in danger."

"Holding the gun makes me feel better."

"Try sucking your thumb instead."

They approached the Bentley, Sharpe leading the way. As they got closer, Walker could see the shape of a man at the wheel and a spiderweb of cracks on the driver's side window, the glass spattered with blood. Sharpe drew his gun.

Walker glanced at him. "What's wrong with your thumb?"

"Cover me." Sharpe moved cautiously toward the passenger-side door and opened it.

Walker came up behind Sharpe and saw the driver, a bullet hole between the eyes, dried blood and brains still dripping from the driver's side window, the shoulder belt holding the corpse in place. There was a gun in the dead man's hand.

Sharpe holstered his gun and said, "Looks like a suicide."

Walker opened the back door. There was a box on the back seat full of real estate brochures for a home called the Epitome. He picked up one of the brochures. On the back was a picture of the dead man in the front seat. His name was Levi Brisker.

"Maybe he was despondent over his $75 million house burning down." He held up the brochure to Sharpe. "This is Levi Brisker. I've read about his place. He's up to his hair plugs in debt."

"He's only been dead a couple of hours, at most. We need to secure the scene and call this in."

"Why do you want to do that?"

"Oh, I don't know," Sharpe said. "Maybe because we're police officers and this is a crime scene?"

"Think about it a minute," Walker said. "What are we securing the crime scene from? There's nobody out here."

"The killer could be," Sharpe said.

"Brisker killed himself."

"I said it *looked* like suicide, not that it *is* one. It's not."

"You're an arson investigator," Walker said, "not a homicide detective."

"He was shot between the eyes. Most people who shoot themselves put the gun to the side of their heads, or under their chin, so they won't lose their nerve looking down the barrel," Sharpe said. "Also, the brain matter is all over the driver's side window. That means he was facing the passenger seat when he was shot. Why would he do that? He'd face forward. Someone sitting in the passenger seat shot him in the face, then put the gun in his hand to make it look like suicide."

"Okay, let's say you're right."

"I am right," Sharpe said.

"What's next? We aren't supposed to be here. You call this in, and then what happens? Do you think they are going to send in homicide detectives and a crime scene unit with two wildfires closing in on us? We'll be lucky if they can even send a chopper to get us out."

"Okay, let's say you're right."

"I am right," Walker said.

"We can't just ignore a murder."

"We won't," Walker said. "We'll quickly take a bunch of pictures to document the scene, then grab the gun and his wallet and hurry on our merry way."

"We can't remove anything from the car. We'll contaminate the crime scene."

"There won't be a crime scene after the fire comes through here, only ashes. Whatever we take will be the only evidence that survives," Walker said. "Assuming, of course, that we do, too."

"Then the smart thing to do would be to go back now with the evidence," Sharpe said. "Because this is a homicide, and that takes priority over a property crime."

"If we go back now, we will destroy our careers for nothing, while Danny Cole gets away with the biggest arson, and maybe the biggest heist, in Los Angeles history. And worst of all, we'll be the only ones who'll ever know that's what happened, because we can't prove shit. That will torture you for the rest of your life," Walker said. "Which can lead to mental illness, alcoholism, hair loss, and impotence—or, in your case, make those existing conditions much worse."

Sharpe took out his phone. "I'll start with the front seat and the body, you shoot everything else. With your camera, not your gun."

"That's obvious."

"Maybe to most people," Sharpe said. "I'm not convinced it's true for you."

They were still documenting the crime scene five minutes later when they heard a new flurry of radio chatter about a couple of teenagers who'd hiked to the Lost Cave to party Friday night . . . and hadn't been seen since.

The wind was blowing harder now, picking up speed as it flowed down the mountains into the canyon. Danny could feel the dry heat of the wildfire and smell its charcoal musk in the brown air, which was thick with tiny embers that winked out like dead fireflies before they could hit the ground.

Danny stood beside one of the palm trees that ringed Roland Slezak's house. The windows of the house were open and the hallways had been splashed with gasoline for the windblown firebrands to ignite.

But he couldn't wait for that to happen, not with this house. He needed to see it himself, to see it burn the way it should have years ago. So he'd asked Alison to go up on the Epitome's rooftop sundeck and send over the Icarus for a strafing run.

Now Danny was joined by the others as the Icarus circled the house once on a dry run, then doing it again, this time hovering over the top of each palm tree and dropping multiple fireballs into their crowns.

Within seconds, the trees burst into flames, spewing embers into the open windows of Slezak's house. The Icarus moved on, igniting one tree after another. By the time the drone flew back to the Epitome, the house was ablaze, massive flames seething out of the windows, generating scalding heat that Danny could feel fifty yards away.

Danny, Logan, and Mertz stared at the blaze with a grim satisfaction that neither Kurt nor Tamiko could appreciate. The two of them hadn't been there when Arnie Soloway died. Kurt's gaze kept drifting back to the Kremlin, farther up the street, as if he could see the cavern of cash underneath it.

"Our job is done. We can go," Danny said and they headed to their three vehicles on the street.

Tamiko got behind the wheel of the patrol car and Danny got into the passenger seat beside her. Mertz and Logan took the fire engine, its storage compartments filled with stolen goods. And Kurt climbed into the truck, his flatbed carrying only the Bobcat and not a single pallet of cash, much to his increasing, nearly unbearable frustration.

They drove off in a caravan, the patrol car in the lead.

They'd done it.

They'd pulled off a heist for the record books, if such books were kept, and were about to make a smooth escape ahead of the wildfire they'd created . . . and without a single police officer aware of what they'd done.

For Danny, the success of this heist gave him a deeper, richer sense of accomplishment than any job that he'd ever pulled off. It wasn't that his complex, incredibly risky plan had actually worked, or that he was leaving Wishbone Canyon wealthy beyond his wildest dreams. It was something else.

This time, he felt an emotional fulfillment that he'd never experienced before and that he knew he never would again.

There was no sense even trying. There was nothing more he could achieve, only more that he could lose.

In that moment, he decided that this was his last heist. And that he wouldn't run any more cons, that he'd only engage in the insignificant lies and simple deceptions that would be necessary to live a rich, peaceful life of world travel and pampered anonymity.

As of now, Danny Cole was retired.

CHAPTER
TWENTY-FOUR

From Walker's position in lower Wishbone Canyon, standing on a fire road that might have originally been cut out by a crew of convict firefighters, he could see a house ablaze on the eastern ridge.

Sharpe surveyed the scene with binoculars. "One of the three houses up there is burning, and I see a fire engine there, but nobody is trying to suppress the flames."

"Because they're fake private firefighters," Walker said. "If we hurry, we can catch Cole in the act."

Sharpe lowered his binoculars. "Those kids who went to the Lost Cave on Friday night still haven't been found."

"We don't know that. We lost radio contact twenty minutes ago. It's a dead zone here."

"Which means that even if we manage to arrest Cole and his crew, we can't call anybody to get us out."

"What's your point?"

"We're at another fork in the road, Walker. We can go up there after Cole, or we can head east, to the Lost Cave, at the southern tip of this ridge, and find those kids."

"Or find nothing except the Topanga Fire coming at us."

"Maybe so, but we're the only first responders who can get to the cave. We couldn't do anything to save Brisker—he was already dead. But we can for the kids."

"We don't know if the stupid teenagers are there," Walker said. "And if they are, we don't have a signal to call for an extraction."

"It's a dead zone here. It may not be over there."

"That's a big gamble," Walker said.

"The way I see it, we can gamble our lives on arresting a bunch of thieves," Sharpe said, "or on saving the lives of two kids."

"If they are still there, assuming they ever were, or that they haven't already been rescued."

"If we make the wrong choice, which worst-case outcome could you live with?" Sharpe asked. "The crooks getting away or the kids dying?"

It was a powerful moral question and the implications brought a smile to Walker's face. "No problem, Sharpe. We can do both!"

Walker started marching east, a man on a mission.

Sharpe hurried up beside him. "I don't see how that's possible."

"You will. But I'll tell you what I don't get. Arson investigation wasn't supposed to be as dangerous as chasing fugitives. That was the deal I made with Carly. And yet here I am, walking into the path of two raging wildfires without any backup or much of a plan. Explain that to me."

"Have you ever considered that it's not the job that's dangerous, it's you?"

"Nope," Walker said.

"You could make delivering pizzas a high-risk job, which, if we survive this, could be our next profession."

"Something to look forward to," Walker said.

◆ ◆ ◆

The caravan of thieves was crossing the road that connected the two sides of the wishbone when Alison's voice rang in their ears.

"We have a problem," she said.

Danny looked out the passenger window of the patrol car at the mountains a couple of miles to the north. The monstrous blaze had crested the peaks and was crashing down the slopes, toppling trees in flames and turning the brush into an inferno. But it was still far enough away that they had time to pick up Alison and Adam and reach the Pacific Coast Highway before the wildfire consumed Wishbone Canyon. So that wasn't the problem. And if the Topanga Fire was coming up fast behind them, he couldn't see any sign of it yet in the rearview mirror. So that wasn't the problem, either.

"What is it?" he asked.

"We're hearing reports that a couple of teenagers were partying at a cave last night in Wishbone Canyon. Nobody has heard from them," she said. "That's right in the path of the fire, but the command staff has determined it's too risky to attempt a search and rescue."

Danny knew the cave from his convict firefighting days. It was at the rocky bottom of the south end of Wishbone Canyon's eastern ridge, the one they'd just fled.

Kurt, from his truck at the end of the caravan, said, "How is that a problem for us?"

Alison said, "We set the fire. If they get killed, it's our fault."

Tamiko said, "Not if it's the Topanga Fire."

"It doesn't make a difference," Alison said. "It's going to become one unstoppable, catastrophic wildfire stampeding to the Pacific."

Mertz spoke from the fire engine he was riding in with Logan. "You don't even know if the kids are actually there."

"But if they are," Alison said, "we are the only ones who have a chance at saving them. We're already on the ground in the fire zone and that cave is not even a mile east of here."

Mertz said, "We've pulled off the heist. If we keep on driving, we can make a clean getaway."

Alison said, "It won't be clean if we have their deaths on our conscience."

Adam spoke up. "It won't be on mine. Shit happens."

It certainly did, Danny thought. Just like it did in Ventura, right after the close of a perfectly executed scheme, the money in their hands and their escape virtually assured. But he knew what he could live with and what he couldn't. He sighed and looked at Tamiko. "Stop the car."

She wasn't happy about it, but she did as he asked, bringing the other vehicles to a halt, too.

"Everybody out," Danny said. "I can't have this discussion over earbuds."

He and Tamiko got out of the patrol car, meeting Mertz, Logan, and Kurt on the road. The scorching wind wailed through the canyon now, heralding the imminent arrival of the army of flames. They drew into a circle by the fire engine, the large vehicle providing some cover from the swirling embers.

"I'm going," Danny said. "I have to know those kids aren't in the cave or trying to walk out of there. But that's a personal choice. I can't ask any of you to go with me."

"Good," Tamiko said, "because I won't."

Danny started taking some firefighting equipment, which had been brought along mostly for show—a helmet, a full-face shroud, gloves, and a Pulaski to cut away brush.

Alison said, "I'm staying here until I know those kids are safe."

"I'm in," Logan said, and he seemed happy about it, too. "In my heart, I'm a firefighter and this is what we do."

"But you're not one," Mertz said. "You're a junkie and a thief. Stealing is what you do. It's what I do, too."

"No, you are a firefighter, too," Logan said as he grabbed equipment from the fire engine. "I've seen you do it. It wasn't just a job you did."

"You were fooled. I'm a survivor," Mertz said. "We've just pulled off the score of a lifetime. I'm not willing to risk losing it, or my life, because some stupid kids decided to party in a cave."

"Me neither," Kurt said.

Danny clapped Logan on the back. "I'm glad you're joining me. Get some helmets, full-face shrouds, and Nomex suits out of the fire engine for the kids." He turned to Tamiko and held out his hand. "I need the keys to the cop car."

She slapped the keys into his hand. "You're being an idiot. You find those kids, what happens?"

"We take them out of here with us and drop them off on PCH." Danny opened the trunk and was surprised to see piles of loose cash inside from Pletov's garage. Tamiko shrugged sheepishly. He began tossing out handfuls of cash, the wind sending them fluttering away. "All the kids will know is that they were rescued by two firemen in a cop car."

Tamiko said, "But what if you and the dumb-shit teenagers can't outrun the fire?"

"We'll take refuge with them and Storm in the underground safe room at the Epitome until the fire passes."

"And then you'll get caught," she said. "And end up back in prison again."

"Maybe not." He took the equipment from Logan and put it in the trunk.

Adam chimed in from the war room. "You definitely will, just like last time you stopped to help some poor schlub. I'm out. No need to stop by the house for me. Just keep on going to the promised land. I'll catch up."

Danny tossed two more loose bills from the trunk, slammed the lid closed, and faced the others. "The Wizard is right. Get out while you can. If you don't hear from me in a few days, give my share to Arnie's family."

"Give mine to my girlfriend, Shauna, and our daughter," Logan said.

Danny and Logan got into the patrol car, drove a short way down the road, then made a hard left onto a fire road into the canyon, the money on the roadway swirling around the three remaining crew members who were standing there.

◆　◆　◆

Mertz swatted a wind-tossed hundred-dollar bill out of his face. "Let's move out."

"Not me," Kurt said. "Not yet." He yanked out his earbuds, threw them in the brush, and gestured to Mertz and Tamiko to do the same. They did. "I don't want the weather lady hearing this. I'm going back for the cash."

"We've got plenty," Mertz said.

"We can have more. Much more." Kurt pointed at the eastern ridge, where Slezak's house was now fully engulfed in flames, the blazing palms highlighting it like sparklers on a wedding cake. "It's right there for the taking."

"And then what?" Tamiko asked. "How do we get it all out of here? The fire will be right on top of us."

"We take the cash back to the Epitome, stay there with it until the fire passes, and then haul it all away."

"How are we going to do that without getting caught?"

"I'll come up with a way." Kurt looked at her imploringly, relying on all the years that they'd risked their lives together, committed crimes together, and occasionally slept together to count for something now, when he really needed her. "Trust me. I can do this."

"You aren't Danny Cole."

"Neither is he anymore," Kurt said. "The weather lady has ruined him. He isn't thinking straight."

"Maybe so," Mertz said. "But Danny was right about leaving the money behind. I'm getting out now with what we've got."

"Me too." Tamiko stepped forward, held Kurt's face in her hands, and kissed him tenderly on the lips. "I'm sorry."

"Your loss, baby. Whatever I take now, I'm keeping for myself." Kurt turned his back to them and climbed up into the cab of the truck.

Mertz shook his head sadly. "There goes the Man Who Would Be King."

Tamiko glared at him. "What's that supposed to mean? You don't know him."

"But I know greed when I see it. Let's go." Mertz got into the fire engine. Tamiko joined him and they drove on toward Wishbone Road. And then it would be on to Latigo Canyon Road all the way to the Pacific Coast Highway, and then up to Paso Robles, not stopping for anything but gas until they reached the run-down farm Danny had found where they could regroup, unload the fire engine, and hide out for a while.

Kurt followed them only as far as the fork in the road on the western ridge, then made a wide U-turn and headed back the way they came, toward an unimaginable fortune.

Only it wasn't unimaginable. It was real. He'd seen it. He'd touched it. And very soon, every last dollar of it would be his.

In the reinforced concrete safe room under the Epitome, Adam Horowitz abruptly stood up. "I'm out of here. Are you sure you want to stay?"

Alison nodded. "I need to know the kids are safe. Besides, the Saint and Smokey will need me to keep them updated on the fires."

"They'll see that for themselves and they won't be able to hear you anyway. They'll be out of our radio range in another hundred yards, if they aren't already."

"I'm staying," she said. "I'll leave when they do."

"If they do," Adam said.

She ignored the comment. "How are you getting out?"

"In style. I'm taking the Aston Martin," Adam said, then pointed to his computer keyboard. "Before you leave, hit control-shift-delete on the keyboard."

"What will that do?"

"Wipe the hard drives and fry the equipment. And I mean that last bit literally, so stand back when you do it."

Adam walked out, closing the door behind him, and went straight to the Aston Martin. He got inside. It felt good. The seat hugged him like a lover. This was how he was meant to live. How he *would* live. He started up the car and sped out of the garage into his new, richer life.

The Aston Martin shot up the ramp and flew into the motor court. He tore around the fountain, executing two perfect drifts that would've made Vin Diesel proud and that probably gave the marble *David* a hard-on, then sped across the bridge, over the moat, and down the long driveway to the road.

And that's when he saw that the end of the driveway was blocked by two black Suburbans, six men with snake tattoos around their necks standing in front of them, and he nearly screamed.

Viboras!

How did they know we were here?

He slammed on his brakes, the Aston Martin fishtailing to a stop, and hoped Alison was still listening to her earbud. "Storm, lock yourself in the safe room. Tell the Saint not to come back."

"They'll die out there," Alison said, clearly confused.

"Tell him the Viboras are waiting for him."

"Who are the Viboras?"

The six men were taking out their guns, daring him to come at them. He wasn't going to take that dare. He had another option. Adam floored it, veered left, and sped off the embankment, high into the air, toward the road below.

The Aston Martin smacked down onto the slope on its wheels, and for an instant Adam thought he'd made it, but then the car flipped over and rolled all the way down to the road, landing upside down in the path of Mertz's huge, speeding fire engine.

◆ ◆ ◆

Mertz yanked the wheel hard, the fire engine clipping the edge of the Aston Martin, sending it spinning. But Mertz kept right on going. He wasn't stopping for anything, and Tamiko didn't object.

◆ ◆ ◆

Adam was buckled upside down in his seat, surrounded by blood-spattered, deflating airbags. He didn't feel any pain, but he was aware of being impaled by something, of broken bones, of failing organs, and of a missing eyeball, which was resting in the gauge cluster, looking at him. With his remaining eye, he could see a Vibora floating upside down and sideways, grinning at him, showing off two gold-capped incisors. It all seemed very surreal to Adam, but also painfully sad. He wanted to cry.

The Viboras swarmed around the car. Their leader, a gun in his hand, squatted beside the car and peered into the shattered windshield.

"My name is Angel," the Vibora said. "Like the Angel of Death. Where is Danny Cole?"

It took all of the energy Adam had left to spit out a mouthful of blood and teeth and say just two words.

"Fuck you."

Angel pointed his gun at Adam's remaining eye and shot him.

◆ ◆ ◆

Alison screamed, horrified by the gunshot, which she'd heard from Adam's earbuds.

She rushed to the safe room door and locked it. The gunshot, and Angel's question, still rang in her ears. The Viboras, whoever they were, wouldn't be able to reach her. And if they didn't give up and run off soon, the fire would get them. She hoped it would.

Alison knew she was safe, that she would survive.

But the Saint—or, rather, Danny Cole—wouldn't and neither would Smokey, or the kids, if they came back here and encountered those killers.

Unless she could warn them to stay away, to keep on driving to PCH without stopping and leave her behind.

On the surveillance screen, she saw two black SUVs heading up the driveway like hearses. She'd expected death to come calling today, but not like this.

Alison went to the mike and hit the "On" button.

"Danny? Can you hear me? Danny?"

All she heard was silence.

But she'd keep asking until she got an answer, if only for the comfort of hearing her own voice.

CHAPTER
TWENTY-FIVE

Danny and Logan drove the fake patrol car to the end of the fire road and walked the rest of the way to the cave along a hiking trail through desiccated oak trees, parched mustard grass, and sagebrush. The winds were roaring through the canyon, clogging the air with smoke, filling their nostrils with the aroma of burning wood.

"Remember the last time we were here, Danny?" Logan asked.

He did. A group of stupid kids came up here to get stoned, started a campfire outside the cave to roast marshmallows, and sparked a wildfire that rampaged through Malibu and destroyed a dozen houses before being put down at PCH.

"I'll never forget it," Danny said.

"We were right up against the flames, cutting a line and hosing fire," Logan said.

"Scared me to death. Made me wish I'd stayed in prison."

"That was the best day of my life."

"It was almost your last."

"Good times," Logan said. "The Park Service should have sealed the cave after that fire if they didn't want kids partying here anymore."

"They would have," Danny said, "but some Native American tribe sued to prevent it, arguing that the cave had historical significance."

"I think the Indians just wanted to see Malibu burn again."

"They got their wish," Danny said.

"So have I," Logan said.

They reached the cave, which was more like a stone igloo, a space created by the collapse of several massive boulders sheared off the ridge eons ago. Two teenagers, a boy and a girl, were huddled together inside, wearing only T-shirts, shorts, and flip-flops, their backs against the rocks. The girl's right leg was bruised nearly black around the ankle and stretched out in front of her.

"Hello there," Danny said. "Your rescue party has arrived."

The girl shrieked with relief and joy. "Oh, thank God! I am so glad to see you. If I could get up, I'd hug you."

She couldn't, but the boy with her did, holding Danny tight. "Thank you, man. We were afraid nobody was coming, that we'd die here."

"That's not going to happen," Danny said, gently extricating himself from the teary-eyed boy. "Why didn't you leave?"

The boy wiped the tears from his eyes and said, "We got really stoned, woke up, saw the smoke, and couldn't get a signal on our phones to call for help. So we ran . . ."

"I fell and hurt my ankle," the girl said. "I told Dusty to go get help."

"I couldn't leave Britney," Dusty said. "And I figured it was safer for both of us to stay in here and hope somebody would show up than get caught out in the open when the fire came."

"You did the right thing, because here we are," Danny said and handed him one of the extra helmets, face shields, and Nomex suits. "Put these on. We have to go . . . there isn't much time."

"I'll carry you on my back." Logan gave Britney the same gear that Dusty had.

She got into the Nomex suit. "Why are there only two of you? Where are the rest?"

Before either Danny or Logan could answer, someone else did.

"We're right here, honey," Sharpe said. "Everything is going to be okay now."

Danny turned and saw two men behind him, a jowly, hound-faced man he didn't know and a big guy in a cowboy hat that he recognized immediately, and who officially became, in that heartbreaking moment, the face of fate to him.

"Hello, Cole," Walker said.

"Marshal Walker," Danny said. "What a delightful surprise."

"It's Deputy Walker now. Los Angeles County Sheriff's Department. This is my partner, Walter Sharpe. He's their top arson investigator." Danny nodded, extrapolating from that fact alone that they'd somehow tracked him by the way he'd started the fires. Walker looked at the other firefighter. "You must be Bobby Logan."

Logan nodded but seemed both confused and worried.

Walker put his arm around Danny. "Can I have a quick word?"

Danny let Walker lead him a few steps down the trail, leaving Sharpe with the others. He was astonished that what had been, only minutes ago, his most successful, career-capping heist had suddenly collapsed around him to become his downfall. But he couldn't see the flaw in his plan. The only explanation he could find was that he'd fallen for a con himself, one crafted by Walker and Sharpe. But even that was hard to accept. "Those two kids look genuinely freaked out to me. I can't believe it was all a trap."

"It was and it wasn't," Walker said. "We came here to catch you and your crew, but when I heard about these two kids, I figured you'd come for them and to us. Your big failing as a crook is that you care about other people. It's what got you before, too."

So it wasn't a critical mistake in his scheme, or falling for a con himself, that had doomed him. It was simply bad luck and a weakness in his character. In some ways, that was easier for him to accept than the alternatives.

"My lawyer calls it my basic decency," Danny said. "She used that in her closing statement to the jury."

"Now she can use it again," Walker said. "You're under arrest, in case that isn't obvious. Are we going to need cuffs on you two?"

Danny shook his head. Walker obviously knew what was going down . . . in a broad sense, if not the specifics. "Let's not scare the kids more than they already are. How long were you waiting for us?"

"Only a few minutes," Walker replied.

"Going to call in the reinforcements now to pull us out?"

"We can't get a signal and I'm not sure they'd come if we could," Walker said. "It's too dangerous. The Topanga Fire is right over that hill and the Chatsworth Fire is charging into the canyon any minute now."

"So, what's your plan?" Danny asked.

"Let's hear yours."

"We've got a car, down on the road. There's a house on the western ridge, a mile or two from here, that's supposed to be fireproof. It's called the Epitome. We can hole up there until the wildfire passes." Danny noticed a strange expression flicker by on Walker's face at the mention of the house.

"Will the rest of your crew be waiting there to jump us?"

"They're long gone," Danny said. "They don't have my big failing."

"Did you kill Brisker for his house?"

"Of course not. Why would you even think that?"

"Because we found his body on our way in," Walker said. "Someone shot him in the face and left him in his Bentley. Any idea who that might be?"

"Probably some debt collectors from the Mexican cartel that invested in his house. Brisker was facing bankruptcy and they were about to lose their money."

"So, you offered Brisker a way out of his jam?"

Hearing the question made another frightening possibility occur to Danny.

"Maybe two ways, only I didn't realize it at the time." But he did now and the implications filled him with a sickening dread. "Brisker might have decided to hedge his bets."

"What does that mean?"

"To convince him of my bona fides, I told him how I took down Diego Grillo." That was a huge mistake. He'd underestimated how desperate, and wily, Brisker was.

"You think he sold you out to the Viboras for quick cash and they gave him a bullet instead."

"If he did," Danny said, "Vibora assassins could be waiting for me at the house."

"Have you got another plan?"

"Yes," he said. "Let's use yours."

"My plan was to use your plan. We'll have to take our chances at the house."

Sharpe trudged over angrily and whispered to the two men, "If you two are done catching up, the wildfire is just over that hill and when it comes roaring down at fifty miles an hour, we won't be able to outrun it on foot." He turned to Britney and offered her his warmest, most reassuring smile. "These two nice firemen are going to carry you. One will have you under the arms, the other by the legs. We can move faster to the car that way."

As Danny joined Logan to lift Britney up, Sharpe whispered to Walker, "That will keep their uncuffed hands occupied on the way to Brisker's house."

"You heard all that?"

"Just me, and maybe the rest of his crew, too. I plucked this from Logan's ear and put it in my own." Sharpe opened his closed fist to reveal a flesh-colored earbud, then closed his fist again so they could continue talking in private. "Cole has one, too."

"I didn't notice," Walker said. "That's some real *Mission: Impossible* shit."

Danny and Logan lifted Britney up and started down the trail as fast as they could go, considering their load. Dusty stepped up to the two detectives. "When's the chopper getting here?"

Walker said, "It's not and we've run out of time. Two fires are about to converge on top of us, so we're going somewhere safe."

Sharpe pulled Walker aside and whispered in his ear, "What happened to not scaring them more than they already are?"

Shit. Walker smiled and addressed Dusty again. "But you have absolutely nothing to worry about. We're professionals. We know exactly what we're doing."

Walker put his arm on Dusty's back and gave him a gentle shove down the trail.

"News to me," Sharpe muttered, then put the earbud in his ear and brought up the rear, taking one last look over his shoulder into the hot wind.

Two hundred yards behind them, the Topanga Fire blew thunderously over the hilltop, detonating a stand of oaks to announce its arrival.

In the underground garage of Arseny Pletov's house, Kurt Sabella used the forklift to lift his eighth pallet of cash onto the flatbed. It was all he could fit on the truck, only a fraction of what there was left to take, which was frustrating, but there was still room in the cab for some loose cash.

He cut open the shrink-wrap around one of the remaining pallets and began stuffing cash into two thirty-gallon Hefty trash bags that he'd found in the house above only minutes before it was engulfed in flames.

It was unnerving working under an inferno, even though he knew he was safely surrounded by concrete, but what really disturbed him, what he couldn't stop thinking about, was that the impending wildfire outside would soon sweep down the ramp and incinerate the millions of dollars he couldn't take with him.

He could close the garage door behind him when he left to keep the fire out, but he'd be damned if he'd save the money from being burned so Pletov could spend it. If Kurt couldn't have the cash, nobody would.

But Kurt knew he wouldn't have any of it, either, if he didn't get his ass out of there now. He couldn't see what was happening outside, but he could hear it, cracking and crunching its way through the trees, like a heavy-footed giant.

Kurt tossed the bulging trash bags of cash into the cab, money spilling onto the seats and floor, then climbed in after them, planting his ass on a few thousand dollars in loose bills.

He started up the truck, put it into gear, and pressed the pedal to the floor, heading for the exit ramp and using the remote he'd found to open the garage door ahead of him.

As the garage door rose, smoke billowed in from outside, temporarily obscuring his view, but once the truck punched through the thick haze onto the cul-de-sac, he found himself in a windstorm of swirling ash and embers.

All three houses were aflame, the hardscape around them a circle where nothing burned, creating an eerie spotlight effect that highlighted the intense fires against the dark, smoky backdrop. The hillside in front of him was alight with what looked like a hundred campfires, but the road wasn't burning. It was an escape path dusted with embers, his own glittering yellow-brick road.

The Epitome wasn't far at all.

He would make it. With time to spare.

Fuck Danny Cole and those other cowards.

Kurt was going to the Emerald City.

◆ ◆ ◆

Danny and Logan eased Britney into the back seat of the patrol car.

Sharpe gestured to Logan and Dusty. "You two in the back with Britney. We'll sit up front. Cole, you drive."

The others quickly piled in. Sharpe walked around the car and got in last, whispering just loud enough for his earbud to pick up his words, "You still have at least one man at the house or you would have gotten rid of these earbuds."

Danny stole a glance at Sharpe as he got in, a look that acknowledged that he'd heard him, then peeled out, the fire chasing after them, igniting everything in their wake. As he drove, he whispered just loud enough for Sharpe to hear on his earbud and Walker to hear on his own.

"We're out of communications range now, but not for long," Danny said. "We'll know soon if the Viboras are waiting."

Danny couldn't believe how wrong things had gone. And it was all his fault. He had to find a way to make it right. For Alison, for Logan, for those two kids in the back seat. Even for these two cops.

Walker took off his hat and adjusted the rearview mirror so he could see what was behind them.

So could Danny. He saw the terrified expressions on the faces of the teenagers looking back at him, but beyond them, he was relieved to see they were putting a lot of ground between themselves and the tsunami of fire from Topanga. A plan occurred to him, almost fully formed, probably because it was the only option he had with the resources and time that were left.

Danny whispered, "There's a safe room in the underground garage. If the Viboras are waiting, I'll drop the five of you off before we get to the house so you can go in on foot and get everyone safely inside through the back door."

Sharpe asked, "What are you going to do?"

"Drive up to the front door and keep the Viboras occupied by giving them what they want."

Walker looked at Danny. "You're sacrificing yourself for us?"

"I really hope not," he said.

"You have a plan?"

"More like an act of pure desperation," Danny said.

CHAPTER TWENTY-SIX

The Viboras stood in the great room, drinking bottles of whiskey they'd found in the pub and watching the two wildfires: the Topanga blaze sweeping away the rubble of the three houses and spilling down the eastern slope, and the Chatsworth flames, rampaging down the canyon. Soon the two would smash together into one explosive, cataclysmic inferno right on top of the house.

But the Viboras didn't seem very concerned to Alison, who was watching them and the approaching fires from a dozen angles on the monitors in the safe room.

The fires worried her more than the Viboras. She was afraid that Danny, Smokey, and the kids were already incinerated.

She leaned into the microphone. "Danny, are you there? Do you have the kids?"

There was a hiss of static. That was new.

"Danny? Do you hear me?"

"We've got the couple and they're fine," he said.

"Thank God." She felt an enormous swell of relief that brought tears to her eyes. "But you can't come back here."

"I don't have a choice. How many Viboras are waiting for me?"

How did he know?

"Six. They're in the house. They killed the Wizard."

There was more static, then: "I'll be out front in five minutes."

"You're unarmed. They have guns."

"I have you . . . and Icarus . . . and they don't know that." And then he told her what he wanted her to do.

Kurt drove on the road through a tunnel of whirling fire toward the western ridge. He knew that he could power through it to the other side and outrun the surrounding flames. His big problem was the fire that he was carrying.

The pallets were ablaze, and in the rearview mirror he could see the flames spreading across the flatbed toward the cab. But there was no way he could stop to ditch the truckload of fire he was carrying through an inferno. He didn't want to anyway. Not all of the pallets were on fire.

His only hope was to keep driving.

It wasn't far. Just to the next ridge. He could make it to the Epitome, to safety. Maybe he could even save the last pallet or two, certainly the bags of cash beside him, if nothing else.

All he had to do was keep driving.

Danny drove alone in the patrol car across the bridge, over the moat, and into the motor court, where the two Suburbans were parked.

The Viboras wouldn't be happy about seeing a cop car outside, he thought, but he'd ease their minds in a moment.

Danny took off his helmet and face covering, got out of the car, and stepped out in front of it, hands at his sides.

No cops here, fellas. Just harmless little me, your friendly neighborhood thief.

He felt like he was stepping in front of a firing squad. Because he was.

The six Viboras, led by gold-toothed Angel, tumbled out of the house, each holding a whiskey bottle by the neck in one hand and a gun in the other.

◆ ◆ ◆

"Hurry! Hurry!" Alison Grayle opened the french doors to the backyard and waved in Walker, Sharpe, Logan, and Dusty, the four men carrying Britney between them. Walker looked over his shoulder as they went inside. He could see the wildfire seething in the canyon now, a river of flame lapping up against the hillside behind the house.

Alison led them down the stairs to the garage, and then across to the safe room. But she didn't go inside. Instead, she stood outside the door and said, "Close the door behind you and you'll be safe. The room is fireproof."

Walker said, "Where are you going?"

"The roof." Alison turned and ran back to the stairs

Walker helped the men set down Britney, then started for the door, but Sharpe stopped him.

"It's suicide," Sharpe said.

"They're armed and Cole's not," Walker said.

"Too bad."

"We're cops," Walker said.

"And you're a father with a child on the way," Sharpe said. "Your responsibility now is to protect the two kids who are here and make it home to your family."

Walker's first thought was that it was a bullshit choice. Sharpe could stay and protect the two teenagers while Walker brought himself and his gun to Cole's unarmed confrontation with the heavily armed Viboras. Walker and Cole would still be outnumbered and outgunned, but Walker would have surprise on his side and could probably take down half of the Viboras before they could shoot back.

But he'd still be risking his life in a gunfight in the middle of a fast-moving wildfire . . . and for what?

A chance to take down the bad guys.

A very slim chance.

But wasn't that why he wore a badge?

But if he didn't make it, and the odds were that he wouldn't, Carly would become a widow and his child would never know his father.

Or he could stay hunkered down here, let the bad guys fight among themselves, and increase the chances that he'd be alive tomorrow for his wife and kid.

It meant he finally had to decide what he was more devoted to . . . his badge or his family.

Walker looked at Sharpe and gave him a slight nod. He was staying. Sharpe closed the door and locked it. Logan began to cry.

◆ ◆ ◆

In the motor court, Danny could feel the heat of the flames, and he could see them, too, through the windows of the house behind the Viboras, rising up in tall spirals, fueled by the canyon brush.

Angel said, "Diego Grillo sends his regards."

"I guess he's mad, huh?"

"You're going to beg to die."

"We really don't have time for begging. There's a fire coming," Danny said. "So if you're going to kill me, get it over with, you dumb, gold-toothed, snake-necked motherfucker."

Angel shot him.

The bullet hit Danny in the left shoulder, spinning him around and bouncing him off the side of the car. He slid into a sitting position on the ground.

Angel aimed his gun at Danny's crotch. "We're going to watch you burn alive."

But Danny's attention wasn't on the gun. It was on a spot behind and above Angel's head.

"You first," Danny said.

That's when the Icarus swooped down over the Viboras, raining fireballs on them.

Two of the men screamed, their heads bursting into flame. Another Vibora caught fire, his whiskey bottle exploding like a Molotov cocktail, igniting the man next to him.

Danny scrambled behind the car as Angel advanced like the Terminator, shooting his gun. But dodging fireballs was throwing off Angel's aim, the bullets hitting either the car or his wailing, immolated friends, who were running around blindly on fire in front of him.

◆ ◆ ◆

Angel whirled around, roared with fury, and shot at the drone, which exploded in the air and spun into the moat. Satisfied, he turned back toward the cop car to finish what he'd started.

Alison stood on the roof, helpless and horrified, as she watched doom advance on Danny.

◆ ◆ ◆

Kurt sped up the driveway, the Epitome right in front of him. He was so close. He was going to make it, riding the bat out of hell all the way.

Only the bat was burning.

The pallets were ablaze and his wheels were spinning whirligigs of fire.

He could see the moat . . . and some people, too.

Fire people.

Maybe he wasn't riding the bat out of hell . . . but the bat flying into it.

The cab window behind him shattered, hot shards of glass spraying the back of his head and igniting the cash all over the seat.

Kurt screamed but didn't let go of the wheel.

◆ ◆ ◆

Angel marched around the car to Danny, who had nowhere to hide. Danny didn't cower and, to his surprise, wasn't afraid.

"Your day really turned to shit," Danny said.

"Not as bad as yours." He took aim at Danny's head and squeezed the trigger.

Instead of hearing an explosion, and then falling into eternal nothingness, Danny heard a dry click.

Angel was out of bullets.

The Vibora looked down at his gun, enraged, and when he raised his head again . . .

. . . he was hit by the blazing truck, which kept on going with Angel caught on the grille, charging past Danny in a comet tail of fire across the motor court, and smashed into the fountain, shearing off the statue and grinding to a halt.

Danny rose up and peered over the hood of the car in shock.

What the hell . . . ?

That's when the entire truck exploded, sending fiery shrapnel in all directions and hurling *David's* marble head through the windshield of the patrol car.

Danny got slowly to his feet and, cradling his limp arm, staggered around the bodies and the burning truck and to the house.

It's all over now, he thought.

He'd pulled off the greatest heist of his life. He'd exacted his vengeance, he'd humiliated CAL FIRE, and Arnie's family would get the compensation they'd been wrongfully denied. He'd even saved the lives of the two innocent kids that he'd endangered with all of this.

So it wasn't a complete disaster.

As he entered the foyer, he saw Alison rushing down the grand staircase to meet him.

"You're alive," she said.

"For the moment." Danny looked past her at the wall of flames rising from the canyon and licking out at the windows of the great room. If he and Alison stayed here and went down to the safe room, they'd probably survive the inferno, but they would certainly spend the next few decades in prison.

And he knew he would have to live the rest of his life tortured with guilt over Alison's imprisonment, which would never have happened if he hadn't gotten her into this scheme by manipulating her grief over her dead husband.

That would be the most painful punishment of all for Danny.

But there was nothing he could do about that now.

Then Danny looked up at the chrome Lamborghini spinning on the crystal-encrusted pedestal, all of it gleaming beautifully in the flickering red-yellow light cast by the inferno, and realized it might not be over yet.

Danny smiled at Alison. "I'm sure glad Brisker didn't go with a Ford Focus."

A few hours later, shortly before sunset, Sharpe, Walker, Logan, and the two teenagers emerged wearily from the Epitome to a postapocalyptic landscape. Although the firestorm had passed, little bonfires remained everywhere, like puddles after a heavy rain. The hills were scorched and stripped, the remaining trees gnarled and charred, just like the twisted, fallen bodies that lay on the motor court amid the burned metal skeletons of two SUVs, one car, and a flatbed truck.

Sharpe and Walker stepped out of the house first, followed by Logan and Dusty, who supported Britney, who hopped along on one foot. Behind them, the house was eerily pristine and intensely white against the smoking coal-black nothingness everywhere else. It was the only structure in sight that was still standing. To their left, the firestorm had descended on Malibu and PCH, creating a wall of smoke that completely obscured the coastline from view.

The two detectives were in a difficult situation. They'd come here to stop a heist there was no evidence had actually happened and to nail the arsonists behind a wildfire they couldn't prove was intentionally set.

The radios that the two detectives carried crackled to life with a stream of dispatcher communications, which Sharpe and Walker ignored. In the distance, from the mountains to the north, they could see a single helicopter coming their way, probably on a routine damage survey of the fire zone in the blaze's wake. The detectives eyed it warily. It wasn't only help coming but also a lot of tricky questions that needed answers, ones that wouldn't destroy their careers.

Walker said, "What's our story?"

Sharpe glanced over at Logan, Britney, and Dusty, who seemed shell-shocked by what they were seeing and the miracle of their survival. "We can't hold Logan. There's no evidence that he committed a crime."

"Besides impersonating a firefighter."

"Not even that. There are no official insignias on that outfit he's wearing. Besides, he helped rescue two kids. To them, he's a firefighter and a hero," Sharpe said. "So is Danny Cole. It's not entirely false. Cole and Logan could have made a clean escape with their loot, but instead they risked their lives to rescue the teenagers. And then Cole sacrificed himself to save all of us. I respect that."

"It was also all Cole's fault."

"Yes, there's that, too. But there's also those 'emotional stakes' you talked about. Years ago, two firefighters were killed doing their jobs and their families were treated horribly in the aftermath. I can understand why Cole and Grayle wanted some measure of justice for that, though their way of getting it was insane and catastrophic."

Bobby Logan noticed the two detectives watching him and it seemed to Walker that the attention made him uneasy. Walker couldn't blame him. He'd be uneasy, too, in that guy's shoes.

"What about Brisker? All these bodies? And that flatbed truck?"

Sharpe regarded the truck, heaped on the fountain and atop the marbled, heavily muscled legs of a male statue, and frowned, obviously having trouble making sense of it.

"I have no idea what the story is with that truck. But I say we pin it all on the Mexican cartel trying to make good on their bad investment on this house," he said. "They stole the drone. They set the fires. They killed Brisker. They tried to escape when we showed up and got caught in the flames. Who alive is going to contradict us?"

"How do you explain Cole and Logan?"

Sharpe shrugged. "Two former convict firefighters who heroically risked their lives to help others in the same mountains where they once served as volunteers."

"What about Alison Grayle?"

"What about her? All we know is that there was an unidentified woman here who let us into the basement," Sharpe said. "We don't know who she was or what her relationship was to Brisker or the cartel. She went upstairs to get something and didn't come back. We owe her our lives."

Walker thought about that. They had the gun that killed Brisker. They had the bodies of the Viboras. They had the wreckage of their SUVs and the drone. A forensic accounting would turn up the cartel's investment in the house.

The evidence would back up Sharpe's scenario, though there were a lot of holes. That was normal. Things rarely got tied up in neat, tidy resolutions that explained everything.

"That actually all holds up," Walker said.

"Because it's pretty close to the truth."

"Only it isn't."

"It's what we can prove with the evidence, and the corpses, that we have," Sharpe said.

"Unless we catch the rest of Cole's crew and recover what they stole."

"If there were any others, and if they stole anything, and if they got away alive with any of it."

"Or, better yet, we could catch Cole and Alison."

Walker could see the markings on the chopper now. It was from the Los Angeles County Fire Department. Dusty and Britney began waving enthusiastically at the helicopter, as if they were survivors of a shipwreck who'd been stuck on an uncharted desert isle for years. Logan wasn't waving. He didn't seem sure of what he was supposed to do and kept glancing nervously at the two detectives for direction.

"If they survived," Sharpe said. "But then we'd have to admit that the story we told was a lie and where would that leave us?"

"At Pizza Hut," Walker said. The helicopter circled low around them, confirming that they'd been seen. The pilot was presumably looking for a spot to land. The moment of truth, or half-truths, or barely truths, was coming.

Logan moseyed over to them. "I'm afraid to ask this. What happens to me now?"

Sharpe shared a look with Walker, who nodded his agreement, then said, "Do you want to be a fireman?"

Logan nodded. "More than anything."

"Okay, so let me remind you what you told us," Sharpe said. "You and Danny Cole were watching the news and saw the fire, out here where you used to work as convicts. You knew the fire department was struggling to deal with it all and you felt this overwhelming desire to help. So you two came out here without asking, to do your bit, and stumbled across these two kids. That's when we ran into you."

What were we doing out here? Walker thought. They'd have to do some work on the answer to that question. But they still had time.

"Yes, that's what I told you," Logan said. "My memory is hazy on one thing, though. Where did we get the patrol car?"

Good question, Walker thought. Where *did* they get it? He didn't want to know, so he offered Logan the simplest explanation. "You found it abandoned on the road, keys in the ignition, remember? You have no clue how it got there."

"Yeah, that's right. It's a real mystery." Logan chewed on his chapped lower lip, which was already bleeding a bit from the chewing on it he'd been doing for the last few hours. "I don't know what happened to Danny."

"None of us do," Sharpe said. "We had no radio signal, so he went for help and didn't come back."

Walker added, "Be sure to thank Cole when the governor pins a medal on you. It will be a nice touch."

Logan nodded, briefly overcome with emotion. The three of them watched the helicopter land on what was once the front lawn, now a carpet of ash. "Why are you two doing this for me?"

Sharpe said, "Some good has to come out of all this death and destruction. Maybe a little redemption, too."

Walker thought about Alison Grayle's dead husband and her bills, and about the dead convict firefighter who'd died here years ago without any acknowledgment of his sacrifice or adequate financial compensation for his family. There weren't any heroes here, not counting himself and Sharpe, of course.

"Thank you. I won't let you down." Logan shook Sharpe's hand, and when he did, one of his sleeves rode up, revealing a glimpse of the watch on his wrist.

Sharpe noticed it. "Nice watch."

Logan tugged his sleeve down over it. "My grandfather gave it to me. It's a family heirloom."

"You wore it into a fire?"

"I never take it off," Logan said. "It's my good luck charm and it worked again."

That was a quick cover story Danny Cole might have come up with, Walker thought. Logan had learned a few things. Maybe he'd learned a lot. Hopefully, he'd learned the right lessons.

A trio of firefighters spilled out of the chopper. Logan hurried over to Dusty and Britney and helped bring her to the first responders.

Sharpe watched Logan go. "Family heirloom, my ass."

"If you really want to pursue that line of inquiry," Walker said, "I can tell you exactly where it leads."

"To Pizza Hut," Sharpe said.

"That's right."

Sharpe sighed. "I have to admit, Walker, you're a natural man-hunter. You got your man."

"Only you and I will ever know it."

"But we do," Sharpe said.

Walker regarded Sharpe for a moment. They'd only known each other a few short days. And yet, somehow it already felt like it had been so much longer. He already trusted him more than some people he'd known for years. "You really are a genius at this arson stuff. You figured out everything. I don't think anybody else could have done it."

"Didn't do either one of us much good."

"We saved those two kids," Walker said. "That's something. Like you said, it's an outcome I can live with."

"Me too," Sharpe said, then held out his hand. "Partner."

Walker shook it. "Gonna get yourself a Stetson now?"

"Hell no."

Walker's phone rang, startling them both. He took it out of his pocket, looked at the screen, and was surprised to see one signal bar and his wife's name on the caller ID. He answered it.

"Hey, honey."

"I was getting worried about you," Carly said. "I haven't heard from you all day. What have you been up to?"

"Just sitting in a room doing nothing while the world burned around me."

"That's what I like to hear," she said. "Are you coming home tonight?"

Walker looked at Sharpe, his new partner, and felt a wave of gratitude wash over him. "Yes, I am," he said.

"Great," she said. "Can you pick up some KFC on the way?"

EPILOGUE

Diane Krepps-Soloway went from standing all day at a cash register at WinCo Foods in Bakersfield to standing at home making dinner for her kids to busing tables at Coffee on Coffee at night. No matter what shoes or socks she wore, or what skin balm she rubbed on her feet each day, or which "advanced" hydrocolloid gel bandages she put on her heels and toes, she still got painful blisters. Some of them were big, ugly blood blisters, too, that horrified her kids.

To relieve the pain on her feet, and to take the pressure off her blisters, she unconsciously walked at odd angles while balancing plates of food, which also strained her back and shoulders. She was certain that she walked, and even stood, like a hunched-over, elderly, arthritic woman stricken with osteoporosis, which she feared she'd be before she was forty.

So she was understandably too distracted by her misery, and too tired from only five hours' sleep a night, to pay much attention to the couple she'd served in one of the window booths. They'd been pleasant enough, not demanding or rude, which ordinarily might have made them memorable, but she'd stumbled on the diner's cracked linoleum coming out of the kitchen and slopped mashed potato gravy all over her uniform. While she was busy wiping off the mess, only succeeding in making it look like someone had taken a shit on her chest, the couple had paid their bill and left.

When she got to their booth to scoop up the cash and clear the dishes, she found a note written on the receipt.

Your tip is in the envelope on the seat.

Diane looked around the booth and found a padded envelope with her full name written across the front.

How did they know my name?

She opened the envelope. Inside was a Lamborghini key fob, emblazoned with the distinctive raging bull logo.

Your car is parked on the street.

It's not very practical, but you deserve it for your excellent service. We really enjoyed our chicken fried steak.

Stunned, she walked outside, ignoring her irate manager, who was yelling something at her about it being "way too soon" for her break. Parked at the curb was a chrome-plated Lamborghini Aventador, gleaming bright even in the moonlight.

She staggered up to the car and saw another envelope with her name on it resting on the hand-stitched Alcantara seat. She aimed her key fob at the car and the distinctive scissor doors rose up to let her inside. Her late husband had been in the exotic and luxury car leasing business, or so she'd thought, and he would have loved this.

It felt like some kind of violation, no, an abomination, to sit in a $500,000 Italian sports car while wearing a dirty, gravy-stained waitress uniform, but she did it anyway, picking up the envelope off the seat as she got inside.

Is this someone's idea of a cruel joke?

Diane tore open the envelope. It contained the pink slip—the State of California Certificate of Title—for the Lamborghini in her name (she had to look twice to be sure she wasn't hallucinating) and another handwritten note with a string of numbers across the top.

The number above is your bank account at Union Bancaire Privée in Geneva, Switzerland. The balance is $10 million.

Live a little, it's what Arnie would have wanted for you and the kids. It's what we want for you, too.

Her chest was tight, and she was having trouble breathing. For a moment, she feared she was having a heart attack. Or a stroke. Or both.

She tried to remember the couple. They were her age, though they'd looked a lot younger than she did, and the man's left arm was in a sling. But beyond that, she couldn't really picture their faces.

Did she know them? Impossible to say now.

Diane didn't question how they knew Arnie. She didn't question where the car and the money came from.

You don't question miracles.

Instead, she lowered the scissor doors, fired up the naturally aspirated V12 engine, put the car into gear, pressed her blister-covered foot against the gas pedal, and with a shriek of pure, ridiculous glee, raced into her new life.

Author's Note and
Acknowledgments

This book is entirely a work of fiction, but those of you who have read some of my other novels may notice this is not the first time I've written about a massive wildfire raging through the Santa Monica Mountains in Malibu. I did it before in my novel *Lost Hills*.

I admit that I am repeating myself.

My excuse, though, is that it's intentional. I am writing about the same fire in both books, though seen from two entirely different perspectives in the midst of two entirely separate crime stories. There are few minor "fictional facts" about the wildfire that don't quite match up between the two books, but that was unavoidable in order to tell this new story, so you'll have to live with them (assuming you notice them at all).

I took a lot of liberties with geography in this book, beginning with Wishbone Canyon, which doesn't actually exist but is inspired by a Malibu canyon that didn't quite suit my storytelling needs, so I made one up that did. Garner's Crossing is fictional as well, though based on a real town in the San Bernardino Mountains.

I couldn't have written this book without the advice of Ed Nordskog, a retired and highly respected arson/bomb investigator with the Los Angeles County Sheriff's Department and the author of the reference books *The Arsonist Profiles: Analyzing Arson Motives and Behavior*, *Incendiary Devices: Investigation and Analysis*, and *Arson Investigation in the Wildlands: Case Building and Practical Analysis* (with Joe Konefal), among others, which I drew from extensively in my research. Moreover, Ed endured countless emails full of dumb questions from me, which he answered in great detail and with limitless patience. But he should not be blamed for any factual, technical, legal, or procedural errors in this book. Those are all entirely mine, and some might even be intentionally made for the purposes of telling my story.

I am also indebted to Ken Andrews, a twenty-eight-year veteran of the Bureau of Alcohol, Tobacco, Firearms, and Explosives and now a certified fire investigator, who gave me a lot of detailed background on arson investigation. In fact, he was so intrigued by Danny Cole's method for igniting the fires, and how such an arson could be investigated and proved, that he conducted his own experiments by setting some fires in his backyard in the same way. He sent me the videos of the experiments, as well as his analysis of what he'd learned. That went above and beyond, and was also very cool.

I also want to thank Tony Knighton, lieutenant, Philadelphia Fire Department; Brandon Dhuey, directed enforcement officer, Brown County Sheriff's Office; and Jason Weber, public safety coordinator, Northeast Wisconsin Technical College, for sharing their experience, expertise, and advice on arson investigation.

A number of books were enormously helpful to me in my research, including *Breathing Fire: Female Inmate Firefighters on the Front Lines of California's Wildfires* by Jaime Lowe; *Kirk's Fire Investigation, Eighth Edition* by David J. Icove and Gerald A. Haynes; *NFPA 921: Guide for Fire and Explosion Investigation* 2021 (National Fire Protection Association); *Fire Investigator: Principles and Practice to NFPA 921 and 1033, Fifth Edition* (Jones and Bartlett Learning); *A Guide for Investigating Fire and Arson* (National Institute of Justice); *Blaze: The Forensics of Fire* by Nicholas Faith; *Setting Fires With Electrical Timers:*

An Earth Liberation Front Guide (May 2001); and finally *Fires . . . Accidental or Arson?* by Richard J. Keyworth, from which I learned about the accidental shampoo and laundry detergent fire scenario that inspired a chapter in this book.

Dozens and dozens of published articles, papers, and essays were very informative resources for me, but I would like to give special thanks to Joshua Daniel Bligh for "Confessions of an Inmate Firefighter," published by the International Association of Wildland Fire; Catie Cheshire, Sinead Hickey, and Miles Green for "Female Inmate Firefighters Build Character but Often Can't Use Fire Skills After Release," published by Cronkite News; Andrew Freedman and Jason Samenow for "Record Strong Santa Ana Wind Event Targets Southern California, Escalating Wildfire Threat," published by the *Washington Post*; Jaclyn Cosgrove for "Firefighters' Fateful Choices: How the Woolsey Fire Became an Unstoppable Monster," published by the *Los Angeles Times*; Matthew Hahn for "Sending Us to Fight Fires Was Abusive. We Preferred It to Staying in Prison," published by the *Washington Post*; and Joseph Serna and Rong-Gong Lin II for "Extreme Red Flag Winds in L.A. Region Are Dangerous, Unpredictable," published by the *Los Angeles Times*.

Finally, I have to thank my wife, Valerie; my daughter, Madison; my brother, Tod; my good friend Phoef Sutton; my long-time publisher Gracie Doyle; my editors Megha Parekh and Charlotte Herscher; and my literary agent Amy Tannenbaum for their enthusiasm and support for this book. Without them, *Malibu Burning* wouldn't have been written.

About the Author

Photo © 2013 Roland Scarpa

Lee Goldberg is a two-time Edgar Award and two-time Shamus Award finalist and the #1 *New York Times* bestselling author of more than forty novels, including the Eve Ronin series, the Ian Ludlow series, and the first five books in the Fox & O'Hare series, which he coauthored with Janet Evanovich. He has also written and/or produced many TV shows, including *Diagnosis Murder*, *SeaQuest*, and *Monk*, and is the cocreator of the Hallmark movie series *Mystery 101*. As an international television consultant, he has advised networks and studios in Canada, France, Germany, Spain, China, Sweden, and the Netherlands on the creation, writing, and production of episodic series. You can find more information about Lee and his work at www.leegoldberg.com.